THE GUILT BUSTERS

GRAEME CANN

WESTBOW
PRESS®
A DIVISION OF THOMAS NELSON
& ZONDERVAN

WestBow Press books may be ordered through booksellers or by contacting:

WestBow Press
A Division of Thomas Nelson & Zondervan
1663 Liberty Drive
Bloomington, IN 47403
www.westbowpress.com
844-714-3454

ISBN: 978-1-6642-1118-6 (sc)
ISBN: 978-1-6642-1119-3 (hc)
ISBN: 978-1-6642-1117-9 (e)

Library of Congress Control Number: 2020921649

Print information available on the last page.

WestBow Press rev. date: 11/23/2020

CHARACTERS IN ORDER OF APPEARANCE

John. Survivor of childhood sexual abuse by pedophile Father Justin McKean.

Marie. Psychologist and widow of Vic, who was killed along with their two children in a car accident.

Helen. A stranger John meets after a counseling session with Marie.

Claire. John's estranged sister, married now to Sam.

Father Vince Patrick. Parish priest of the church attended by Claire and her family.

Father Simon. A retired priest who Father Vince sees as his mentor.

Tim Parnell. A son of the church choir mistress. Tim was also abused by McKean.

James Churchill. Solicitor acting for eleven sexual abuse survivors involved in the McKean case.

Margaret. Met both John and Tim in the psychiatric hospital. Another victim of McLean.

Phil Hansen. A key person in Father Simon's testimony.

Bishop Paul. Vince's bishop.

Rev. Carol Mustafa. Prison chaplain.

Kaye. The woman jailed for causing the deaths of Marie's husband and two daughters.

Sally. Margaret's estranged grandmother.

Allan and Anna Jennings. Allan was the first person to read his witness statement at the sentencing of Father Justin McKean.

Father Justin McKean. Found guilty of the sexual abuse of eleven children.

Father Michael O'Shea. The priest who covered up McKean's abusive behavior.

FOREWORD

The author of the *Guilt Busters* is a pastor and counselor who has been my mentor, friend, and confidant for more than thirty years. He is a wise and experienced leader, a man of faith and humor, and one I describe as having a PhD in life. He himself experienced sexual abuse as a child and for more than fifty years has been involved in caring for those who have been impacted by the same experience.

While all the characters in this multidimensional story are fictional, every situation and circumstance that the author writes about is common to child sexual abuse survivors all over the world. It is written for both survivors and those who support them and explores the individual and relational consequences of having been groomed and abused by a pedophile.

Written in the shadow of the Australian Royal Commission into Institutional Response to Child Sexual Abuse, it provides understanding and insight that will affirm survivors and give them hope of recovery. It will equip counselors and others who support them and strengthen the resolve of those who seek to prevent child sexual abuse from occurring in the church context.

I believe that it achieves all these goals, and I warmly commend it to all those who have traveled this journey and to those who support and care for them.

—Roger Dingle, Dip. Civil Engineering; Dip Ed; B.Ed. (admin); Grad. Dip Arts (Soc Sc.); Grad. Dip. App. Psych.

PREFACE

The young man sat across the room from me, staring at the floor. He had made the appointment, he told me, to talk about his struggle with depression. As he had spoken about the seasons of dark despair that he had experienced for most of his life, he had begun to weep. The weeping had stopped now, but he could not lift his head as he repeated over and over, "I am ashamed. So ashamed." When I asked him if he was ashamed because he was depressed, he shook his head and mumbled, "No! I am depressed because I am ashamed." For the next hour, he spoke of the childhood sexual abuse he had suffered at the hands of a man he had loved and admired.

His story was painful for him to tell. In almost every one of the hundreds of sexual abuse stories I have heard over fifty years as a counselor, and in my own story as a survivor, the main elements were eerily similar. The pain of being deliberately and cynically groomed by the perpetrator, the skillful emotional manipulation that left him feeling guilty and ashamed, and the burden of the inevitable debilitating consequences that he lived with every day of his life were tragically evident in every word he spoke and every tear and every sigh that punctuated his story. The only time he lifted his head and looked me in the eyes was when he firmly declared that the whole sordid story of abuse was his fault—that he was irreparably broken and that he deserved to suffer.

This young Australian man was one of more than sixteen thousand people who contacted the Royal Commission on Institutional Response to Child Sexual Abuse. The commission found that of those who were abused in religious institutions, 61 percent were abused in Catholic institutions, 14.8 percent in Anglican institutions, and 7.2 percent in Salvation Army institutions. The remaining 17 percent of responders were abused in institutions managed by other Christian and religious organizations. The commission found that 41 percent of responders were abused while being in out-of-home care, 31 percent were students in schools, 14.6 percent were involved in religious activities, and 8 percent were in youth detention. As shocking as these statistics may seem, it is generally believed that 90 percent of all sexual abuse of children occurs in their own homes.

This book not only highlights the importance of keeping children safe, but it is about addressing the destructive consequences of child sexual abuse. All the people in this story are fictional, but every circumstance and situation that I describe has occurred thousands of times in every nation of the world. The shame that most survivors live with does not belong to them but to those who abused them and to a society that monumentally failed to protect them. My prayer is that survivors who read this book will find a pathway to healing and that the present and future generations will provide the most vulnerable members of our communities the protection that is their right.

ACKNOWLEDGMENTS

Many people have contributed to the writing of this book. Among them are the many mentors, friends, family members, church members, pastors, and counselors who—in too many ways to document here—have spoken into my life over eighty years. I am grateful to you all for being a rich source of encouragement, education, and inspiration, especially in the sixty years that I have had the privilege of serving God as a pastor and counselor, where I have traveled with hundreds of people who have allowed me to hear their stories and share both their pain and their joy. It is from you that I learned many of the ways that people's lives are affected by child sexual abuse, and it is because of your courage and resilience that I believe so strongly that, despite the indescribable suffering that child sexual abuse causes, there is hope of complete recovery.

I am grateful also to my wife of fifty-eight years, Julia, whose love, encouragement, and life has strengthened, inspired, and challenged me throughout our whole journey together. Her support in writing this book and the hours she has invested in editing the manuscript have been invaluable.

To my incredible children, grandchildren, and great-grandchildren, I dedicate this book, because not only are you a source of great joy and pride to me, but you represent both the present and future generations who must continue to confront the issues addressed in this book, so that your children grow up in loving and protective families and communities.

Finally, I want to thank God, my heavenly Father with whom I have enjoyed a rich relationship and from whom I have learned and received the blessing and healing of forgiveness.

1

LOST

The dreaded question:
How are you?

How to answer?
Long form

Shocked.
Horrified.
Unbalanced.
Desperate.
Splintered.
Anguished.
Fearful.
Broken.
Sick.
Apprehensive.
Aching.
Worried.
Angry.
Guilty.
Tired.
Sad.
Sad.
Sad.

Or short form,
Fine, thank you.

How do I answer that
sometimes pro forma,
sometimes loving,
but always dreaded question?

—Warren Cann, 2018 (with permission)

A Room in St. Kilda, Melbourne

Dear Dad,

I should have told you what I am about to tell you when I was twelve, fourteen, or even sixteen years old. I guess it was my fault that I didn't do that, but I was always afraid that you would only see the evil in me and punish me further for what happened. I was already being punished by a man I thought was my friend and, in my mind, by a God I thought was everybody's friend except mine.

It might surprise you to know that some of my antisocial behavior that you did not understand came out of my futile attempts to avoid continually hurting the people I loved. Dropping out of university rather than continuing and disappointing everyone when I failed to succeed. Avoiding conversations rather than becoming argumentative and aggressive. Choosing to avoid family occasions rather than disrupting them by my objectionable and sometimes drunken behavior. Spending time alone, drinking or playing games online, to avoid what I felt was your judgmental attitude toward my behavior. All these decisions did not seem like choices to me. These, and many others like them, seemed to be my only options.

You often wondered aloud why I did not ever speak to someone about "what was bothering me." I was never sure what you meant when you said that. I did not feel that I was being bothered by anything, or at least anything that I could talk to anybody about. I just felt worried, angry, tired, and sad. What I knew that no one else could know was that I was different from everybody else. I saw people who were obviously happy, when I knew happiness was an impossible dream for me. I saw people who believed they had an exciting future, while I lived with a painful past. I saw people secure in their relationships, while for me, the idea of being in a relationship filled me with crippling fear. I saw people happily recalling memories, while I was tormented night after night by unspeakably horrific nightmares.

The painful past I have lived with revolves around events that occurred when a man I trusted sexually molested me. He was a friend of yours and was always in our home. He was a friend of God's because he was our parish priest, and therefore he was my friend too. He was the friend of the other boys my age as well. He took us on camping trips, he coached us at basketball, and he led us through our confirmation classes. He invited us to visit him in his house, where we played video games, listened to music, and ate takeaway. He was knowledgeable, kind, fun loving, and generous. When he first touched me in what I now know as an inappropriate way, I accepted it as an expression of affection. But when one night in a tent, in a riverside camping ground, he raped me, I was frightened and confused. I was frightened because of the degree of force that he used and confused because when he finished, he became angry, telling me that God would punish me if I ever told anyone about what happened. So began a life of excruciating secrecy.

This secret world in which I now lived was made all the darker and foreboding by several perceptions that I had about myself. I was aware that I was a child and he was an adult with position and power. This perception led me to the unshakeable belief that I had committed a dreadful sin not only against God but against this "good man," and this clearly meant that I was evil. I also perceived that if anyone were to discover what I had done, I would be punished and rejected not only by my abuser and God but by everyone else. The third perception was perhaps the most painful. It was that at no time is it safe to trust myself or another person because relationships are dangerous, and friendships will always have a painful end.

As an adult, these perceptions have not only remained but have indeed intensified. Isolating myself from others, drinking to excess, viewing pornography, and visiting prostitutes has done nothing to alleviate my pain. I dread the nights and have become addicted to sleeping pills in a desperate attempt to sleep. Six weeks ago, I had had enough. I could bear my brokenness and my pain no longer, and in what I know now as the darkest moment in my entire life, I overdosed on sleeping pills. The man who lives next door found me and called for an ambulance. In the hospital, I was placed in the psychiatric ward and put in the care of a psychiatrist. On my discharge, I have been referred to a psychologist. Tomorrow will be my second session with her.

Dad, I am not sure why I am writing this letter since you died three years ago. Perhaps it is the nagging feeling that I have had since I left home, that if I had told you all this when it happened, things might have been better between us. I always felt distanced from, and somewhat disapproved of, by you. I am not sure why. Maybe it was a combination of your attitude toward me and my imagination. You certainly had good reason to disapprove of many of my behaviors, and when you punished me physically for them, I seemed to feel okay with that. I had crossed a line or broken a rule, and it was just and right that I should be punished. But later when I was too big to spank and you just withdrew from me in disgust, that was painful.

I wish now that I had spoken to you about these things long before I left home, and sometimes I rehearse the opening paragraphs of what I would have said. "Dad, I know I am a pain in the neck, and I don't blame you for getting mad at me. But have you ever stopped to think about why I am so angry and rebellious? Has it ever occurred to you that you and Mum were not the only significant adults in my life? Have you ever thought that some other significant person in my life might have wounded me so badly that I can no longer trust and love you the way I want to? Dad, this man encouraged me to believe that I was intelligent, clever, and witty in a way that you never did. He showed me physical affection in a way that you had been unable to do. I realize now that I craved these things from you, but you never gave them to me. I have sometimes wondered whether you were happy to abdicate the father role and delegate it to another. The man you hand-balled me too was a monster dressed in respectability, and when he had

had his way with me, he dropped me like a hot scone."
I never did get the courage to have that conversation,
but I wish now, with all my heart, that I had.

Dad, I do not know what the future holds or
even whether I have a future. I am unemployed, as
I have been for most of my life. The truth is that
I am unemployable. I am untrained in any field; I
have no work experience to put on my résumé and
no references. I live in one room. I have no friends.
I live alone, watch television alone, and drink alone.
Cutting myself off from the family many years ago
means that I do not see my sister, Claire. I do not even
know where she lives, but even if I did, it is unlikely
that she would want me to contact her now. Well,
Dad, that is my story.

John

When he had finished writing, he rose from his chair and stretched.
He crossed to the dressing table and glanced at the mirror. "Well,
John, my boy, tomorrow we continue a journey to who knows
where," he said to his reflection. He was startled when he realized
that he obviously had not shaved for many days. The rough half
beard and the puffy eyes, bloodshot from sleeplessness and too much
alcohol, made him look much older than his thirty-two years. Living
alone and eating only takeaway, mostly pizzas, had taken its toll on
his body. Hot pizza for dinner and cold pizza for breakfast and lunch
washed down with copious cups of strong black coffee and more
bottles of beer than he could remember was the reason a potbelly was
where his slim waist used to be. The forty cigarettes a day accounted
for his hacking cough and yellow teeth. Funny about that. He had
never smoked until his stint in hospital. It was Margaret that got him
started. Poor, sad, wafer-thin Margaret. *I wonder what her story was. I
wonder if she has ever written a letter to a dead father.*

His time in the hospital and meeting other patients like Margaret had been an eye-opener for him. He had sat one sunny afternoon in the garden of the psychiatric hospital, observing his fellow inmates. There was, of course, chain-smoking Margaret. She sat alone, seemingly unaware of anyone else, just staring into space. Then there was Alex. He was never still. He paced from the veranda to the front gate and back again, over and over, ceaselessly. He smoked his cigarette aggressively, as if it were some live thing that needed to be destroyed. And Jenny, an attractive but furtive figure, darting from one person to another, asking if she could get them something and then rushing off to wash her hands every few minutes. Then there was Barry. Big, obese Barry, who rarely moved from wherever he sat. He never stopped talking. It mattered little that no one was listening. He just kept talking. It was the kind of talking that didn't need a listener, because the thoughts and sentiments came from deep within his spirit and were meant to justify to himself the pain and confusion that completely enveloped him. And then there was Jim and his girlfriend, Amy. They had met each other at the hospital and had immediately fallen deeply in love with each other, as both had done countless times before with others they had met in similar circumstances. To John, it seemed that neither of them felt that they were alive unless they were attached, leechlike, to another living being. He had wondered about each of them. What had brought them there? What demons did they struggle with? Had they, like him, been abused, and had they ever reached a place in their lives when they knew that the pain they fled from would never, of its own volition, cease attacking them unless their lives were suddenly to end? In a way, he was comforted in the hospital by the realization that he was not alone in his mental illness. But there was another sense in which this place frightened him. It was as if he and the other patients were at the same time both alive and dead—alive to the unbearable suffering that each of their journeys had brought them, and dead to the hope that life would ever be any different.

His conversations with Margaret were the most surprising. While almost everybody else who bothered to engage him in conversation talked endlessly about his or her own life and pain, Margaret just listened, never saying a word, except occasionally asking a question. Margaret's questions were always perceptive. They weren't probing, inquisitional types of questions but rather gently encouraging questions that affirmed that she was listening deeply and that she understood. He had never met anyone like Margaret before. She never assumed that he was okay simply because he smiled, or that he was being rude when he wanted to be on his own. She responded kindly to who she knew him to be, quietly accepting the fact that there was a part of him that she might never know.

Each day, John had looked forward to his appointment with Dr. Jefferies. For the first time in his life, he felt that in Dr. Jeffries he had met a man, a doctor, who could not only envisage a life and a hope for him beyond what he had now but was willing to do everything he could to convince John of that too. They had, of course, talked about the depression that had brought John to the suicide attempt and had discussed the medication that would help John in the immediate future. But Dr. Jeffries had also spoken about the need for him to begin a journey with a psychologist and referred him to a Marie Forsythe. Two weeks ago, after his discharge from the hospital, he had had his first appointment, and tomorrow he would see her again.

2
ASHAMED

A Counseling Center in Carlton, Melbourne

Marie Forsythe was a pleasant-looking woman in her early forties. Her hair was brown, her eyes were emerald green, and her smile was warm and genuine. She had studied psychology at Melbourne University and for the past seven years had practiced counseling in the inner suburb of Carlton. When Dr. Jefferies referred him to her, he had said she was well qualified and very good at what she did. She welcomed John warmly, and they sat opposite each other with a small coffee table between them. It was a comfortable room, John thought. One wall was lined with books, and on another was a picture of Marie, with a tall, smiley man and two small girls, obviously twins. The windows looked out into a pleasant tree-filled garden that acted as a buffer between the building and the busy street. As she had done on his previous visit, she now waited for him to speak.

John took a deep breath and began. "Last week, you suggested that I should write down the most common painful emotions I was aware of. I sat one evening on the St. Kilda pier and wrote them down. I feel angry, fearful, ashamed, depressed, worthless, hopeless, broken, sick, apprehensive, and sad. I can sometimes mask some of those feelings with alcohol and sleeping pills, but whenever I am fully aware of who I am, the pain of those emotions drives away any hope of happiness and leaves behind only despair."

"I am not surprised, John, that you describe your emotions in the way that you have, but I am surprised by the omission of the one I imagined you would mention first. From what you told me last week, I had presumed that the overwhelming emotion you live with constantly is guilt."

"I did not include it, Marie, because I do not experience guilt as a feeling. My guilt is not a feeling; it is a fact. A blind man does not feel blind; he is blind. A left-handed woman does not feel left-handed; she is left-handed. Disabled people do not feel disabled; they are disabled. A person who has behaved in an immoral way does not feel guilty; they are guilty." As John spoke, his voice rose, his face reddened, and his head dropped. The final time he used the word *guilty*, he thumped both fists into his thighs. "Can't you see, Marie?" he continued loudly. "You psychologists might be able to help us change our feelings, but there are no therapies and no magic that can turn guilt into innocence. I have been pronounced guilty by a man of the cloth. I have been treated as guilty by the condemning eyes of the people I meet, and I affirm that condemnation every time I look at myself in the mirror."

Marie sat silently, sensing the depth of his pain and waiting for him to begin again. She glanced at the smiley man and the two girls on the wall and remembered how painful it had been for her to be defined by her loss. Ever since their deaths, she had felt an overwhelming sense of guilt. You know, the incessant questioning that always starts with "What if." *What if I had had the foresight to discourage my husband from driving home on that wet night? What if I had told him that even though I missed them greatly, they should not rush home?* Was it her selfish need of them that caused her husband to drive through the storm to be with her? She remembered the torment of those unanswerable questions. She remembered also the counselor who had encouraged her to see the guilt not as fact but as a feeling that materialized whenever she tried to make sense out of the tragedy that had robbed her of her family.

When John at last spoke, it was in a voice so soft that she had to lean forward to catch his words.

"I don't have anything else to say, except that I know the shame and the self-loathing I have felt ever since I was twelve years old is a direct consequence of the dreadful, irreversible wrong that I have committed. The man that abused me was a good man. He told me he loved me, and he always wanted to be near me so that I would always know what real love was. He said that he was sorry that my father did not love me as much as he did. I loved him too because he was fun loving and kind. I chose to let him touch me. I chose to sleep in the same sleeping bag. I chose to inflame his passions so that he raped me. I realize now that I corrupted him because of my own selfish neediness. No, Marie, I do not feel guilty. I am guilty."

Despite her awareness that she was in a therapeutic relationship with John, and the rules of her profession always demanded her responses must be nothing but those that one would expect from a therapist, Marie found herself fighting back the tears. They were not the tears of sympathy but tears of anger. She knew, as one who had sat often with both men and women who had been abused by a person who used position and power to victimize them, that John was not just a victim of sexual violence but also the victim of a vicious and soul-destroying lie. When John raised his head, Marie spoke gently. "John, you have made a judgment about yourself that is very severe and that you see as correct. Maybe it is correct. Maybe it is wrong. Why don't we test it out? Let's put twelve-year-old John in the witness box, and I will be the prosecutor, and you can be the jury, and we will test the evidence. I will cross-examine you, and you will give me the answers your twelve-year-old self would give. Will you give it a try?" John nodded his head, but the expression on his face and the visible tension in his body were clearly not in agreement.

Marie rose, stood behind the office desk, and comically placed her glasses close to the end of her nose. Then with an exaggerated "Ahem," she began. "John you are hereby charged this day with, at the age of twelve, having deliberately and knowingly corrupted your parish priest. How do you plead?" John looked bemused but went along with the charade.

"Guilty, Your Honor."

"How old were you, John, when your friendship with this man began?"

"About ten, Your Honor."

"How old was he?"

'I don't know. About forty I guess."

"What position of power or prestige did you hold at the time?"

"None of course. I was just a little kid."

"What position of power and prestige did this man hold?"

"He was my parish priest."

"So, this forty-something man who was powerful and respected chose a ten-year-old boy to be his best friend?"

"Yes! I guess so."

"And he told you that he loved you in a way that your father did not?"

"Yes!"

"How did he know that your father did not love you as much as he did?"

"He told me that if my father had loved me, he would want to spend time with me."

"And you believed him?"

"Yes! I did."

"So, when he touched you in what you now know to be an inappropriate way, you understood that he was being loving?"

"Yes!"

"Did this inappropriate touching happen more than once?"

"Yes! But I knew that he was a good man, so therefore it must be what men and boys do."

"Did he ask you to touch him?"

"Yes!"

"More than once?"

"Many times."

"And you did?"

"Yes! I hated it, but I did it."

"You knew it felt wrong, but because you trusted your abuser, you did what he asked?"

"Yes!"

"If you, as a twelve-year-old, thought that such sexual contact between an adult and a child was wrong, is it possible that your abuser, as an adult, knew that it was wrong also?"

"I did not think that at the time."

"What do you think now?"

"I know that sexual activity between an adult and a child is called pedophilia, and an adult that seeks and engages in such activity with a child is called a pedophile."

"And then he suggested, when you were twelve, that you go on a camping trip together?"

"Yes! I went on several such camps."

"And on this occasion, he suggested that you sleep with him in his sleeping bag?"

"Yes! It was a very cold night. We both had shorts and shirts on. I thought that it was okay."

"Would you today, as a grown man, make that same suggestion to a boy of twelve or to anybody other than a spouse?"

"No! I think that is wrong."

"And when he raped you, did that feel like he was being loving?"

"No! It hurt. He was very rough. I was terribly scared."

"What happened after he raped you?"

"He told me that I was not to tell anybody about what had happened between us, and if I did, God would punish me."

"Did you ask him why you would be punished?"

"Yes! He said that if I had not tempted him and raised his passions, it would never have happened."

"So, it was your fault?"

"Yes! He then got very angry and grabbed me by the shoulders and screamed that I had been tempting him for two years, and he had known that he should walk away, but he had not wanted to hurt me."

"Then what happened?"

"He told me that if I was to avoid God's judgment, I should leave the church and the basketball team and keep my mouth shut for the rest of my life."

"And you did that?"

"Yes! I did."

"How hard has it been keeping what happened to you a secret?"

"It wasn't hard not to tell anybody, if that is what you mean. But the knowledge of what happened to me was not a secret to me. The pain of his betrayal did not go away just because I didn't tell anybody. The condemnation that he pronounced on me has been repeated by an accusatory voice in my head every day of my life since."

Marie smiled at John. "In a court of law, after all the evidence has been gathered, both the defense and the prosecution address the jury. If I were to do that, based on what you have told me both last time we met and now, this would be my closing address.

"Ladies and gentlemen of the jury, this man, John, stands before you as a self-condemned man. In his childhood and throughout his teenage and adult years, he has accepted as a fact that he is guilty of corrupting his parish priest, even though the events he believes he was completely responsible for have seemingly ruined his own life. Let me remind you of the salient points of his evidence.

"One. When first befriended by this man, who I will refer to as his abuser, he was only ten years old. The attention given to him seemed to be the attention that he was craving from his own father. The abuser, in fact, according to John's clear recollection, compared his love for the boy with his father's inattention. I put it to you, ladies and gentlemen of the jury, that this friendship and attention was nothing more or less than grooming.

"Two. Young John trusted his abuser absolutely, and when on a number of occasions he touched John inappropriately, it did not raise any concerns for this trusting boy who had confidence in his abuser, because he was a priest.

"Three. When John's abuser suggested that the boy touch him inappropriately, John knew in his own mind this felt wrong, but that thought was canceled out by his love and respect for the abuser.

"Four. It is a well-attested fact that a person's guilt is often demonstrated by their behavior immediately after the event. After what was undoubtedly the preplanned rape of a twelve-year-old boy, the man deliberately set about establishing that the boy, the victim, John, was responsible.

"Ladies and gentlemen of the jury, you have been asked to decide whether or not, in your opinion, and beyond all possible doubt, the evidence before you proves that John is guilty of corrupting his parish priest. Now, you must retire and consider your verdict. Next week, you must express your opinion on whether this twelve-year-old boy was, and is, still guilty."

For a long time, John sat staring at the floor. He was stunned. In just a few minutes, Marie had demonstrated that no court of law would ever find him guilty of criminal behavior. As grateful as he was to Marie for this amazing revelation, all he wanted now was to be on his own. Marie seemed to instinctively understand this and said gently, "I think that is enough for today."

As they both rose from their chairs and John moved toward the door, Marie said, "John, I understand what you said about guilt being a fact and not a feeling. However, in a court of law, the accused is assumed innocent until he or she is proven guilty. The facts must be examined, as we today have examined what you have always regarded as fact. You see, there is false guilt as well as real guilt. False guilt is guilt that has been projected onto us by someone else. It happens all the time in everyday life, but when it happens in circumstances like yours, the consequences can be devastating and far-reaching. As you consider your verdict, you must seek to understand the type of guilt you have labored under in the past twenty years."

As John walked to the bus stop, he wondered, in light of his answers to Marie's questions, how he had ever come to the decision that the guilt he carried was his and not his abuser's. He had never heard about projected guilt before today, and for him, it was a revolutionary thought. He suddenly realized that he could never in a thousand years accuse a twelve-year-old boy of having for two years knowingly pursued a good man with the intention of doing him evil. It is possible, he thought, that a young child might make an unwise choice in choosing to love another person, but it could never and would never be an evil choice. And if he had been the exception to the rule and had been evil in his pursuit of the priest, why, when he had at last succeeded in corrupting him, had he felt so fearful, and when he had been rejected, why had he felt so wounded and alone? No, Marie was right. Whatever the projection of guilt meant, that was what his abuser had done to him. But why? Had McKean not told John many times that he loved him? That he would look after him always? Yes, but what if, John thought to himself, what if he had lied? For a twelve-year-old boy, it would have been unthinkable that a priest would have lied to him. But as a thirty-two-year-old man, John knew that pedophiles were people who lusted after children and would go to immense lengths to stalk and groom a child for the purpose of committing a sexual act against them. Marie was trying to show him that, to his abuser, he had been nothing but a target.

Hot tears rolled down his cheeks, and as he hurriedly wiped them away, he realized that they were happy-sad tears. They were tears that came from a dark, sad, and gloomy place, yet it was as if they were joyful tears because they pointed to a new way ahead. In the past, he had looked in the mirror and had seen a bad boy, but now he knew that boy was not bad, but rather he was a good boy who had been used by a bad man. Almost immediately, John knew he had an enormous decision to make. He could choose to feel sorry for himself, drown in self-pity, and live the rest of his life in the twilight of victim-making questions, which all started with the words "what if," or he could reject the notion that he was a victim and find his purpose and his motivation for living in his hatred of McKean.

Intuitively, he rejected the prospect of continuing to live in a twilight world where he was always half-drunk and half-sober, half-dead and half-alive, half-awake and half-asleep. Nor did he want to continue to hurt the people who loved him by projecting his self-hatred on to them. And yet his new realization that his abuser was the sole cause of his pain had unleashed in him an anger that burned hotter than any he had ever felt before. What would he do with his rage? Would he simply push it down inside so that it became as destructive as his self-hatred had been? Would he search until he found his abuser and exact some terrible revenge on him? Would he direct his anger at the church, or even at God himself?

John stopped walking. He could no longer see through his tears.

He sat on a nearby seat and buried his head in his hands. His body shook with the sobs that came from deep within his spirit. He was completely unaware of the people passing by who would have seen a grown man sobbing like a child. He was also unaware of the woman who stopped and then sat on the same seat and quietly waited for his crying to cease. After a long time, he blew his nose and began to wipe away his tears, and as he did so, the lady who shared his seat moved a little closer.

"I am sorry," John said.

"Don't be sorry," she replied. "I sat here because I did not want you to be alone when you stopped crying. I lost my ten-year-old daughter two years ago, and I am always grateful for people who have sat with me when I cry and then let me talk when the crying stops."

John stared at her. She was about his age. Her soft blond hair framed an attractive face. Her blue eyes were kind, and her voice gentle. In her, he saw his sister. The beautiful Claire who had always been so puzzled by his fits of rage as a teenager. Claire, who he had not seen since he had left home.

"I apologize for staring," he said, managing a smile, "but you remind me of my sister who I have not seen for sixteen years. Thank you for stopping. My name is John."

"My name is Helen. You don't have to tell me anything if you don't want to. I stopped because I just didn't want you to be alone when you were feeling so much pain."

John turned his body to face Helen. "Can I ask you, when you lost your little girl, did you feel angry as well as sad?"

"Not at first. My first feelings were of overwhelming grief. I felt like my heart had been torn from my body, and for many weeks, I felt that I was drowning in a sea of sorrow. Some months after my daughter died, I became aware of being angry at people close to me. I was angry at God and my husband and my little boy and my sister who was living with us. I was angry at the ambulance officers and the police and at mothers who had not lost a child. I was even angry at my daughter for dying. But most of all, I was angry at myself. I guess I knew her death was not the fault of those I was aiming my anger at. So then it turned inward. I became very depressed. I was convinced that my family would be better without me. It was a long time before I realized that my depression was not only the result of my internalized anger but also the terrible sense of guilt I carried. That is when I started to cry."

"That's it, Helen," John said. "I have just come from my counselor, and she has helped me to see that for more than twenty years, I have internalized anger and masked it with projected guilt, and it has robbed me of my life. As I started to see that I needed to find a better way to deal with my anger, I just began to cry. Now I feel empty. Abandoned! Like there is no hatred that will restore my life. No vengeance that will take away the anger. There is nobody that I could love enough or who could love me enough to make me feel unbroken. I don't want to go on deadening the pain with alcohol and sleeping pills only to wake up and find that it is still there."

"John, let me tell you about my guilt," Helen said quietly. "My daughter did not die in a hospital with an illness that could not be cured. She was strangled in the car of the man who abducted her after he had raped her numerous times. I can't imagine the terrible pain she suffered and how terribly afraid she must have been. For most of the past two years, I have been tortured by terrible dreams. In the dreams, she was screaming for me to help her. She needed me, and I wasn't there. Just like I wasn't there that day when she came out of school and waited for me to pick her up. You see, she would never have been abducted and raped and murdered if I had arrived at the school on time. It had to be my fault, and the guilt I carried till just recently was tearing me apart. It was like I was living in the dark and being tormented by a thousand demons. I could not imagine living for the rest of my life knowing I had been responsible for her death. I realize now the guilt was preventing me from grieving her loss.

"Everybody in my life scalded me for carrying the guilt for her death, but that didn't help. One day my pastor told me that if I believed that I was responsible for what happened, I better do something about it. I was surprised and asked her what she meant. She asked me would I have forgiven my husband if he had been the one who had been five minutes late to pick up my daughter. I realized that I would have, and she simply said that when I was ready to forgive myself, she would be happy to help if I wanted her to. Sometime later, I went to her and asked her to help me, and now I know that it is possible live with grief, but no one can survive under a mountain of guilt and anger."

John's eyes were so filled with tears he could barely see. They were not tears of grief as much as they were tears of hope. If this young mother could find relief for the terrible guilt that she had lived under, then maybe there was hope for him. As they both stood up, she smiled and asked, "Can I give you a hug?" and before he could answer, she did, and then turning, she walked quickly away.

ENLIGHTENED

Shock tells me
my world ended.
Pain tells me
I am broken.
Entitlement tells me
I am a victim.
Anxiety tells me
there is no hope.
Despair tells me
I will never know happiness again.

Lies.
All lies.

Deep longing tells me
I know what love is.
That is the truth.

—Warren Cann, 2018 (used by permission)

In a Room in St. Kilda

McKean,

I cannot bring myself to call you Father, because
now I have come to believe that you were in fact the

antitheses of all that a priest should be. I cannot even call you Mr. because that is a term of respect that belongs to men like my dad. I am not sure that I will even send this letter, but the writing of it will help me crystallize the thoughts that are torturing me. My counselor has challenged me to examine whether the guilt that I have assumed is mine for nearly twenty years is indeed mine or, in fact, is projected guilt that really belongs to you. She has triggered a myriad of questions that I myself must answer, so here I go.

Did you, as you often said, really love me and enjoy my company, or were you just grooming me for sex? For nearly twenty years, I have convinced myself that it was love you felt for me, not lust, but today I am daring to ask, Could I have been wrong? When I answer that question as a twelve-year-old boy, it is easy to answer it the way I want the truth to be. Why else would you want to spend time with me when my father seemingly ignored me? Why else would you choose me to be your camping partner? Why else were you so kind and gentle and understanding? Of course, you were concerned for a child you deemed to be neglected. You invested time and energy in me because you could see potential in me that others could not. I want everything you said about me to be true, because I ached then, and still do, to be loved and valued by an adult. Such affirmation and kindness came to me from nobody else.

However, I am no longer a twelve-year-old boy. I am a thirty-two year-old man, and although those kind and affirming things you said to me are still the only kind and affirming things that had ever been said to me until recently, I now have the courage to see them as lies.

If you did really love me, I could almost rationalize my being raped by you as "just one of those things." But as an adult, I cannot equate your brutality that night with love. I cannot see love in the angry face I see in my nightmares almost every night. I cannot hear love in the sneering, accusing voice I hear again and again in my head, threatening me with the wrath of God should I ever tell anyone about our secret. Nor can I imagine why someone who loved me would reject me from that night on and pour their affections out on another.

Not until today has it begun to dawn on me that I am in fact one of those thousands of men and women who are so-called survivors of institutional child sexual abuse. That is what it comes down to. I am a statistic. The one out of five boys who have been abused in their childhood. I am the recipient of those fine-sounding apologies delivered by politicians and bishops. I am the topic of all the talk shows on radio, debating whether I deserve to be compensated. I am represented on all those documentaries as a shattered shell of a man who will never recover, never be capable of sustaining a relationship, and never be able to make a worthwhile contribution to society.

Well, I want you to know, McKean, that I have decided that I will no longer carry your miserable guilt. I will no longer blame myself for an evil that you perpetuated. I will no longer fear the wrath of God for what has happened between us, for his wrath will be poured out on you, not me. With the help of my counselor, I have taken hold of the blame I have borne for twenty years and placed it where it really belongs. The shame I feel is no longer a result of your carefully and wickedly planned victimization of me. The shame I feel now is that for so much of my life, I have let the behaviors that flow from my painful emotions wound others who did not deserve to be hurt. But because that guilt is real and not projected, I hope, in time, I will be free of that shame also.

Hear me, McKean. I will no longer be defined by your intentionally destructive behavior toward me. I refuse to be a statistic or a topic for discussion by do-gooders. I am a person, and albeit years later than it should have been, I choose to be a healthy adult. As a child of ten, I needed protection. I needed the protection that a mother and a father should instinctively provide. I needed the protection of decent people who not only saw my vulnerability but also saw, with joy and anticipation, my innate value as a person. I no longer need protection, although I must admit that every step I take toward a healthy adulthood is formidable. In the safety of my own space and on a good day, I dream of unwrapping that potential and value through which maybe I might still bless the world in which I live.

However, now I am left with other questions that only you can answer. Why did you abuse me, and maybe other children like me? I cannot believe that you entered the priesthood with the intention of ruining the lives of children. I am sure you must have been originally driven by some altruistic desire to serve God and do good. Even now I remember some of your sermons. Did you believe what you preached? Is there a God? If there is, did He sanction what you did to me? Has He rejected you for abusing children? Has He rejected the children you have abused? Has He rejected me? Do you sleep well at night or do you hear the sobs of children whose innocence you have stolen?

Let me tell you what else you have stolen from me. The joy of being a child, my sense of humor, my trust for others, my ability to make and maintain close relationships, my faith in God, my self-respect, and my appreciation of my sexuality. I am determined, with the help of those who truly love me, and even with the help of God, who you demonized in my mind, to take all those things back.

When I was a child, my faith in God was important to me. The only truly exciting time of my life was preparing for, and presenting for, my first communion. Even as I sit here right now, I can remember some of the questions and answers in the confirmation study guide.

"Who is the Holy Spirit? The Holy Spirit is God, the Third person of the Trinity."

"When does the Holy Spirit come to us? He first comes at our baptism when we receive sanctifying grace, or God's very life within us."

"How does the Holy Spirit help us? The Spirit strengthens us and makes us holy. The Spirit enables us to love, spread and defend our faith."

And the last one that I can recall is "Who is a Christian? A Christian is a follower of Jesus Christ." What am I to do with this now, McKean? For twenty years, I have told myself that these things are true for you and all the good Catholics out there but not for me. I am evil because I seduced you. You told me that yourself. But now I know that is not true, so do I accept that the Holy Spirit came into my life at baptism? That God really does love me? That, far from going to hell, I am here to love and defend and spread the faith? Or is it all nonsense? Just stuff made up hundreds of years ago by a pope who was busy grooming and using boys for sex.

O God, if you exist, save me from this torment and confusion.

4
REAL OR UNREAL?

A Counseling Center in Carlton

Marie sat at her desk, her day diary open and her hands folded in front of her. Her head was bowed, and as was her custom before her day's work began, she prayed for each of the people she would see that day. As she finished, her eyes went to the smiley man and the two little girls in the photograph on her wall. It was almost two years ago today when a horrific accident on the Maroondah Highway stole them from her. She grieved for them every day, and the indescribable loneliness she felt was, and had been for two years, her painful new normal. Her greatest source of pain was the sense of having lost what she had always considered as her highest purpose. Ever since she was a teenager, she had longed for the day when she would be a mother, and when that day came, it was like the fulfillment of all she had been preparing for during her whole twenty-five years. The so-called parenting chores were always, without exception, a source of great joy to her, and as much as she enjoyed counseling others, nothing would give her as much pleasure as being a wife and mother.

John's arrival brought her back to the moment. As he entered the room, she was immediately struck not only by the fact that he was clean-shaven but because he uncharacteristically looked at her eyes when he greeted her.

"I need you to help me understand what is happening to me," he said as they settled into their chairs. "All my life, I have blamed myself for my abuse, and yet at the same time, I have viewed myself as a victim. I have felt like a victim, and I have viewed the world through the eyes of a victim. Now at last I have moved the blame for my abuse on to my abuser, acknowledging that he knowingly groomed me with the purpose of perpetrating sexual violence against me. I have ceased taking any responsibility for his actions, which means that he is the perpetrator and I am the victim. What I do not understand is that, for the first time in my life, I do not feel like a victim."

"Your parish priest, John, abused you by grooming and molesting you. By threatening and finally rejecting you, he also victimized you. He singled you out in order to subject you to cruel and unjust treatment. The most cruel and unjust part of his behavior is that he skillfully manipulated the way that you would forever see the abuse. The most painful and destructive aspect of the past twenty years for you has been the self-condemnation caused by him succeeding to convince you that you were responsible for what he did to you. Although you were his victim, when you now cease to wrongly accuse yourself, you cease to feel like a victim. You have confronted and exposed the lie. You have taken the first step toward assuming control over your life. You are no longer a victim, John. You are a survivor."

Marie paused as John, with his head bowed, began to weep. Twenty years of pain rose to the surface. His weeping escalated into body-shaking sobs. It was like the breeching of a dam wall. Marie had seen the outpouring of pain and grief like this before and indeed had been to this place often herself. She would sit with him till the sobbing ceased.

When John at last raised his head and looked at Marie, he smiled a sort of sad-happy smile and said softly, "Thank you. This is the second time I have wept like that. The first time was after our last session. What you did for me then is too wonderful for words. You gave me an instrument with which I could free myself from the shackles of projected guilt.

"I have come so far in the past few weeks. Releasing myself from the blame for the abuse has brought me unbelievable peace of mind. For these twenty years, I have believed that it was what he did to me that night that destroyed my life. Now I understand the real issue is that since that night, I have been trapped in a web of self-loathing, condemnation, secrecy, and lies. I thought I needed to reverse what happened to me in the past, knowing of course that was impossible. Now I know what I needed to do was to change how I have responded to what happened. In the course of a few weeks, I have gone, in my own mind, from being evil to normal and from being a victim to a survivor."

"There are a number of tasks that need to be performed on the way to total freedom, John, and you have completed the first one. That task was to make the sort of choices you need to make to free yourself from the shackles of irrational, projected guilt. You have done that, and I am very happy for you, but there are still a number of other tasks ahead."

"That's true, Marie, and that explains my tears just now. Those tears came from the realization of what, in my pain, I have done to members of my family. I was thinking of my mother who died six years ago. Officially she died of breast cancer, but I know, she also died of a broken heart. She had tried so hard to love and help me, but so great was my anger that after causing her much pain, I walked out of her life sixteen years ago and did not even return home for her funeral. It seems as I reflect on it that I may have had more hatred for her than I did for my abuser. Come to think of it, I hated her as much as I hated myself. I not only blamed myself for the abuse, but I also blamed my mother. She was the one who was supposed to protect me from danger, and she failed. She and Dad loved the priest and spoke so highly of him that I might have imagined that they were somehow implicit in his behaviors toward me.

"I feel ashamed as I remember the way I treated her. How I screamed at her when I was upset. How even as a sixteen-year-old, I would return home drunk late at night, and on more than one occasion, I struck her with my fist. I humiliated her in front of others. I put her down and ridiculed her. I stole from her, crashed her car while driving it without her permission, and actually paid a prostitute with her credit card. She was a good woman, Marie. She did not deserve to be treated like that. She would have had no idea where my anger was coming from. While I was lost in self-loathing and self-pity, she was also paying the price for my anger and pain."

Marie sensed that the real guilt John was feeling for the way he had treated his mother had the same power to destroy his life as the false guilt he had carried for so long. He could not shift this guilt as he had the false guilt. It was his to bear and to resolve.

"John," she said, "there are a number of steps that lead to being deeply healed from pain like yours. You have taken the first one by shifting the blame for your abuse to where it belongs. Now you are beginning to enter the second stage. Becoming aware of all the people you have hurt as a result of your anger is very painful but also helpful. You can no longer love your mother and father and build a healthy relationship with them, and you must grieve that loss. But you do have the opportunity to forgive yourself. The true meaning of forgiveness is to *put something away* or to *set something loose*. You will discover how to do that, and when you do, you will have taken another step toward true freedom."

Later that day, John sat on his favorite seat in the St. Kilda Botanical Gardens pondering what Marie had said about the guilt he was feeling in relation to his treatment of his mother. He had learned from her, that guilt, be it real or projected, became destructive when you internalized it. She was encouraging him to externalize it by speaking it out and by exploring ways by which he might be absolved from it. It occurred to him as he sat there that somewhere in Melbourne was a woman who had observed his relationship with his mum more closely than anyone else. Claire, his younger sister, would be in her late twenties by now and quite possibly married with children of her own. He recalled a dreadful night when, as a sixteen-year-old, he had arrived home late one night very drunk. A terrible row had erupted between him and his mother, and he had begun striking her. Claire, who was a slightly built girl in her early teens, had imposed herself between him and their mother, and when he had hurled her roughly aside, she had fallen, striking her head on the table as she went down. She had fallen to the floor unconscious, but he had not waited to check on her. He had simply run from the room. Thirty minutes later, an ambulance pulled up at the house, and through his bedroom window, he had watched the paramedics stretcher Claire to the waiting vehicle. His mother had climbed in beside her, and as they drove away, his father had followed them in his car. The very next day, he left the family home never to return. In the years since he last saw her, his guilt had been unrelenting. He had thought of her often but presumed that the anger she must have felt toward him would be far too intense for them ever to reconcile.

John felt a great grief rising from somewhere deep inside himself. Would it ever end? How many others had he hurt, maybe in some cases irreparably? Could he ever build bridges with the people he only now realized that he loved and needed? Would meeting Claire lead to a healing of the pain that was between them? Would she even want that, or would she be too angry or too afraid to even consider meeting him? Nevertheless, he needed to at least try. If he was going to take back what McKean had stolen from him and his family, reaching out to Claire was one of the things he had to do.

5

RECONCILED

The St. Kilda Botanical Gardens

He had asked her to meet him in the Botanical Gardens at St. Kilda. He would be waiting for her by the Alistair Clark Memorial Rose Garden. She had hesitated at first for two reasons. Her memories of being with her brother when she was ten and he was twelve were far from pleasant, and a meeting would be made more difficult because they had not seen or spoken to each other for sixteen years. Not since that awful night when she had been taken unconscious to the hospital. When she woke later in her hospital bed, she did not remember much of what had happened. What she could remember was their father's anger and their mother's tears. She had thought that her family had been irreparably damaged that night, but remarkably, her mother did not. Until the day she died, she had clung to the hope that he would one day return and the family would be healed.

She had attempted to contact him when her mother became ill but without success. In fact, until she had received his email last week, she was not even sure he knew that both their mum and dad had died. She had married since he had walked out of the family home, and he had not met her husband or their two boys. Through a common acquaintance, she had heard of his suicide attempt and, in fact, had gone to the Alfred Hospital to see him. He was in an induced coma at the time, and she was assured that he would recover, and from there he would be transferred to a psychiatric care facility.

As she approached the seat where John sat, he rose and greeted her. She was shocked to see that he moved like a man much older than his thirty-two years. He was overweight, his complexion was an unhealthy gray, and his hair was streaked with silver.

"It is good to see you, Claire," he said quietly. "It has been a long time, but that is my fault, not yours. I chose this spot in the gardens because I remember that you loved roses, and this is a magnificent display." She smiled shyly and sat beside him on the seat.

"So much has happened in the past sixteen years," she said. "As you know, Mum died five years ago, and Dad two years ago. I married about eight years after you left home. You would like Sam. And you have two nephews, John, who is six and is named after you, and Mark, who is four. We live in Elsternwick, not far from here."

John looked at her closely as she spoke. She hadn't changed much, and although this meeting must have been a little awkward for her, she was making a real effort to make it less so.

"Claire, I have asked you to meet me here not because I want anything from you but because I want to apologize for everything I have done to you. The very last time I saw you, you were lying unconscious on the floor because I shoved you. I was so angry and self-focused that I left you there and walked out of the room. I am so sorry for that and for leaving you to look after Mum and Dad when they were sick, and to manage their business affairs after they died. I have been an ungrateful, self-absorbed person, and I want you to know that I am sorry."

She smiled again as she said, "Yes, there have been lots of times when I have called you those things and a lot worse. I sure could have done with some help, especially when Mum and Dad died. I tried to find you, but it was like you did not want to be found. I guess I am hoping you have asked me to meet you here because you want things to be different from now on."

"I do" he said quickly, "but that decision might be yours rather than mine."

For the next two hours, John shared his story with Claire. He told her about his relationship with the priest, who she remembered well. He told her about the grooming and the rape. He described how he had taken the responsibility for the abuse. He recalled the wasted years living in a murky haze of self-hatred, fortified by alcohol and drugs. He brought her up to date by telling her about Marie and how she had helped him to understand that he could deal with both the projected guilt that had ruined his life and the real guilt that he carried in relation to those he had hurt. He took responsibility for the way he had behaved toward her and their parents and especially their mother. He shared his grief that he had missed the opportunity to reconcile with his parents before they died, and he asked her forgiveness for treating her the way he had. Claire listened, her eyes wet with tears. She was deeply shocked by his revelation of his childhood abuse and expressed the anger she now felt toward the abuser, whom she also had trusted.

When he had finished, she told him that not only did she forgive him but that she was certain that their dad and mum had forgiven him also. They had never given up hope that he would come back. Their dad never changed his will in which John was an equal beneficiary with her. They had harbored no bitterness toward him, only deep sadness and concern.

"John, let me tell you about Mum. She was a woman with a deep and quiet faith. She prayed for you and me all the time. You were not alone in hurting Mum. You do not know this, but when I was eighteen, I found that I was pregnant. My boyfriend at the time, who was the father of the baby, left me for someone else, and I took myself off for an abortion. Mum was devastated, but even though she would have advised me against the abortion if she had had the chance, she supported me through my recovery. I went through a time of deep depression and dropped out of university. I was racked with guilt about the abortion and shattered by the rejection I had felt by the father of the child. Mum loved and nursed me through it all, and I will be eternally grateful to her for that.

"Not long before Mum became ill, she spoke to me about you. She told me that you were a dream of a kid until about halfway through your first year at secondary school. She said that the change in your behavior was so dramatic that she had gone to the principal to speak to him about it, thinking that something must have been happening at school. It never crossed her mind that you had been abused by the priest. Your abusive and rebellious behavior puzzled and wounded her, and she sought help and advice from the very same priest. He told her that your behavior at basketball had also deteriorated, and that is when he had banished you from that and other church activities that you had been involved in up till that time.

"When she became ill, all she wanted was to see you, so I contacted anybody who might have known where you were living but could not find you. She made me promise her on her deathbed that when I found you, I would tell you how much she loved you and how sorry she was that she could not have been a better mother to you."

John took a deep breath. "Claire, I am not sure what I am asking for when I ask for forgiveness. What is it? Why does forgiving someone who hurt you seem so hard and so unfair? And why is it so hard to forgive myself for the pain I have inflicted on you and our parents and others?"

"Let's walk around the garden," Claire suggested. As they came near the lake, Claire began quietly. "Following my abortion, I became extremely ill. Mother visited me in hospital. I was embarrassed and ashamed, and I could not look at her. She quietly reminded me of a game I used to play when I was little. I would close my eyes, and because I could not see her, I thought that I was invisible to her. Mum used to giggle and pretend that she could not find me. Then I would open my eyes, and she would say, 'I see you,' and pounce on me. She remembered how delighted I was to be found. In the hospital, she told me that I could pretend that I was invisible, but the truth was that she could not only see me but that I was the same Claire that she had always loved and of whom she had always been proud. I asked her how she could possibly love me after what I had done, and her answer changed my life. She said that she had a father who not only loved her unconditionally, but when she did something that was hurtful to him, he forgave her straightaway. She said she had learned how to love and how to forgive others from the way he loved and forgave her. I was astounded at first because I knew that her father had abandoned his family when our mother was just a baby. Then I realized that because she had never had an earthly father, she had always thought of God as her father. She told me there had been a time when she had done something that had permanently damaged a relationship with a very good friend. I asked her how she got around to forgiving herself for that. She said that her 'father' told her that she could not go on hating someone that he loved so much. So, she gave up hating herself and got on with her life. John, Mum forgave you in the same way that God forgave her, and when she died, she died at peace with herself."

They walked together for a long time in that beautiful garden. Fittingly, the only witnesses to their heartfelt reunion were the breathtakingly magnificent roses. When Claire was leaving, they arranged to meet the following Sunday, at the Fawkner Crematorium and Lawn Cemetery, where they would visit their parents' graves. After that, they would go to McDonald's and catch up with Sam and the boys.

As John walked alone through the gardens, he paused again at the lake. In the middle of the lake was a fountain, and near it was the statue of a man with an umbrella. *Rain Man* had stood there since 2005, holding an umbrella to protect himself from the spray that came from the nearby fountain. John saw himself in the *Rain Man*. Instead of standing a safe distance from the fountain, he sought protection under a fragile umbrella. He, too, for twenty years had stood too close to a fountain spewing out the foul waters of self-condemnation, but instead of distancing himself from it, he had raised an umbrella of self-protection that had failed to keep him safe. Well, he thought to himself, those days were behind him now.

6
BROTHERS

A Parish Rectory in Melbourne

Father Vince Patrick, a big man in his midthirties, was dark complexioned and had kindly brown eyes. His black hair was neatly cut, and he was clean-shaven. He had welcomed John warmly and had motioned him to a comfortable armchair in his study. The middle-aged woman who had opened the door to him placed a jug of water and two glasses on the low coffee table that sat between them, then left the room.

"Thank you, Father, for agreeing to see me. I am not a member of your flock, and I am sure that you are terribly busy. I have recently reconciled with my sister, Claire, who I had not seen for sixteen years, and her husband, Sam, whom I had never met. They are active members of your church, as my mother also had been till her death some years ago. In a conversation at MacDonald's last weekend, Sam and Claire encouraged me to speak to you. Hence my phone call last Tuesday."

"I remember your mother well, John. She was a great lady. She once told me that she had a son that she no longer saw, but she felt assured that one day you would be reconciled with her and the family again."

"I am afraid, Father, that I have left it too late."

"Oh, I don't know, John. It all depends on whether you believe in life after death. Your mum sure did, and she was certain that if she did not see you again in this life, she would see you in the next."

"When I was a child, I attended this church with my mother and was involved with the basketball team. I was also confirmed and partook of my first communion here." John paused, took a deep breath, and then plunged into his story. He told Father Vince about his relationship with the priest, whom he named as Justin McKean, who had become his abuser. He told him of the guilt and shame he had carried ever since. He told him about his behavior as a child and the damage he had inflicted on his family. He told him about dropping out of school and of his dependence on alcohol and sleeping pills. He told him of his suicide attempt, his admission to a psychiatric ward, and the help he had received from both the psychiatrist at the hospital and the psychologist to whom he had been referred. Finally, he spoke of how having ceased to blame himself for the abuse, he was now possessed by a burning, unrelenting anger toward the man who had violated his trust, robbed him of his innocence, plunged him into a world of self-condemnation, took away his future, and tore apart his family.

Vince sat through John's story, his head slightly bowed, and his folded hands held up near his chin. His eyes for most of the time that John had spoken were filled with tears. He did not reply straightaway. John sensed that he was stunned and simply sat and waited. When he did speak, his voice was low and his words halting.

"Thank you, John, for being open and transparent with me. I have over the years heard stories like the one you have just told, and each time, I am starkly reminded of the terrible consequences of such an abuse of trust and position. I do not know what to say to you. Of course, I am terribly sorry, but that does not seem enough. You have been made to see yourself as the guilty one in this series of events, and that is unbelievably cruel. Your anger is a very appropriate reaction and is clearly justified. I am very relieved that you are receiving the help you need, and that already it has led to your reconciliation with your sister and her family. However, there is also an issue of justice here, and by telling your story to me, I have become part of the equation. The man you have named as your abuser is still practicing as a priest in country Victoria. Other stories that I have heard that have involved sexual abuse in this parish have caused me to have my suspicions about him, but in those cases, the abuser was never identified. Now that you have spoken up, I suspect that at least three other men your age will also identify him as their abuser. I will of course give you all the support I can, but I am also happy to leave the task of counseling you to your psychologist. I clearly have two tasks to undertake. First, I must take this matter to the bishop, who in turn will advise the priest that he has been named as an abuser. Second, although I am not legally bound to do so, I believe that I should directly report this matter to the police."

The two men sat in silence. John eventually spoke hesitatingly.

"Vince, I am a bit taken aback by your response. I guess I expected you to rise to the defense of the man I have accused. I expected you would have demanded that I present you with watertight evidence. I even thought that you might simply offer excuses for your colleague, or even worse, reaffirm my guilt. Why have you simply taken what I have told you at face value?" Vince did not reply but slowly rose from his chair and crossed to the filing cabinet. He withdrew a letter and came back to his chair.

"What I am about to show you, John, must stay between us for the time being. This is a letter to my father, written by my parish priest in 1995, when I was twelve years old. The young transitional deacon referred to in this letter is the same man you today have accused of abusing you. Here, read it." John chose to read the letter aloud but almost immediately regretted his decision.

> Dear Mr. Patrick. I have considered the matter you brought to my attention last week, and here is my response. The man you accused of sexually molesting your son, Vince, is a trainee priest who is fulfilling his training requirement in the role of a transitional deacon. As you are aware, this is necessary before he can ultimately be ordained as a priest of the church. If, as your son alleges, this man acted toward him in an inappropriate way, it is most unfortunate. Given the

immaturity and inexperience of the man concerned, and the general unreliability of a child's evidence, I am treating this matter as minor. However, because you and your family are loyal members of the church, I have decided forthwith to transfer the person concerned to another parish. I trust that this meets with your approval.

Yours Sincerely,
Father Michael O'Shea (Parish Priest)

P.S. As your spiritual adviser, I urge you to instruct your son Vincent as to the seriousness of accusing someone without evidence to support the accusation.

John folded the letter. "I had no idea, Vince, honest. Man! I am sorry."

"It's okay, John. You could not have possibly known. Nobody knows. Father McKean had groomed me for some months just like he groomed you a couple of years later. Then one night, he molested me in his house. Obviously, I told my father the very night it happened, and he went the next day to the parish priest. When he received the letter you have just read, he was angrier than I had ever seen him before. He confronted Father O'Shea the following Sunday and caused a very nasty and embarrassing scene. He refused to allow any of us in the family to go back to that church again. Dad wanted to go to the police straightaway, but I begged him not to, and my mother took my side. Instead, he made a written record of what I had told him, his interview with the parish priest, and the original letter from which this copy was taken. The papers are with his solicitor with strict instructions that I am the only one who can access them. Guilt affects different people in different ways. You became angry and self-destructive, and I became obsessed with the need to do penance and make amends. I came to believe that the only way of dealing with my terrible sense of shame was to become a priest. At first, my father opposed the idea, but finally he came on board. Although Mum and I continued to attend a church in another suburb, Dad never went to church again. Shortly after my abuse, his business failed, and he was bankrupted. He was so full of despair that he eventually took his own life. My mother found him dead one morning. He had hung himself in our garage. Despite struggling with obsessive-compulsive disorder, I threw myself into my studies, was finally ordained, and more latterly gained my Master of Divinity degree. Not once in my life have I felt led by God to serve him, but rather, I have been driven by guilt to placate him. I have always felt that God could not forgive me for being a stumbling block to a godly priest unless I lived a life of penance."

"That must have been very difficult, Vince," John said quietly, "but from my position, I see that today, in this very meeting, you have not placated God; you have served him by listening to me and telling me your story. I do not know whether I believe there is a God or not, but I sure am glad that you do. You have some work to do when it comes to being driven by guilt, but your faith has kept you soft and gentle and enabled you to give help to others when in fact nobody has ever helped you."

"I am so glad you have told me your story, John," Vince said finally. "It has been very difficult for me to listen to it but thank you for what you have just said. While you have been telling your story, I have realized something for the very first time. I now know that, of course, God has forgiven me, but I have never forgiven myself."

Vince sat without speaking for an exceptionally long time, but both men felt comfortable in the silence as they reflected on what this conversation meant for them both. John was greatly relieved and deeply comforted by the lack of judgment and defensiveness that came from Vince. It was like, after all this time, someone with real authority was affirming what in the past few weeks he had been discovering. Vince, on the other hand, was aglow with hope. He knew John was right in refusing to carry the blame for his abuse any longer, but in affirming that, he was saying the same about himself. Right now, it seemed to Vince that John was a messenger of hope, sent after decades of fervent prayer. The message was that he no longer needed to be driven by guilt but that he was free to make whatever choices were right and good.

"Tomorrow, John," Vince finally said, "I will go to the bishop, and with your permission, I will tell him your story. I will also, for the first time, tell him my story. I will ask him to act, by standing the priest in question down and by reporting the matter to the police. He will undoubtedly want time to think about his decision, but if he ultimately refuses, you and I will go and see the police together. Whichever way it goes, this is going to be a terrible bun fight. It will be very public. Some church members will be truly angry at us. Everybody will have their own opinion about why the matter has taken so long to come out and why it has come out now. I may lose my position as parish priest. You may be pestered by the media. Our abuser has enormously powerful contacts in the church, and they may well see us as the enemy." When John and Vince parted later that afternoon, each felt that he had gained a brother.

7

CONFESSION

In John's Room in St. Kilda

"Parish Priest Surrenders to Local Police," screamed the headline of a Melbourne daily newspaper.

> Father Justin McKean, a parish priest in a rural diocese in Victoria, handed himself into the police yesterday. It is believed that Father McKean had been given an ultimatum by his bishop two weeks ago after complaints were made by two Melbourne men who claimed that they were sexually abused by McKean in two different parishes when they were both twelve years old. It is also understood that McKean, who is cooperating fully with the police, has given them the names of nine other people, who he admits to having abused over a period of ten years while they were children in his care. He has been charged with multiple cases of rape and other charges relating to the sexual abuse of minors. He has been remanded in custody until his court appearance next month. The diocesan officials declined to comment other than to affirm that each of the persons identified by McKean would be offered counseling assistance and be eligible to receive a financial settlement from the Catholic Church.

The twenty-four-hour news channel carried the same story. There was footage of McKean being ushered from a police car into the police station, where, according to the young reporter, it was expected that charges would be laid. In fact, she reported breathlessly that unnamed sources had confirmed that as many as thirty charges may be laid against the fifty-five-year-old priest. The bishop, who declined an interview on camera, stated in a written statement that Justin McKean would plead guilty to having abused children, both as a trainee priest and indeed throughout the first ten of his twenty-five years as a priest in parishes in both the Melbourne and Victorian rural dioceses. He would neither confirm nor deny that one of the original complainants was, all these years later, himself a priest.

John laid down the paper and called Vince. They were taken by surprise by the action McKean had taken and were relieved both for themselves and the other survivors. There would be no bun fight. McKean would, on his guilty plea, be given a jail sentence; each of the survivors would be interviewed by lawyers for the diocese, and financial settlements would be offered. If any of the survivors wished to take the route of civil action against either McKean or the diocese, that would be an individual and private matter.

That morning, John chose to go to the Botanical Gardens and on his arrival sat on his favorite seat by the lake. Things had moved quickly and positively, but he was now conscious of a deeply concerning emotional struggle. With Marie's help, he had been able to free himself of the burden of self-imposed guilt. What he was left with was a mountain of red-hot anger. He was angry not only because of his own suffering but because of Vince's suffering and the suffering of the nine others that McKean had victimized. He had asked himself this morning as he had read the paper whether the punishment that McKean would receive was enough retribution for the suffering he had caused. Would the embarrassment of having his personal life exposed to the public and the pain of a long prison sentence be just punishment when compared with the almost immeasurable damage he had caused his victims? But, then, what would be an appropriate punishment? he asked himself. And how would he or any of the other survivors resolve their anger if a satisfactory punishment were never administered?

On impulse, he rang his sister. Claire had read the newspaper report, and when she heard John's voice, she wept. She wept from the relief she felt that what could have been a frightful public issue had been resolved so easily. But she wept too for John. She wept for his grief over the lost and damaged years of his life. She wept for a boy who had longed for love and seemed now to be so utterly alone in his pain. She wept for what she had only just understood to be the apparently insatiable anger that now inhabited his soul. John wept too. He was suddenly deeply aware that another feeling so unlike any that he had ever experienced was, despite his rage, establishing itself deep in his psyche. It was an inner strength that seemed to come from several different directions all at once. It came from the realization that, for the first time, he was known and loved for all that he was. It came from not being alone in the anger and confusion he felt, and it came too from the knowledge that his pain was shared with others. It might be imagined that a telephone conversation that consisted of no words, just the sounds of two people weeping, would have been a very unsatisfactory interaction. In fact, the opposite was true. The two people engaged in this tearful exchange, having had until recently been separated for sixteen years, and having now been reunited, were experiencing the wonder of being known and being loved. So wondrous in fact had been their reconciliation that words were inadequate and weeping together was richly appropriate. There was something about the poignancy of this moment that left John with the distinct impression that he would not always be a prisoner of anger and hatred.

As he walked back to his room, John realized that he was deep into what Marie had called the second stage of his healing process. Having understood that McKean was fully responsible for everything in relation to his abuse, he had begun to see that the blame for his own angry and aggressive behavior, which had so wounded his mother and father and sister, could not be laid on McKean. He himself was solely responsible for his choice to punish his mother for what McKean had done to him. They were *his* angry words that struck her in the heart. It was *his* lack of self-control that led to him destroying his mother's belongings, stealing her credit card, and striking her with his fist. It was *his* choice to walk out on his family, never to go back even when he knew that first his mother and then his father was dying. It was not McKean who had made the choice to drown his pain in copious amounts of alcohol, or to avoid meaningful relationships, or to deal with his sense of sexual inadequacy by using prostitutes. It was not McKean who decided to take an overdose of pills because he could not bear the pain anymore. As difficult as it was for him to own these choices, he knew that logic demanded that he did.

When he reached his room, he sat down at the small desk, opened a pad, and took up a pen and began to write. "It is an amazing twist of logic that for so long I have blamed myself for the way McKean treated me but excused myself for the way I treated my family. Even now when I am able to blame McKean for the abuse, the temptation is to conclude that he is therefore responsible, twenty years later, for my choice to wound the people who love me. It is not true. What is true is that the perpetrator is always responsible for the event, but the survivor is responsible for his or her response to the event. I can choose to destroy others by projecting my internalized anger on to them, or I can choose not to. My dilemma is, however, if I choose not to punish others out of the anger I feel toward McKean, and if I choose not to internalize my anger, what do I do with it?"

With his pen still poised over the writing pad, he reflected again on his meeting with Claire. If his parents and his sister knew that his behavior was what had wounded them, would they not be justified in being angry at him? Would they not be within their rights to want him to suffer for the hurt that he caused them? Was he not guilty of criminal behavior toward his mother and Claire? Could not his mother have had him arrested for theft and with assault causing grievous bodily harm? The answer to all those questions was yes, of course. But had not Claire said, "I am sure that Mum had forgiven you long before she died, and she desperately wanted you to know that"? What did that mean? Did it mean that his mother had decided that what he had done did not matter anymore? It didn't matter that the little boy she had carried, given birth to, and nurtured was now the monster who abused her, rejected her, and hated her, seemingly without cause? Had she concluded that the pain she had felt when he rejected her didn't really hurt? No, of course it mattered. And, of course it hurt. Did Claire mean that his parents had just explained it away as something that some kids do and that they just needed to see it for what it was? No, they had neither trivialized nor condoned any of his behavior. Claire said that her mother had forgiven him in the same way that God had forgiven her. Was that possible for her because she was religious? What would it take for him to forgive himself for what he had done to his mother and father and Claire? He started to write again. "If my mother could die in peace after so much pain and grief had been inflicted on her by others, I need to know how."

8
SIMON

An Aged Care Facility, Melbourne

The old man sat looking out his bedroom window. Two nurses were busy making his bed. The younger one said teasingly, "Now, Father Simon, here you are expecting visitors, and you have not combed your hair since you got out of bed."

"No, Sister," he said with a mischievous twinkle in his eye, "I haven't. If I look too well cared for, it might discourage them from kidnapping me and getting me out of this place."

"Well, we wouldn't want that, would we, you old rascal." She laughed and straightened the tie he always insisted on wearing.

"Will it be family that are visiting you then?"

"No, just two young men full of respect for a retired priest of the church, unlike you impudent young women who insist on heartlessly teasing a defenseless old man." They all laughed. He was happy here. The staff were like family, and although his visitors were few, he was always greatly heartened when young people came seeking advice and counsel.

An hour later, Matron knocked softly on his door and announced, "Father Vince and his friend have arrived." They were ushered into the room, and he stood slowly and painfully to greet them. Vince, who had spent many wonderful hours with this sunny old man, introduced him to John, and they sat down, bathed in the sunlight that streamed through the window.

Vince had visited the old priest a week ago to prepare him for this visit. He had told him about the circumstances that had drawn him and John together. He had told him also how John had helped him understand the importance of refusing to carry the blame for his abuse as a child and move it to where it belonged. This he had done, and the release he experienced had been indescribable. It was during that visit that Vince had told Simon for the first time that he had always felt that rather than having been called into the ministry by God, he had entered the ministry to placate a God who he believed was angry with him. The old priest's reply had amazed him.

"Vince, whether one's initial call to ministry can be substantiated or not is of little importance. What is important is whether one's call has been demonstrated by the humility of his spirit, the quality of his servanthood, and his faithfulness to God. I have been a priest for a very long time, and rarely have I met a man whose humility, gentleness, love, and obedience to God have been such an authentic reflection of the Christ you follow, as I have found you to be. However, I think that it is an appropriate time for me to share with you one nagging concern I have had for you ever since we first met. I see that beneath and behind the Christlikeness that is clearly visible for all to see is a dark, and up till now indefinable, shadow. I now understand what it is. The guilt that you have carried was not only false, but it served to mask the anger you feel toward your abuser. It is a credit to you that you have not allowed it to negatively affect your ministry, but now that you no longer live under the cover of the guilt and shame, it will. Vince, to be able to continue to be the man of humility, gentleness, and love that you have always been, you must find a way to resolve your anger."

After a few minutes of reflection, Vince had responded. "Yes, Simon, you are right. That indefinable shadow that you can see has been there all my life. Now, since making the choice to resolve my guilt issue, I understand the shadow expresses itself in three painful and very tangible ways. The first way is depression. I have never told you before, because I guess I was ashamed, but I frequently experience the deepest, darkest depressions you can imagine. These times most often come upon me at the end of a day's work. They are characterized by a complete loss of energy, a feeling of absolute exhaustion, and an attitude of self-loathing and shame. If I were not on medication, I am sure that these depressions would completely incapacitate me for much longer periods of time. However, after a long sleep, often assisted by sleeping pills, I can propel myself into another day. My thinking till now is that the depression is linked to my having done wrong. I suspect that the truth is that the depression is the result of having internalized what you call red-hot anger.

"The second way that the shadow you can see expresses itself is in a complete lack of self-esteem. All my life, when mixing with others, I have felt this overwhelming sense of inferiority. It does not matter whether the other person is an adult or a child, in less than a minute after being in their presence, I find myself feeling inferior to them. I know that it is irrational, but at the time, to me, the feeling of inferiority seems to be appropriate. The third way in which this shadow expresses itself is in a lack of trust. I have no close friends, and logic tells me that it is not because people don't like me and don't want to be my friends. I feel unsafe when I get too close to another and am afraid they will get to know who I really am."

Father Simon had listened intently, and now he sat in silence, waiting for Vince to continue.

"Both my new friend, John, and I find ourselves in the same place. We have both taken a giant step forward by refusing to carry false guilt any longer, but in doing so, we have left ourselves without a way to deal with our anger."

"There is a way, Vince. Bring your friend John with you next week, and we will explore it together."

John had jumped at the opportunity to meet with Simon, and so now they all sat together in his sunbathed room. Simon spoke first.

"I believe that both of you have come to explore with me a way of resolving your anger toward your abuser. You have already discovered that seeing him jailed deals with the justice issue, but it does not help with your anger. Of all the life tasks you will ever undertake, resolving justifiable anger will be one of the most essential and the most difficult. In a very real sense, anger is vengeance orientated. It is a drive to make the wrongdoer suffer at your hands for what he has done to you. So, he, being sent to prison by the authorities, does not necessarily help. Anger demands you inflict the punishment yourself. The problem is the anger has been internalized, and instead of it forcing your abuser to pay the appropriate price for his actions against you, it has exacted a huge punishment on yourselves, and in some cases, others also. The depression, the self-hatred, and the physical exhaustion are all symptoms of misdirected anger. Now, for the first time, both of you have directed your anger in the right direction, but so deep is the suffering that his abuse has caused, no price that you or the justice system demands will be enough. No punishment devised by man is enough to atone for the fear and sense of loss that this man created in you when you were young boys. Nor is any punishment able to restore the innocence that he stole from you or lift the projected guilt and shame that he caused you to carry. All you have been left with is rage that can never be placated.

"If this rage cannot be placated, it will ultimately destroy you, but it does not have to end that way. You both know that there is a verse in the Bible that says, 'Forgive one another then, as God through Christ has forgiven you.' Let me explain to you what I think that means. Jesus Christ was God, who became a man, to provide the answer to the very problem you are currently faced with. He lived for thirty-three years and in that time did not sin against God or society or individuals. At the end of his life, he allowed himself to be falsely accused of breaking Jewish law and was tortured and ultimately nailed to a cross by Roman soldiers. Among his last words before he died were 'Father, forgive them, for they do not know what they are doing.' Because Jesus, an innocent man, bore the most horrendous suffering and ultimately death, for every man, woman, and child who lived and would ever live in the future, God has chosen to offer forgiveness to those who seek it, on the basis that the price for all sin has been paid once and for all.

"What that means, my young friends, is that for as long as you carry and internalize your anger, you are paying a price for your abuser's sin. A price that has already been paid by Jesus, long ago. Forgiving your abuser does not in any way absolve him of his crime. Christ's sacrifice means that you now have a reason to cease being angry. You have no need to seek some punishment for him that will be equal to his crime against you. Let me say it again: that price has been paid. Your forgiveness of him is not about absolving him from what he has done to you; instead, it is about setting yourself free at last.

"Letting go of your anger is exceedingly difficult. It feels like your abuser is getting off too lightly. It might even seem like, having suffered for all these years, you are being victimized all over again by being asked to forgive him. But listen carefully. This forgiveness is not for his benefit but for yours. It will not take away his guilt, but it will liberate you from his influence over your lives. If you allow yourself to be imprisoned by the very human compulsion for revenge, he will have the power to control and even destroy you. But as soon as you give up that right, on the basis that the price for his criminal actions against you has already been paid by Jesus, you are free to get on with your life. You do not have to act on what I have said. You may not be ready to do that yet. It will always be your choice. But in all my years, I have not found a better way to deal with victim anger than to believe that the retribution I am demanding has already been made. If you want to cease being a victim, projecting your anger on yourself and others, this, I believe, is the only way."

John listened to every word the old priest spoke and knew that he was speaking about the forgiveness that his mother had practiced. Quietly, he said, "Father, my mother was a woman of great faith, and the way of forgiveness that you have described is the way she understood forgiveness also. As a child, I too was a believer, but I am no longer. I was taught that the priest was a reflector of who God is, and that belief has been shattered." Simon reached out and laid his hand over John's hand.

"Then, my son, you were taught incorrectly. Jesus, not the priest, is a reflector of who God is. Priests will fail to live up to your expectations. Jesus will always connect you to the Father. Now I am tired, and you must go. God bless you both."

His eyes had already closed by the time they had risen from their chairs. They quietly and very thoughtfully left his room. After signing themselves out of the aged care facility, they walked without speaking to Vince's car. "Why don't we get a coffee. I know just the place," Vince had said. As he drove the short distance to the café, they were both lost in thought. The coffee was served to them in a comfortable outdoor dining area at the back of the little shop.

It was John who spoke first. "I feel like we have been in the presence of an ancient prophet or guru. What an experience! I have never in my life met a man like him or heard anyone say the things that he said. He was right, you know. He affirmed that it was important that, as a survivor, I do not carry the guilt that really belongs to my abuser. But he made it clear that on its own, that transition is not enough to set me free. I certainly know that I have not been feeling free since I decided that I was not responsible for what happened when I was a child. I have felt relieved, but instead of feeling free, I have been feeling like a prisoner who has simply been moved from one prison to another. For twenty years, I have lived in a prison of guilt, and McKean has been my jailer, and now I am in a prison of anger, and he is still my jailer. Dealing with guilt was in a sense easier than dealing with anger, because it was unreal, projected guilt, not real guilt. But the anger is real and is completely justified. I have all the right in the world to be angry and to demand that he suffers as I have suffered. I was impressed that Father Simon did not say that it was wrong to be angry. But I also realize that I have no right to demand that others pay for my anger. My father, my mother, Claire, all of them have paid dearly for what I have believed to be justifiable anger."

Vince nodded. "That's right. What I understood he was saying was because the anger I feel can only be satisfied when I have made my abuser suffer as I have suffered, then I will be in this prison forever, unless I find another way. And I was thinking that that sounded unfair to me. For the first time in my life, I have begun to understand that McKean was a monster who targeted and then groomed me with the sole purpose of gratifying his own twisted sexual urges. I have a right to be angry. He deserves to suffer. He molested boys who trusted him."

"I agree with that," John said. "But, Vince, you are a priest. What do you make of what Simon said about Jesus having already paid the price for McKean's sin?"

"He was talking about what we refer to in theology as *substitutionary atonement*," Vince replied. "It simply means that Jesus voluntarily died as a substitute for others, or, if you like, instead of them. This teaching is based on biblical statements such as 'Christ suffered for our sins, once, for all time, He never sinned, but he died for sinners to bring you safely home to God.' A less technical way of understanding this is that Jesus, through his death, did for us that which we can never do for ourselves. We Catholics celebrate this every time we celebrate the Eucharist, and Protestants do the same when they celebrate Communion, or what some call the Breaking of Bread. What Simon was saying was that by continuing in our anger, we are demanding a price that has already been paid by Jesus and accepted by God as being enough. My problem with that right now is if that applies to us, it equally applies to McKean. I can't cope right now with the possibility that McKean thinks that God has totally forgiven him for ruining the lives of so many boys."

That night as he tossed in troubled sleep, John dreamt a disturbing dream. He saw his mother kneeling in a radiant beam of light. She held her hands in an attitude of prayer, and she was speaking, John presumed, to God. She was clearly upset. "If only I could set him free," she cried bitterly. "If only I could somehow take his anger on myself, somehow feel his rage and carry his pain. I bore him in my body, I gave him life, I nurtured him as a babe. When he hurt himself, I comforted him; when he had a fever, I cooled his tongue with ice water; and now that anger seeks to destroy him, I cannot prevent it, even though I am in the presence of a powerful and loving God." In his dream, John watched his mother weeping.

Then he heard a voice in his dream saying, "My daughter, do you remember when this son of yours broke your heart with his rebellious behavior? Do you remember when at sixteen years of age, he struck you with his fist? Do you remember how he left your home, never to return in your earthly lifetime?"

"Yes, I remember," his mother said through her tears.

"Then how was it that you were able to forgive him?"

"I remembered the nail prints in the hands of your son, and the crown of thorns on his head, and the spear wound in his side, and I knew that if you had paid such a price for his sin against me, then I had no option but to set him free."

"My daughter, one day your son will know that too, but the choice will always be one that he must make."

9
DISCLOSURE

A Catholic Church in Melbourne

Father Vince was presiding over the early-morning mass in the Church of St. Francis. Some two hundred or so members and a handful of visitors made up the congregation on this Sunday. Sitting near the back was an unusually neatly attired John, and beside him was his sister, Claire, and her husband, Sam. The set scripture had been read, and Vince stepped to the small lectern to deliver his usual homily.

"Many of you will already know that a former priest of this parish has handed himself into the police after being confronted by our bishop about claims made by two men who, as boys of twelve, had been sexually abused by him. He has confessed to having abused eleven children over a period of ten years and is cooperating with the police in their inquiries. What you do not know is that I was one of the men who brought my complaint to the bishop. Let me make two things clear at this point. The first is that I was not sexually abused in this parish, and the second is that I cannot speak warmly enough of the prompt and appropriate action taken by our good and godly bishop. My intention this morning is not to comment on the matters that are being investigated but rather to make a frank confession.

"For more than twenty years, I have lived with the belief that I was responsible for the abuse that occurred to me and that God was angry with me. I entered the priesthood believing my only hope of relief from the terrible guilt that I carried was to placate God by being totally submissive. In my ten years as a priest, I have listened to hundreds of confessions, many of course in this parish, and have offered to each one the grace of absolution. I have always envisaged people going away feeling forgiven. But my overwhelming guilt remained. I am theologically trained. I have a master of divinity degree, and I can very ably preach a sermon on the substitutionary atonement of Jesus, but I could not bring myself to believe that God could forgive me for what I have always believed to be my sin. Sometimes I fasted for days at a time, denying myself all the normal comforts of eating good food, watching television, and even sleeping on a comfortable bed. I have wept literally buckets of penitential tears, but nothing took the soul-eroding guilt away.

"Recently, a newly acquired friend who had not been to church since he was twelve years old told me that the most destructive aspect of my sexual abuse was not what physically happened, as bad as that may have been, but the fact that the abuser had further victimized me by convincing me that I was responsible for my own experience of sexual abuse. That, coupled with his threats of God's judgment and punishment, succeeded in blinding my spirit from ever being able to recognize where the blame really belonged. My friend showed me how incomprehensible it was that I, a small boy of twelve, could have understood I was being groomed for sex. He helped me understand how unsuspecting and unguarded I, as a boy of twelve, would have been on that night when my abuser used me to satisfy his own sexual needs. You will have to make your own decision whether I had the right to inform on a fellow priest, but I am here today to say that I will no longer carry the guilt he projected on to me. Nor will I continue in the ministry just to placate an angry God. I will instead serve a God who loves me with an everlasting love and who has the power to heal broken lives.

"In April 2013, the first public hearing of the Royal Commission into Institutional Response to the Sexual Abuse of Children was held. On that occasion, it was announced that a definition of child sexual abuse had been formulated for the guidance of the commission. That definition was that child sexual abuse includes any act that exposes a child to, or involves a child in, sexual processes beyond his or her understanding, or contrary to accepted community standards. Sexually abusive behaviors could also include voyeurism, exhibitionism, and exposing the child to, or involving the child in, pornography. It includes child grooming, which refers to actions deliberately undertaken with the aim of befriending and establishing an emotional connection with the child, to lower the child's inhibitions in preparation for sexual activity with the child.

"During the days between that first public session and when the final report was handed down, I understand the commission received 42,041 calls and 25,964 letters and emails. They conducted 8,013 private interviews and made 2,575 referrals to authorities, including the police. I share this with you today because I want you to know that this is not just about me, or Father McKean, or this church. This is about thousands of children who have been failed by the very institutions that are meant to keep them safe.

"We would agree, I am sure, that the sexual abuse of a child is a terrible crime and among the greatest of personal violations. It is a crime committed against the most vulnerable in our community and is a fundamental breach of the trust that children are entitled to place in adults. It is one of the most traumatic and potentially damaging of human experiences and can have lifelong, adverse consequences.

"Tens of thousands of children have been sexually abused in many Australian institutions and thousands more in their own homes. Whatever the actual number, it is a national tragedy, perpetrated over generations within many of our most trusted public institutions and in the most trusted institution of all, the family.

"The Royal Commission into Institutional Response to the Sexual Abuse of Children found sexual abuse of children has occurred in almost every type of institution where children reside or attend for educational, recreational, sporting, religious, or cultural activities. Some institutions have had multiple abusers who sexually abused multiple children. The reality is that society's major institutions have seriously failed to protect the children in its care, and in many cases, these failings have been extended to an inadequate response to the abused person. It is difficult to comprehend the collective influence on the whole community of such a widespread and life-shattering abuse on the children of our nation.

"People of the Church of St. Francis, if we do not rise up and demand justice for the abused and thorough accountability for all those who have the responsibility of caring for children, we are no better than the very worst of the institutions investigated by the Royal Commission.

"As I close, I would like to extend an invitation to anyone who was also abused, either in this parish or another, to come and see me or go directly to our bishop. We cannot reverse what happened to you, but we may be able to assist you on your road to recovery."

There was a deathly silence in the church, and then suddenly some whispering and movement from the rear of the building. The congregation watched, mouths wide open, as a frail old man was wheeled to the front of the church. The man who pushed the wheelchair parked it beside Vince and walked back to the front pew.

"Most of you know me, but for those who do not, my name is Father Simon," he said in a firm voice, and then turning to face Vince, he went on. "Please, Father, may I say a few words?" Vince nodded, too stunned to speak. Never had someone interrupted a service he was conducting. The old man spoke again.

"Vince has not asked me to speak today, but I have decided to do so because I know, from over sixty years of experience as a priest, that many of you will feel confused by what you have heard. Many of you will know the former priest in question and will remember him as a good man who in a myriad of ways served you and your families. He would have baptized many of you, overseen your confirmations, officiated at your weddings, and conducted the funeral services of your loved ones and friends. In fact, when you read of him in the paper last week, you probably did not believe the accusations that had been made. There may be others here this morning who themselves, or perhaps a family member, was abused by the same or another priest, and you will be relieved that justice is being done. Father McKean has not been charged because of accusations that have been made against him but rather as a result of the confessions of guilt that he himself has made. It is further proof that when we leave unholy hungers unattended, they will ultimately reveal themselves in unholy, and in this case criminal, behaviors. The thing that is most at risk today as a result of these revelations is the unity we enjoy as a congregation. Father Vince is right in bringing the matter into the open, but revelations like these have the potential of causing division and conflict. At times like this, we need to understand that the universal church is the Body of Christ and that his prayer was that we would all be one as he and God the Father are one.

"There are four reasons for us to weep tears of great sorrow today. We must weep tears for the children, now all adults, who were groomed and assaulted by a priest of this church. They have not only experienced the pain and indignity of being abused, but their ability to trust the church and its priests has been in some cases permanently destroyed. We must weep for our own parish priest, Father Vince, whose great courage has placed him in danger of being abused again by the church he loves. We must weep for the church, not the great universal gathering of Christ followers that Jesus calls his church but the visible institutional church, with all its frailties and foibles. Finally, we must weep for ourselves, for as members of a local congregation in which children have been abused, we cannot pretend that it has nothing to do with us. I am ninety-two years old, and I have never in my lifetime witnessed such fine spiritual leadership as we have seen today. Father Vince has done three things this morning that every Catholic person should be eternally thankful for. First, he has been transparent and open with us. Rarely does a congregation experience such transparency from the pulpit. Secondly, he has demonstrated that the appropriate response to disclosures of abuse is compassion for the abused, and thirdly, he has made it possible for abused members of this congregation to come forward, knowing that they will be supported by their parish priest.

"Father Vince, do I have your permission to lead the congregation in prayer for you today?" Vince nodded, and Simon beckoned him to come close to his chair. Vince knelt by his chair, and in a voice so empowered that he had no need of a microphone, Simon prayed.

"Our Father in heaven, today we come to pray for Father Vince. Heal the wounds that have been criminally inflicted on him in his boyhood. Confirm the truth that he was not in any way responsible for what happened to him. Fill him with the Holy Spirit so that as he ministers to us, we will know the unlimited grace and unconditional love of the Father. And, Father, bless your body, the universal church and congregations like us who seek to love and follow you with our whole heart. In Jesus's name, amen."

Vince was at the door as the congregation left that morning, and as might be expected, there were some awkward moments. Brian French, a well-known businessman and generous donor to the church, muttered as he shook hands with Vince, "Terrible shame about McKean. In my opinion, he was the best priest we have ever had here. Pity he wasn't here to defend himself."

Mrs. Handley was heard to say loudly to nobody in particular, "It is those psychiatrists, you know. When they don't know what's wrong with a nutcase, they blame it on sexual abuse."

"You wouldn't call Father Vince a nutcase," chimed in Mrs. Symonds.

"Well, Mrs. Symonds, Sunday Mass is no place for a priest to air his dirty linen, if you ask me." And with a haughty shrug of her shoulders, Mrs. Handley went home.

As John, Claire, and Sam reached Vince, they all hugged him warmly.

"Wow," exclaimed John, "I wasn't expecting that this morning."

"I wasn't expecting you here this morning either, but thanks for coming. I do expect a call from my bishop, however, summoning me to an audience. I will let you know how it goes."

As Vince was leaving the church later that morning, the choir mistress, Jenny Purnell, was waiting for him on the steps of the Church of St. Francis.

"My son Tim was one of the boys McKean abused, Father. I guess he may want to speak to you after what you said this morning. He does not come to church anymore. I would imagine his very first question for you would be how could you have possibly become a priest after what that man did to you."

"You tell your son, Jenny, that I would be happy to see him."

"I will, Father, and thank you very much for what you said this morning."

10
RESPONSIBILITY

The Counseling Room, Brunswick

Marie listened intently as John brought her up to date. He told her about his reconciliation with Claire, his relationship with Vince, his visit to Father Simon, and Vince's homily on Sunday. She could sense a new energy in him as he spoke, and she was thankful that each of those events were having a positive impact on him. When he had finished, she asked him where he thought he was up to in his own emotional and psychological journey.

"Well, Marie, you told me that the first step was to free myself from the projected guilt that up till now has defined who I am. I have done that, and what's more, Vince says that I have helped him do that as well. My reconciliation with Claire helped me understand how deeply I had hurt others by my angry behaviors, and now I know that I need to accept responsibility for those behaviors. That was a very painful thing for me to do, but having blamed McKean for the abuse, logic demanded that I needed to accept responsibility for my own actions. However, this admission led to a great sense of guilt and shame, particularly for the way I had treated Dad and Mum. Claire said that she knew for a fact that Mum had forgiven me, and Claire has also. My issue, Marie, is how do I forgive myself. Father Simon spoke to me about God's forgiveness and said that it was possible for God to forgive me because Christ's sacrifice was an acceptable offering for my sins. I guess that sounds great, but it sounds too easy, you know, like too convenient. What do you think?"

Marie smiled. "Well, it certainly is biblical teaching, and the concept of Jesus dying for our sins is the core value of both Protestant and Catholic Churches. I am sure that your friend Father Simon would say that such forgiveness sounds too easy only to someone who does not understand what that forgiveness cost God. However, there is something else that you should remember. When you understood that your guilt about the abuse was destroying you, you were able to direct it to where it really belonged. If it is also true that real guilt has the potential of destroying your life, and someone was to say, 'Give it to me, John,' would that not be a welcome invitation? The alternative decision is to continue to punish yourself for something your mum, your sister, and God have all forgiven you for. Does it make sense for you to punish someone who the people you love the most have already pardoned, regardless of how they have come to that? Ceasing to punish yourself is in fact forgiving yourself."

"Marie, I know what you are saying is right, and it is indeed helpful to see guilt and internalized anger as being related to both self-punishment and the punishment of others. Until recently, I had not understood that. I had seen my self-harm as a response to my abuse, not as self-punishment. I know that I cannot change an historical event, but I can choose to nurture and love who I am. I suppose you are going to tell me that this is the next step."

Marie waited for a moment and then said, "Yes, but I prefer to think of it as the next task. First deal with projected guilt and then deal with real guilt. However, clever theories don't help. What helps is when you start to put feet on statements like, 'I need to nurture myself.' It would be helpful if you could identify the ways that you habitually punish yourself and what you might need to do to turn it into a nurturing behavior."

"I think I know what you mean," John said thoughtfully. "Like when I put myself down or when I withdraw into drunken isolation or when I choose to see myself as unlovable. You are saying that if I were to see them as punishing behaviors, I could choose to turn them into nurturing ones."

"Okay, John, how might you turn drinking in isolation into a nurturing behavior?"

"Perhaps by inviting someone to share a social drink and a conversation with me!"

"What would prevent you from doing that?"

"Maybe believing that nobody would want to be with me when I am feeling morose, which is probably the truth."

"But what if it is the isolation in the first place that makes you feel that way?"

"Yes, that is probably true, especially because I have been unemployed all these years. By the way, Sam's employer has offered me an interview for a job in his large construction business. They need an assistant quantities surveyor, and he is looking for a student or someone who would be willing to work three days per week and attend TAFE the rest of the week, with the purpose of attaining the qualifications to become a quantities surveyor. I have done one year of an engineering degree at university, and if he thinks I could handle the job, he would employ me. I feel anxious about it because I have never had a real job, but I know that working and being financially independent is another one of those choices I now need to make."

"John, despite the fact that there are still some important steps for you to take before you are at the point where your experience of abuse no longer has a negative impact on your life, there is something very important and special happening for you."

"What do you think that is, Marie?"

"Your intimacy circle has gone from zilch to several in the past few weeks."

"What do you mean by intimacy circle?"

"A group of people who are interacting with you in a positive and supportive manner and with whom you are increasingly sharing your life."

"That is true, Marie. That circle now includes Claire, Sam, and the kids. And Vince and Simon. But why is that so important?"

"It is generally accepted in the psychological community that men and women who have a number of people in their intimacy circle are usually healthier than those who are relationally isolated. The more emotionally wounded we become, the more likely it is that our intimacy circle will shrink. The consequence of a shrunken or nonexistent intimacy circle is that we become more and more self-absorbed, and this generally promotes emotional and psychological ill health."

"So, you are saying that even without deliberately focusing on this as an issue, the result of reaching out to others has significant benefits?"

"That is exactly what I am saying. The challenge now, John, is to remember that life is also about them and not just about you."

John smiled ruefully. "Yes, that is the challenge," he said.

"When you first came to me, you hated yourself to the point of suicide. Is that a fair comment?"

"Yes, certainly."

"How would you describe yourself now?"

"Well, I don't blame myself for the abuse, so to a great extent, that hatred of myself has gone. I do not any longer have suicidal thoughts, but I have two new situations in my life that I may or may not be able to resolve."

"What are they?"

"My sense of guilt over how I treated my family, and to some extent myself, and the hate and anger I feel toward McKean."

"Which of those do you want to tackle first?"

"I suppose if I am going to feel good about myself, then I need to forgive myself. Vince said that I need to love myself if I am going to truly be able to love others. On the other hand, my anger tells me that I will never be free until I get even with McKean for what he did to me."

"I have a question for you to think about this week, John."

"Yeah, what is it?"

"What will you do with your anger after you get even?"

11
TIM

A Café in St. Kilda

John stared at Vince in disbelief. They had met for a coffee the day after Vince had been to see the bishop. "You can't be serious, man."

"I am afraid so, John. The bishop was sympathetic toward me and said that he understood my felt need to say what I did, but in the eyes of many in the parish, I had displayed disloyalty to the priesthood and the church. His office had more than twenty phone calls on Monday alone, and the majority of those were from people who believed that I had abused my role and were asking that the bishop take some appropriate action against me. He said that given the significant number of people who were threatening to leave the church and go elsewhere if I remained the parish priest, he had little option other than to look for a parish that would accept me. In the meantime, he has suggested that I take my long service, which is due to me. I have agreed to do that and to go without a fuss, on one condition. My condition is that I am given the opportunity to address a congregational meeting, chaired by the bishop, to which all members would be invited. I also asked that I be allowed to invite at least two other men, who were boys that McKean abused, to speak. The bishop agreed, providing McKean's sentencing has occurred first."

"Of course, he would agree. Don't you see, Vince? He knows that this is not just about McKean but it is also about a church that just moves abusive priests from one parish to another. He is going to use that meeting to whitewash the church and make it look squeaky clean."

"Maybe you are right, John, but the church has already been looking pretty shabby through the Royal Commission. It's far too late to pretend that the church managed this stuff well in the past, and at least this diocese, under the present bishop, has signed on to the compensation agreement. I did make it quite clear to the bishop that I would not be accepting a transfer. If this congregation does not want me, I will resign from the ministry."

"Wow, that's heavy. By the way, who are you going to ask to speak at the congregational meeting?"

"I would like you to be one of them. After all, it was your story that moved me not only to seek justice but to challenge a church that would protect its reputation rather than protect and love its people. The other one is a guy called Tim. I have invited him to join us today so that you can meet him. Just let me warn you, John. You think you are angry about your abuse. You have not seen angry until you meet Tim."

Twenty minutes later, they were joined by a tall, painfully thin young man whose appearance shocked John. He was almost two meters in height and had long black hair and a straggly beard. There was a prominent scar on the right side of his head, and his mouth was crooked in a way that made John wonder whether he had had a stroke. He walked slowly with a pronounced limp, and as he slumped into the chair, he grunted rather than spoke a greeting. He glanced first at Vince and then stared at John.

"Are you a priest?" he snarled.

"No, Tim, I'm not. From what Vince has told me, we are here because we have all been abused by a priest."

"He was no priest." Tim's words were slurred. "He was a stinking monster. As far as I can see, in the church there are only stinking monsters and spineless bishops who let them ruin kids' lives. Vince here shouldn't be a priest. He is one of us, not one of them. I am not surprised that those hoity-toity pew warmers at St. Francis want to sack him. He is too good for them. He should be one of those social workers, not a priest."

Vince rose from his chair. "Tim, you have told me your story, but I was wondering whether you would be happy to tell John. Then maybe if he has the time, he will tell you his story. I must leave you because, surprised as you both may be, priests don't only work on Sundays."

As Vince left the café, Tim said, "There goes a real good bloke. He came to see me the other day out of the blue. I was drinking in my shed, and I saw he was a priest, and I just started screaming at him. I used language that even I am ashamed of having used. He just stood there. I was cursing him and cursing God and cursing the church, and he didn't say a word. Then suddenly, I felt overcome with sadness. And believe it or not, I started to cry like a baby. And do you know what he did? He came and sat beside me and put his arm round my shoulder. Then I realized he was crying too. A priest, crying with me! He kept saying, 'I'm really sorry, Tim,' repeatedly, and I knew he meant it. Then after a while, he said, 'I am not only crying for you, Tim, but for myself also. That monster did it to me too.'" Tim paused and took a deep breath.

"I was born in St. Kilda thirty-two years ago. My birth mother worked the streets for a living and had a drug habit, so I ended up first in a baby's home and then in an orphanage for toddlers. That is where I think the abuse began. I can't remember any specifics, but I have nightmares every night about being abused, and in some of those nightmares, I am just a little guy. Since listening to the things that have come out of the Royal Commission, I have decided that something traumatic happened to me then. It was while I was there that Mr. and Mrs. Purnell fostered me. They are magnificent people, and they were very loving and understanding. I loved them very much, and for the first time in my life, I was happy. Mum Purnell led the kids' choir then, and of course I was part of that. I soon became known as the boy with the velvet tonsils. You wouldn't believe it now, John, but I got to sing all the solo parts. Then McKean came to our parish. The rest is history. He befriended me, and one night when I was only eleven, he molested me. I told my mum and dad that night, and Mum got all hysterical and said that I should be severely punished for telling such terrible lies. I don't blame her for that. It must have been an awful shock. But my dad believed it all right. Two nights later, McKean was found in that laneway next to the church. He was unconscious and had a smashed nose and a broken jaw. No one was ever arrested for the vicious attack, but just before he died two years ago, my father told me he did it. He said, 'I wanted to kill him, son, and I am sorry now that I didn't.'"

"You're not kidding! Wow! You know, Tim, that might be an incredibly significant key to something I haven't been able to understand."

"What do you mean, John?"

"I couldn't work out why McKean abused eleven people in ten years, and then suddenly he stops. I can see now. It was the beating your dad gave him. Your dad might have done it for you, but maybe without realizing it, he saved lots of other kids. Sorry, mate, I didn't mean to interrupt your story. Please go on."

"All my life, I have been a loner. At school, I was bullied, first because I was a foster kid and then later because I was in the choir. I was an overly sensitive kid, and I cried a lot, especially during the time I was being abused by McKean. It was like I was in pain all the time. I remember one day at school, standing alone and saying to myself, 'I will not feel pain ever again,' and it was like something snapped in my head. That's the last thing I remember about my childhood. My mother and my psychiatrist have told me that that day I had some sort of complete mental collapse. A teacher found me wandering in the schoolyard, and apparently I did not know my name or where I was. I never went to school again. I refused to leave home, and my bedroom became my whole world and reading books my only pleasure.

"At the age of fifteen, I began to hear voices in my head. Sometimes the voice I would hear would accuse me of being a demon. On other occasions, the voice would tell me to kill myself. I began to suffer hallucinations and engage in bizarre behavior and self-harm. My condition was diagnosed as schizophrenia, and in the last fifteen years, I have spent probably more than seven years in a hospital. I have had many electroconvulsive therapy treatments and am constantly on antipsychotic medication. Three years ago, before my father died, I broke into his gun cabinet and stole the pistol he used at his gun club. I shot myself in the head, and unfortunately, I survived. Every day since then has been a nightmare, until Vince came by my house last week. When he told me that McKean had handed himself into the police and that he, you, and I might get the opportunity to give victim impact statements, it was like the sun shone for the first time. I only hope that he goes to jail for an awfully long time."

John reached across the table and laid his hand on Tim's arm.

"Thanks, Tim, for telling me a little bit of your story. I am sorry that you have suffered so much, but I want you to know that you are not alone now. At present, there are the three of us, and we are fairly sure that other men will come out of the woodwork before long."

"Not only men, John, but women as well."

"What do you mean?"

"The last time I was in the psyche ward, I met a girl called Margaret. She was a great listener, so I told her that McKean had abused me as a kid, and she just started bawling. She got sort of hysterical, and the nurses took her away and gave her an injection."

"Was this Margaret a really thin girl with blonde hair?"

"Yes, why do you ask?"

"I know her."

"Well, anyway, before I left, she told me that McKean had abused her as well."

"Wow! I never guessed. I told her a bit about myself, but I never mentioned McKean. I knew something traumatic had happened to her. My goodness, I can't believe it."

John and Tim sat in silence for a long while, and then John said, "Tim, the good news, as Vince probably told you, is that McKean has made a full confession and has given police the names of everyone that he abused in those ten years. The list starts with Vince and ends with you. He also has described in detail the nature of each grooming and sexual assault offense. The police will speak with all of us to confirm that what McKean has confessed to, he really did. There is also a possibility that we might get the opportunity of sharing publicly at church in defense of Vince's decision to inform the congregation, last Sunday, concerning his own abuse."

"That's good, John. Thanks for listening to me. Have you got the time to tell me your story?" For the next hour, the two men sat together, and when they parted, they did so with the promise that they would meet again soon.

12
JUSTICE

A Solicitor's Office. Collins Street, Melbourne.

When James Churchill entered the conference room in his legal firm's plush office, ten heads turned, and ten pairs of eyes watched him walk to the end of a long table where an empty chair awaited him. He was a short, stout man of about fifty years of age. His ginger hair was streaked with gray, and his green eyes swept the room, his steady gaze stopping for the briefest moment on each face. His expression showed little of what he may have been thinking or feeling as he settled in his chair, unpacking his briefcase and placing a file in front of himself on the table. He made a mental note that one person had not yet arrived.

Each of the people in that conference room that morning had received a personal letter from James's legal firm, saying that they were acting in the interests of all those who had been named by the accused, Justin McKean, as having been people that he had knowingly and intentionally abused while they were children, trusted to his care by their parents. The details he had given, relating to the specifics of the grooming and sexual behavior perpetrated by him against them, were included in each letter. Each of them was invited to make a personal appointment with James to discuss the contents of the document, and in the past few weeks, each of them had done so. Justin McKean had entered a guilty plea and was to be sentenced sixty days from today, and the judge was offering each of the survivors an opportunity to make a victim impact statement.

James welcomed them and explained that making a victim impact statement was optional, and under no circumstances whatsoever would any of them be put under pressure to do so. The purpose of this meeting was for him to explain what a victim impact statement was, what it should and should not include, and how it would be presented. Should one, or some, or all of them decide to make a victim impact statement, then members of his staff would be available to give them whatever assistance they might need. All the costs relating to the advice and assistance would be covered by the Catholic Church.

James began his explanation by telling the group that in Victoria, victims of crime can participate in the sentencing hearing through the provision of a victim impact statement, which they could read themselves or have someone else read. The victim impact statement is a sworn statement to the court, made by statutory declaration that outlines the impact of the offense on the victim and any injury or loss suffered by the victim as a direct result of the offense. The impact statement must be written and filed with the court at least thirty days before the sentence hearing, and copies would be made available to the offender and the prosecution.

Using a PowerPoint presentation on a screen that they could all see, he made the following points:

1. Your statement must describe in detail the particulars of the impact of the offense on you and detail any physical or psychological injury or damage that you have sustained. Any documented evidence that relates to physical or psychiatric illness, or any other disability, would be useful to include.
2. You may include in your victim impact statement any photographs, drawings, or poems and other material that relates to the impact of the offense on you.
3. Should you include any material that does not causally relate to the impact of the offense on you, the court will reject part or all of your statement.

James spoke in some detail, pausing to take questions when one of their number needed clarification. He finished by informing them that normally their statement could be tested by the offender or his lawyer, and that the person making the statement could be cross-examined, but in this case, the offender had chosen not to have legal representation, had foregone the right to cross-examine the victims, and had asked only that after the victim impact statements had been read, he might have the opportunity to address the court. After a brief pause, James opened the meeting to any who had further questions they needed to ask or comments they wanted to make.

Vince spoke first. "My name is Vince Patrick. I am the parish priest of the Church of St. Francis and a sexual abuse victim of Justin McKean's when he was a trainee priest and I was a twelve-year-old boy. We are all here today because John, sitting on my right, came to me and told me his story. His courage and his willingness to name Justin McKean as his abuser led me, for the first time in my life, to disclose my abuse and tell my story. It also led me to visit the bishop of my diocese and share with him both of our stories. As a result of that, the bishop confronted Justin McKean, and two weeks later, McKean handed himself into the police. I think that for all of us, it could be an important part of our recovery to write a victim impact statement. We may not all wish to read our statements in court, but simply writing them could be very therapeutic."

Throughout the meeting, John was painfully aware of one attendee who sat with her head bowed, avoiding eye contact with everybody at the table. She had arrived after James had begun to speak, and even though her once blonde hair was now black, John recognized her immediately. She had sat in a vacant chair beside Tim, a few seats to John's right, and therefore was out of his line of sight during the meeting. As the meeting closed, he glanced toward where she had been seated, but she had already left. Tim made his way to where John stood and handed him a note.

"Margaret was here," he said. "She left quickly but asked me if I would give you this."

"Thanks, Tim," John said as he took the note. "What did you

think about the meeting? Are you planning to write a victim impact statement?"

"I would like to, mate, but I am not much of a writer. I was wondering whether you could help me. I have got a heap of reports from my psychiatrist and other evidence that I could use, but I have no idea how to put it together."

"I think I could help, Tim. Give me a call next week, and we will make a time to get started.

As John left the solicitor's office, he found himself drawn urgently to read the note that Margaret had written. He had thought of her almost every day since Tim had mentioned that she had also been molested by McKean. He had been puzzled by the feelings that thinking of her aroused in him and surprised by the feeling of elation when she had entered the meeting room. He made for a nearby coffee shop, ordered a skinny latte, and found a table where he could be alone. Opening the note, he saw that it was extremely brief. Just six words, "Could I meet with you? Margaret." Underneath the message was her mobile number. He picked up his phone and, after three or four rewrites, he sent her a message. "Sure. Would St. Kilda Botanical Gardens at 2pm this afternoon be okay?" Almost immediately the reply came, "yep." Wondering at the warm feeling the prospect of meeting her gave him, he wrote, "See you by the rose garden."

MARGARET

By the Rose Garden, St. Kilda Botanical Gardens

He had arrived early, but as he walked toward the Rose Garden, he could see Margaret walking slowly toward him from the opposite direction. John had carefully rehearsed his opening gambit, but as they met near the park seat where he and Claire had sat a few weeks before, his memory went blank, and all he could say was a soft "Hi." She smiled. He had never seen her smile before. For a moment, all the tension and pain that he could remember seeing on her face at the hospital disappeared, and in that moment, it seemed like she was as glad to see him as he was to see her.

"Hi to you too," she said. "You sure know how to pick a nice place. It is beautiful here."

"Do you want to sit here or in the café?" he asked her.

"Is it okay if we sit here for a while? I don't handle closed spaces too well. It was torture sitting in that meeting this morning. I am glad that you could make time to see me."

"Time is what I have plenty of now."

"Me too! It's a few months since we talked as patients at the hospital, John, and just by looking at you, I can tell a lot has happened for you. I guess I would like to hear your story."

"How long have you got?" he said, laughing, and she marveled at the lightness in his voice and manner. Once when describing to Tim the impression John had made on her, she had said that he was like a man who carried a load that was far too heavy and painful for any one person to bear. But now she had the clear impression that he was like an ex-convict experiencing his first days of freedom.

"Well, Margaret, as you know, I was not a voluntary patient in the hospital. I did not want to be there. I was there because I had failed to take my life. I was angry and resentful. I think one day I told you that the only real goal I had was to succeed in ending it all. If hell is torment, that is where I was. I dreaded the nights because all the demons of shame and guilt would scream their accusations at me all night. Getting drunk only made it worse. There was no relief and often no sleep. Mornings brought no relief either. Only more shame and hopelessness. I was sure that no one else could ever understand the dark evil that had penetrated every part of my life and every fiber of my body. I raged at the night and cursed the day that I was born.

"Only two things made my time in the hospital almost bearable. One was the two or three conversations I had with you. It must have been difficult for you, and I am sure that I wasn't being very sensitive to your needs. But the incredible thing is you listened to me. You were the only ordinary person that I can remember who had ever bothered to listen to me. And then there was the shrink, Dr. Jefferies. I wasn't a great fan of shrinks, but Dr. Jefferies was different from the others. He seemed to genuinely believe that there was hope for me, and he encouraged me to believe it also. He encouraged me to think of myself as a person faced with many tasks, and as I found the courage to tackle them one at a time, I would grow stronger in my belief that I could be different. He didn't tell me what those tasks were but referred me to a psychologist who he said would help me to identify them. After I left the hospital, I made an appointment with Marie, and it turns out that my first task was to decide who was responsible for my abuse."

"Did you take it on?" asked Margaret.

"Yes, I did."

"And what did you discover?"

"I was made to confront the reality that there is absolutely no logic by which you can arrive at the conclusion a child is ever responsible for their own sexual abuse. The perpetrator is always fully aware of what they are doing, and their attempt to transfer the blame to the child is just further abuse. I had to face the possibility that the alternative truth to believing I was responsible was to acknowledge that my abuser had succeeded in victimizing me by convincing me the abuse was my fault."

"And?"

"And I realized over time that was the truth, and Marie has been helping me understand that the guilt I have carried all these years is false—or, if you like, projected guilt—and I needed to move the guilt and shame on to my abuser where it really belonged."

"Was that difficult?"

"Exceedingly difficult. There was something in me that did not want to do that. I felt very afraid. If an adult who said he loved me, and who I also loved and respected, had knowingly hurt me, completely aware what he was doing was a criminal offense, how would I ever be able to trust another person again?"

"You are different, John, since you left the hospital. I am pleased for you because you seem to be making progress. But it is not like that for me. I have always known that the abuse that I experienced was not my fault. It is not shame and guilt that tear me apart, that drive me to self-medicating and torments me until I cannot cope anymore."

"What is it then?" John asked gently. Margaret did not answer but simply sat staring at the ground. Her hands moved nervously, and the expression John saw on her face was one of great anguish.

"You don't have to talk to me, Margaret, if it is too difficult."

"No! I want to. I feel like there is a tiger trapped inside of me. A vicious beast who if he ever gets free will destroy me and everyone I love." She was fighting back the tears. Her fists were clenched, and her whole body was trembling.

"Can you name the tiger?" John's voice was very soft now.

Margaret suddenly sprang to her feet. Both her hands covered her face. "No! No! You must not ask me to do that."

"It's okay, Margaret." He stood beside her now. "Just let's walk around the garden for a while. I always come here when life gets too difficult." To his relief, she walked by his side, and soon they were chatting about other things, like where they had grown up. They were both surprised to find that they had attended the same church at the same time, although neither had any memory of meeting the other. They stopped at the canteen and bought a takeaway coffee. They stopped by the lake, and John told her about how for him, looking at the *Rain Man* had helped him understand things about himself that he had never understood before. She simply smiled, and they walked together toward the gate.

As they stopped, she said, "Thank you, John, for telling me some of your story. I am sorry that I interrupted you with my own garbage."

"It wasn't like that, Margaret. I would like to catch up again."

"I would like that," she replied, smiling again. "I am to be discharged from the hospital next week."

"I will call you," he promised. "I don't know whether you would like this," he said, handing her Marie's business card. She took it, thanked him again, then turned away and walked toward the gate. He watched her go and wondered what the name of the tiger might be.

14
GRIEF

Counseling Center, Carlton

The phone on Marie's desk buzzed. "A call for you, Marie, from a psychiatrist, a Dr. Francis," the receptionist said.

"Put him through, Nancy."

"Mrs. Forsythe?"

"Yes."

"Dr. Francis from the Monash Medical Center."

"How can I help you, Dr. Francis?"

"We have a patient in our psychiatric ward who is about to be discharged. She has been a long-term patient, and in this past week, she has been free to go out during the day if she wishes and then return at night. She has given us your professional card and has asked whether we might be able to make an appointment for her with you. Her name is Margaret Adams."

"I don't know her. Did she say that she was a client of mine?"

"No, Mrs. Forsythe. She said a friend she caught up with last week gave her the card."

"Yes, I would be happy to see her, Dr. Francis. When will she be discharged?"

"Tomorrow afternoon after she has seen the residential psychiatrist."

"Where will she be living?"

"I understand that she will be living with a friend in Caulfield for a while."

"All right. I will pass you back to my receptionist, and she will make the appointment. Thank you for your call, Doctor."

Marie replaced the phone, remembering that John had mentioned a Margaret. She wondered whether the girl she would see next week was the same person. No doubt she would find out sooner or later.

John had been to see her last week and had shared his experience writing his victim impact statement. "It was like an out-of-body experience," he had said. "Marie, as I thought about the impact of the sexual abuse on my life, it was like I was sitting in a cinema watching a procession of people crossing the screen. The first one was a little boy, then came an adolescent, the next was a teenager, and following him, a young adult and finally a mature man. As each one moved slowly across the screen, a drama played out, and in each of the enactments, there was a different cast of characters. For instance, the little boy bounced across the screen, full of life and happiness. His mother was there participating in his games and sharing in his happiness. His little sister was trying to throw the basketball through the hoop, and he laughingly tried to help her. They rolled on the lawn, picked flowers from the garden, and waved to strangers who passed by on the street. It was a scene of great happiness and safety.

"Then the scene changed, and the boy who crossed the screen was about twelve. His head was down, and he kicked the ground angrily as he walked. His mother watched him from afar, and his sister stayed close to her, as if she were afraid. His father was walking out of the gate, going somewhere. Then the scene changed again, and this time a sixteen-year-old boy was walking down a city street with an overnight bag. He had tears of anger rolling down his cheeks. He checked a rubbish bin for food. There was no family in this picture, just strangers—some of them judgmental and threatening, some aloof and uncaring, and some kind and compassionate.

"The next scene was a young man sitting alone in an almost empty room. There was a bed, a chair, and an empty wine bottle. He sat on the bed rocking backward and forward while he hugged himself. All the while, his bloodshot eyes tried to focus on a word scrawled on the wall opposite his bed. Written in something that looked like blood was the word *Guilty!*

"Then, Marie, came the last scene. A mature, aged man was striding along what looked like St. Kilda beach. He appeared to be purposeful and confident, like he was going into a battle that he had reason to believe he could win. Walking with him was a group of people who seemed to be as focused on the same objective as he was. He smiled at other walkers and greeted them by raising a hand, but it was clear that he would allow nothing to distract him from his purpose.

"As I watched the five scenes, I tried to capture the word that best described each one. The word I thought of as I watched the first scene was *innocence*. The second scene I described as *rejection*, and the third as *anger*. The word that came to me in the fourth scene as *self-hatred*. The final scene, so astonishingly different from all the others, conveyed the word *hope*."

As John had spoken, Marie had been taking notes. Now, five days after their appointment, as she thought about their conversation, she extracted from his file the notepaper on which she had written as he had talked. She pondered the words *innocence*, *rejection*, *anger*, *self-hatred*, and *hope* and pictured John's life from childhood to manhood as a crazy ride to the bottom, down the steepest of mountainsides. But suddenly it was as if finding that he could go no lower, he had pulled out of his fatal dive and landed on the pathway of new hope. But it was no accidental landing. He was now living with new hope because he had made three momentous decisions. The first was to stop blaming himself for his sexual abuse. The second was to shift the blame to where it really belonged, his abuser, and the third was to find a way to forgive himself for the pain that, in his hurt and anger, he had inflicted on those he loved, and in particular, his mother. It was to this goal that he now so purposively strode. He had discovered that his mother had found a way to forgive him, and he now was in search of a way to forgive himself. She marveled at the turnabout in John's life trajectory and thanked God that she, his sister, Claire, her husband, Sam, Father Vince, and Father Simon and perhaps

Margaret, who she was still to meet, had been there at the time he needed to make those choices.

As she left the counseling room and sat in the beautiful garden that surrounded her house, she began to consider the choices that she still needed to make. It was almost three years since her husband, Vic, and her two beautiful daughters, Fiona and Grace, had died in a horrific car accident. Their sudden loss had been unbearable. Every moment of every day was like a horror movie. At night in bed, she would have the sense that Vic was there beside her, and she would reach out to touch him, but he wasn't there, and his death would once again become a terrible reality. Some nights she would wake with a start, and they would all be there sitting on the bed smiling at her. In that moment, she would feel overjoyed, and then they would be gone again. Often during the day, she would hear the girls giggling in their bedroom, and she would call to them, but they would not come. The pain was excruciating. She could not bring herself to leave the house. She could not bear seeing families together or to hear the laughter of children. She avoided the times when her own extended family gathered. She ceased going to church. She was encased in a cocoon of loneliness and never-ending tears. And then there was the guilt. The overwhelming, ever-present guilt. *If only I had been there to protect my beautiful girls. If only I hadn't insisted that they drive home that night instead of sleeping at his mother's house.* The thought that she, not the drunk woman driving the other car, was responsible for the accident on that fateful night was, she knew, irrational and illogical, but it was so powerful that it threatened to destroy her. This guilt stood at the intersection of good grief and unhealthy grief, preventing her from embracing the reality that all she now had of her family were memories, and one day those memories would sustain her and enable her to live her new normal. Instead, the memories tormented her with the insistent thought that she had failed to keep her little girls safe.

Nine months after the accident, she returned to work, not because she thought she was ready but because she needed to. To keep this beautiful house that at the same time was a sanctuary full of memories of laughter and love and a torture chamber of grief and guilt, it was necessary for her to work. Sometimes she hated the house with a vengeance, but she could not bring herself to leave it. Vic had been so excited when they had set up her counseling rooms so that she could do what she loved, and now she realized that it still offered her the chance to help others and to provide an income to pay the bills. She had made a choice to begin taking clients again, and one of the first to come was John. Now she wondered whether he had been sent to help her face the truth, that she needed to make more choices than to simply go back to work. She knew that she could not make the grief go away, but she also knew that she needed help to escape the terrible guilt. Taking sleeping tablets to help her sleep and even counseling others through their pain, something she loved doing, only distracted her for a time.

Marie remembered then that on the only occasion that she had met John's new friend, Father Vince, he had handed her a business card. It was not his but belonged to a Father Simon. He had simply said, "This is the man who is saving my life," as he handed her the card.

"Well, Father Simon," she said to herself, "I might just pay you a visit."

15
FELLOW TRAVELLERS

A Café in St. Kilda

She had eagerly accepted his invitation to have dinner with him. It had been a significant day for both of them, and they looked forward to hearing how each had fared. After they had ordered their meal, Margaret asked John about his first day at work.

"Well, as you may imagine, it was a bit nerve-racking; not so much because of what the job itself entails but because I have never held down a permanent position in my life before this. Sam met me at the entrance of the building that houses the offices of Fenwick Constructions and introduced me to the lady who is my immediate boss. She is a highly qualified engineer and struck me as being a very competent one at that."

"What is she like?"

"I guess she is in her early fifties, tall, handsome rather than pretty, a migrant from Europe, friendly enough but with a definite no-nonsense air about her. She was an engineer when she came to Australia and was employed almost immediately by Fenwick. She was the only female engineer in the firm for the first fifteen years. Now there are many, and I think she regards herself as a trailblazer for women. She introduced me to Lance, who is the quantity surveyor I will be working with. I have a desk and a filing cabinet in an open-plan office. Lance explained that I will be expected at the office on Mondays, Tuesdays, and Fridays, and I will attend lectures at Swinburne Institute on Wednesdays and Thursdays. I am nervous about it all and still very afraid of the anger that is just bubbling below the surface. In the casual and very temporary jobs I have had in the past, it has been my anger that has always brought on my demise. Hopefully now that I am seeing Marie, I might be able to handle that better. But what about you, Margaret? How did you do today?"

"Well, I kept my appointment with Marie this morning. I hadn't slept very well, worrying about it, and thought seriously about not turning up but did anyway. She seems like a nice person."

"She is a genuinely nice person. Did you see the photograph on the wall?"

"Yes. I asked her about it. She just said it was her husband and daughters."

"You mean late husband and daughters."

Margaret was stunned. "You mean. … you mean, they are all dead."

"Yes, killed in an accident about three years ago. I looked up the news reports that were published at the time, and the subsequent coronial reports, and found that his car collided with another driven by a drunk driver. The driver, a woman, was later jailed for manslaughter." Margaret sat staring at John. Her hands almost covered her face, but he could see that she was ashen.

"Oh, John, that is awful. I had no idea. And she sits in that office and hears other people rabbit on about their problems. I told her my story, and it begins with the death of my mother. I had no idea of what she must have been feeling. Oh, I am sorry. I am so deeply sorry."

John waited as Margaret struggled with her shock. Then he quietly said, "Margaret, I think she counsels others because she loves people, but perhaps it also helps her cope with her own pain."

Margaret wiped the tears from her face, blew her nose, and weakly smiled. "It certainly makes you admire her. It is amazing that even after another human causes her so much loss and pain, she still loves people enough to do what she does."

Their meal arrived, and they ate in silence for a few moments, and finally Margaret laid down her knife and fork and began her story.

"Let me share with you what I told Marie. I do not remember my early childhood at all so can only tell you what my grandmother has told me. Till I was five months old, I lived on the Gold Coast in the state of Queensland with my mother. Apparently, she gave birth to me when she was seventeen years of age. She had run away from home at sixteen, and by the time I was born, she was well and truly addicted to heroin. She insisted on raising me herself and refused to return to her own mother's house in Melbourne. One day when I was still a baby, she killed a young woman in a drug-fueled fight. She then took an overdose, and the police found both the women dead in their flat. Apparently, the other girl had a baby too. My grandmother raised me as her own child from that day. My childhood was a happy one until I turned fifteen. Like lots of teenagers, I was a Facebook devotee and was always talking to my so-called friends. One day a post appeared written by a girl of similar age who I did not know. It said, 'So you miss your mother. Too bad! I miss mine too. Your mother took her from me, and I will never leave you alone until you pay for what she did to my mother.'

"As you can imagine, I was very afraid. From that day, posts from this girl would appear about once a week. Each time, she would tell me some sad thing about her life and then deliver a tirade against my mum. Sometimes she would tell me what she would do to me if she could find me. I was so upset that I took my phone to Father McKean, who was my parish priest, and showed him the posts. He was very sympathetic and asked me to come by his house the next day on my way home from school, and he would show me how to block the posts. Well, I did go, and while I was talking to him, I began to cry. He put his arms around me and took me to his couch. He embraced me and began touching me inappropriately. I struggled, but he held me tightly and began kissing me and telling me how much he loved me. I think I must have passed out or something because when I came to, I was lying on the couch half-naked, and I knew from the pain that I was feeling something awful had happened to me. McKean had gone, and I rushed out of the house, afraid that he would come back and hurt me again. When I got home, my grandmother was not there. I washed my stained underwear and changed my clothes. I never told her what happened to me. I was very, very afraid and ashamed. Every Sunday, I had to go to church. I hated being there. I feared McKean, and I hated myself. Apart from enduring school and church, I became a recluse. I had no friends. I never went out, and as the days went by, I hated myself more and more. At sixteen, I took an overdose of Grandma's sleeping pills and ended up in a psychiatric ward. I was ultimately diagnosed as having a personality disorder and have spent the past fifteen years in and out of the hospital.

"The Facebook posts ceased, but almost every night, I still dream of being chased by a little girl with a gun. In my nightmare, she is screaming, 'You killed my mum!' I run as fast as I can, but she is catching up. I am running up a pathway toward a house, and just as she gets close enough to shoot me, the front door of the house opens, and Father McKean is standing there, and he says, 'Come inside. You will be safe in here.'" Margaret stopped talking and began to weep into her hands. The café was almost empty, and none of the few remaining patrons or the staff showed any interest in the couple at the corner table. When the weeping stopped, she lifted her head, wiping her eyes. John's anger toward McKean rose like bile in his mouth. He did not trust himself to speak.

"Last time we spoke, I told you that I felt like I had a tiger trapped inside of me threatening to destroy me, and you asked me if I could name the tiger. Marie asked me the same question, and for a long time, I could not answer. I have felt for many years that if I named the tiger, it would be like giving it permission to destroy me. I told Marie that, and she said, 'Margaret, perhaps if you name the tiger, you may be able to befriend it.' I found myself panicking. In my mind, I could see the girl and my mother and McKean daring me to tell Marie that I hated them all, and I screamed at her, 'You cannot make a friend of hatred!'

"'Is that the tiger's name?' Marie asked me. I told her it was, and instead of losing control, I felt relieved, even peaceful. Marie suggested that I should write about this hatred and share what I come up with when I see her next week."

"Are you glad that you kept your appointment?"

"Yes, I am, John."

"Did she give you a sense that there is a good reason for you to hope that one day you will be free?"

"She did. She told me that the longer we internalize deep feelings like hatred, the greater the effect those feelings will have on our behaviors. As I was leaving, she asked me if I remembered the moment that I decided to end my life. I said that I remembered it well. She then asked me who I hated the most that night. Was it my mother? Was it the girl who stalked me on social media? Was it Father McKean, or was it myself? She told me not to answer yet, and then she said goodbye."

"Marie is extremely wise. I will never be able to thank her enough for showing me that the guilt I carried was not mine. I am glad that you are seeing her."

They lingered over their meal for an enjoyably long time, talking and listening like two people who were hungry to get to know each other. When the staff of the restaurant made it clear that it was past closing time, they rose to leave. John paid the bill, and as they left the café, he asked, "Can I see you on the weekend?" She agreed. He kissed her on the cheek, and they parted.

16
PREPARATION

A House in Elsternwick

Tim had welcomed John to his mother's home and ushered him into the small lounge room. It was a cluttered room, with a dining table at the far end littered with papers.

"I am glad that you are able to help me with my victim impact statement. I haven't known how to get started. Didn't do much schoolwork when I was a kid, and I find writing something like this pretty difficult."

"That's okay, Tim. The first thing we need to do is draw up an outline, and then we can fill in the details." They sat at the table, and John took a pen and wrote on the top of a sheet of paper, "Outline for Victim Impact Statement." Then under the heading he wrote, "1. Introduction."

"What the judge will want to know, Tim, is your full name, your age now, your address, whether you are married or single or divorced, and whether you are employed or not." Tim nodded and gave John the information. He was thirty-one years of age, lived with his mother, was single, and had been permanently unemployed.

John then wrote, "2. Details of the Abuse."

"You cannot of course tell the whole story, but just give an outline of what happened." Tim picked up the solicitor's letter from the table.

"This is what McKean has said in relation to what he did to me."

John took the letter and read it. It included a statement from McKean describing his grooming and abuse of Tim.

"Do you agree with what McKean says here, Tim?"

"Yes, I do."

"Okay, you just need to copy this into your impact statement."

"I can do that."

"Good. The third part of the statement needs to detail the impact of the abuse on your life till now."

"That's easy, John."

For the next hour, the two men talked and read school reports and psychiatric assessments. When they reached the point at which Tim attempted to take his life with his father's pistol, Tim could go no further. His sobs filled the room. Between the sobs, John could hear Tim groan, "A wasted life, such a wasted life. I hate myself. I hate him," repeatedly.

When the sobbing ceased, John asked, "Tim, who do you blame for your abuse?"

"I always blamed myself. McKean told me it was my fault. Then I met Margaret at the psych hospital, and she helped me understand that it was McKean who was completely responsible. I know that now for sure. But I am caught in a dilemma again, John. I can forgive myself, but the anger I feel toward McKean gets deeper and more powerful every day."

"I know exactly what you mean, Tim. I am stuck there too, and so, I think, are Vince and Margaret and maybe all those others that McKean abused. For me, the journey has been first to understand that the guilt I had carried was not the result of doing something wrong but was the result of being convinced by McKean that I had done something wrong. That was a huge relief. The second thing that my counselor helped me see was that some of my guilt was the result of knowing that, in my pain, I had hurt people who loved me. When those very people were prepared to forgive me, I realized that it must be possible to forgive myself. But like you said, Tim, both those steps that I have taken have left me with nowhere to go as far as my anger toward McKean is concerned."

"Tell me more about the guilt you felt, John. Sometimes when I look in the mirror, I feel disgust. I feel dirty. I know in my mind that I was not to blame for my abuse, and yet I cannot shake the feelings of guilt and self-condemnation. Why does it seem impossible to stop feeling guilty?"

"My counselor introduced me to the idea that there are two types of guilt."

"Two types of guilt?"

"Yes! There are the feelings of guilt I have when I know that I have done something wrong. She calls that real guilt. In these cases, you are guilty of wrongdoing, and you feel guilty as a result."

"That's the only one I have ever heard about."

"Then there are the feelings of guilt I have when someone convinces me that I have done something bad when I have not. She called that projected guilt. That is, I have come to believe that I am guilty of doing something that I have not done."

"So, that is why it is so hard to deal with?"

"Yes! The projected guilt that I carried for all these years was so all-consuming that I argued with my counselor that it was not a feeling but a fact. I did not feel guilty, I told her; I *was* guilty, and that was that."

"So how do you deal with projected guilt?"

"Marie, my counselor, helped me see that the real abuse I had suffered was being convinced by McKean that I was guilty."

"You mean that causing you to feel guilty for something he was responsible for was as abusive, if not more abusive, than the actual molestation."

"Yes! This is perhaps the greatest violation of all. This is, I think, the reason for my anger. It is one thing to sexually abuse a child but another thing completely to destroy any hope of wholeness and happiness that they might have had by making sure they carry the burden of guilt for what their abuser has done."

"So, John, McKean confesses to grooming and raping us, but you are saying that's only half the story."

"I guess that is why we are being encouraged to write our victim impact statements, Tim. This is our opportunity to describe the damage we have suffered by being led to believe that we were responsible for the abuse."

"I can't tell you how much you have helped me, John. I see now that I need to stop beating myself up for something McKean was solely responsible for."

"Good luck, mate. You sure deserve a break."

It was time for John to leave. He rose from his chair, indicating that their time together had finished. Tim's eyes were filled with tears as he opened the door and took John's hand. As he shook it, he simply said, "Thanks."

17

ANGER

The Counseling Rooms in Carlton

Marie welcomed Margaret and suggested that because it was such a nice day, they could sit in the garden. Margaret welcomed the suggestion, as rooms and other tight spaces tended to make her feel like she might suffocate. They sat together on a padded bench seat, enjoying the fresh air faintly scented by the roses that were in full bloom. Margaret was unsure about how to say what was on her heart. "Marie, I did not realize last week, when you spoke to me of Vic and your little girls, that they were no longer with us. John told me about the accident. I am so sorry!"

"Thank you, Margaret. I guess it would be less difficult for the people who come into my office if the photo were not there. I have thought of moving it. But it would not seem right somehow. I don't go to work to forget them. I have heard some grieving people say that after a time, they found themselves struggling to remember what their loved ones looked like. I am determined that they will be part of my everyday life. So, I keep the photo there."

"And so you should!" Margaret paused for a while, knowing that she should begin to focus on why she had come but found herself reluctant to move out of this moment she found herself in.

"I suppose you would like me to share with you how I got on with the homework you gave me last week. I am sure that you are not a bit surprised to hear that I have cried a lot these last few days. The strange thing was when I tried to write about why I hated the little girl from my nightmares, I realized it was not really hate that I felt toward her. Instead, I felt fear. Fear, because she hated me. I know she has every reason in the world to hate me. I am the daughter of the woman who killed her mother. I survived when her mother didn't. It crossed my mind that she may feel that she cannot take her hatred out or get revenge on Mum because she is dead. So, I am her target, and it is the heat of her anger, and to a large extent the validity of it, that fills me with fear. It is the same with my mum. She doesn't overtly threaten to hurt me, but the reality that I have become like her in my addictions and the probability that if I had a daughter, I might also endanger her life, is the source of great fear. And then there is McKean. As I began to write about how I hated him, I realized that the truth is, like the other two, it is not hate I feel but a terrible, indescribable fear. Marie, I discovered in order to survive, I have turned my fear into hatred. My aggressive and sometimes violent behavior toward others is not driven by hate but by fear. My deep, dark depressions are not the consequence of internalized hate but rather of the fear that up till now I have refused to admit to. The tiger's name, Marie, is not hatred but fear. I am afraid of a girl who is threatening me out of her grief. I am afraid that I will be like my mum. I am afraid of men. I am afraid of living, and I am afraid of dying. Turning that fear into anger and hatred is the only thing that enables me to survive, and when it fails, I take drugs, and withdraw into psychotic episodes, and flee to the safety of the psychiatric hospital."

Marie had listened to Margaret without comment. Now she smiled, and with a twinkle in her eye, she said, "I do believe, Margaret, that you are your own psychologist. I could not have done a better job myself. I happen to think that fear is a primary emotion, along with shame, and all our other painful emotions are secondary to them. In my experience, people who believe that they have an anger problem will often discover, like you have, that their real problem is fear, and their anger is an expression of that.

"Years ago, Vic would have described me as a total controller. My anxiety levels went up and down depending on how in or out of control of my circumstances I felt at the time. I learned through therapy that my whole life was built on the need to succeed. Even my marriage and my motherhood. The trouble is that a drive to succeed, rather than a preference to succeed, soon becomes a fear of failing to succeed. And one of the ways I found of reducing that fear was to control everything. I tried to control my husband, my girls, my circumstances, my colleagues, and the dog. The only one who didn't seem to mind was the dog. And when all the important people in my life, except the dog, refused to be controlled, then I would be overwhelmed with anxiety."

"I understand that, Marie, but in my life, there is nothing that I feel I can control. I do not have a home or a husband or kids. I do not have a job or an income other than a pension. I can no longer control my addiction to drugs, nor have I found a way to control my mental health condition. I can't control my nightmares or the reality that I am a sexually abused person. So, I am guessing that you are going to tell me that because there is nothing I can control, when it comes to dealing with my fear, I bypass control and go straight to anger or withdrawal."

Marie smiled again, and laying her hand on Margaret's, she said, "Well I wasn't actually going to tell you that, but I was going to ask you whether you know what you do when you are fearful or anxious. I don't need to ask you that now because you have already told me."

"So, Marie, where do I go from here?"

"The first step is that you have a decision to make. For many years, you have, without thinking about it, dealt with your fear in a certain way. The question is whether or not you want to continue to deal with fear like that or do you want to find a better and healthier way."

"Why would you ask that? Why would I choose to keep behaving in self-destructive ways? Do you think I like who I am and how I live? Don't you think I would want what you have? A job, a house, a fa—" Margaret stopped in midsentence, "Oh, Marie. I am sorry. I was getting so upset. I forgot." She buried her head in her hands, and between her sobs, Marie heard her say, "Oh, I am so ashamed!"

Suddenly, she leapt to her feet. "I have to go! I am deeply sorry! Thank you for your help! I won't be back!" Marie stood facing her with a warm smile, and Margaret was dumbstruck.

"You can go if you must but let me tell you something first. I can understand that you feel embarrassed, but I am not upset. Actually, I am pleased!"

"Pleased?" Margaret managed to gasp through her tears.

"Yes! Pleased. If you would sit for a moment, I will tell you why."

"I can't imagine why you would be pleased. If I were you, I would be very offended." For a moment, Margaret looked as if she were about to leave. Then, to Marie's relief, she sat down.

"Why are you pleased after I said something so thoughtless and awful?"

"I am pleased because you have demonstrated beautifully why my question was relevant and why your answer will be important. I asked you whether you really wanted to find a healthy way to deal with your fear, or will you just simply go on dealing with it by being angry and aggressive. My question made you afraid. Afraid because you might have to give up the only strategy you have for controlling your anxiety. Because you were afraid, you acted in the way you have always done. You got angry with me. In asking you to tackle your fear, I am facing you with a huge task. I will help you, but I need to hear from you that you really want to change your responses. If you want to find a healthy way to deal with your fear, you will find it, but there is some hard work ahead, or alternately, you can avoid the hard work and continue as you are."

Margaret's face was still wet with tears as she stared at Marie. She twisted her handkerchief in her hands, and when she finally spoke, her voice was soft, almost childlike, and her eyes were those of a person who knew that she may never again have this opportunity and was pleading for help.

"Please, Marie, I need your help. You have been so loving to me, and yet, in my fear, I could have destroyed our relationship before it has really begun. Come to think of it, that is what I do almost every time someone reaches out to me. John told me that you said healing comes as we engage in several tasks one at a time. I think I am ready for the first one."

"Last week, Margaret, I asked you to write about your hatred. In doing so, you identified that what you needed to confront was the fear out of which your hatred and anger comes. Now it is time to begin to explore your fear and to discover its core. One way of doing that is to begin to write a journal each day, recording what you are learning about yourself through your behaviors and reactions. We will meet in a fortnight, and you can, if you like, share what you have written with me."

As Margaret left, she embraced Marie. "Thank you again for caring," she said.

18

BLAME

An Aged Care Facility in Melbourne

Marie had spent an hour with Father Simon in an office made available to them by the matron. She had been deeply moved by the peace that emanated from this frail old man. He had greeted her with a welcoming smile and had listened intently to her story. She finished by describing the deep sense of guilt that troubled her. At first, he sat in silence. She could see that he had tears in his eyes. Then he said, "My daughter, your story is almost too much for an old man to handle."

"I am sorry, Father."

"No, no, I am sorry. I am sorry for your indescribable loss. I am sorry for the loneliness you feel, and I am sorry that you carry so much guilt for something that you are not responsible for."

"But I am responsible. Vic would have stayed at his mother's that night, but I encouraged him to drive home."

"Because …"

"Because I did not want the children to miss a day at school and because I missed them."

"Were you responsible for the other driver drinking till she was drunk?" he asked gently.

"No! Of course not."

"Was it your fault that she decided to drive that night?"

"No! Father, it was not."

"Would the accident have occurred if she had not been driving at high speed and if she had not swerved on to the wrong side of the road?"

"No, Father." Her voice was so soft Father Simon had to lean forward to hear her.

"If she had not been driving erratically that night, because she was under the influence of alcohol, would your husband and children still be alive?"

"Yes, Father." Her head was in her hands now, and she was weeping.

"Then this woman killed your family?" There was no answer, just a gut-wrenching groan. Three years of grief began to surface. Father Simon sat quietly. He would not move or speak until she lifted her head. When she did, Simon asked her, "What are your feelings toward the driver of the vehicle that slammed into your husband's car?"

"Until today, I felt nothing toward her. For nearly three years, I have focused only on my own responsibility. Now I am thinking about her, I am thinking about her celebrating at a work function. I am thinking about her drinking till she could hardly stand up. I am thinking about her deciding to drive in that condition. I am thinking about her continuing to live while my family is dead. I am thinking of her coming out of jail into the arms of her family in less than two years from now."

"But what are you feeling about her now?"

"I should be angry, I know. But I don't have any feelings but the feelings of guilt. I am numb. I weep not because of grief but because of guilt. I live with facts, not feelings. The deaths of my husband and children are facts. My loneliness is a fact. My having to get on with my life is a fact. My guilt is a fact. They are facts not of my choosing. They make up my new reality."

"You say that the death of your husband and the death of your children are facts not of your choosing."

"Yes."

"What elements of your life are of your choosing?"

"I eventually chose to go back to work."

"Why of all the choices you could have made did you make that one?"

"I suppose there were a number of reasons really, not the least of which was financial."

"Was it a way of making your new normal more bearable?"

"Yes, I guess."

"Do you have other choices you need to make?"

"I need to make a choice to reconnect with my extended family and my church."

"What is preventing you from making that choice?"

Marie did not reply; instead, she just stared into the weathered face of this loving and gentle man. She knew the answer to his question, but she also knew instinctively that the answer might well be the catalyst that would change her life forever. Drawing a deep breath and locking her eyes onto his, she said, "My shame makes me avoid the good people in my life. I have been so convinced that I am responsible for the deaths of my husband and my children it is easier just to avoid mixing with people who might judge me."

"Will they judge you, or disagree with your opinion that you are responsible?"

"The latter, I imagine."

"And you do everything you can to avoid that?"

"Yes!"

"Why?"

"Because if they convinced me that I was blaming myself rather than shifting the blame to the other driver, I would no longer be able to survive."

"Why do you say that Marie?"

"Can't you see, Father? If I blame myself, I have no more questions to ask and no more answers to find. I do not have the energy to ask questions. I am afraid that if I do what you are asking me to do, I will destroy myself."

"What am I asking you to do?"

"To stop blaming myself and to start blaming the other driver."

"And you are too afraid to do that?"

"Yes!"

"What if I said that you could trust God to give you the courage to ask the questions you are too afraid to ask?"

"I am a believer, Father. I want to believe that God will give me the strength. But I don't know if I can."

"What if I promise to support you for a while with counseling and prayer?"

"Thank you, Father. Can I come back again next week?"

"Sure, you can." As Marie left the little room, she wondered how long she would have to live to be as wise and nonjudgmental as Father Simon.

19
FORGIVEN

In the Parish Rectory

Father Simon was delighted. Trips away from the aged care facility where he lived were few and far between. Vince had arranged for Simon to join him for afternoon tea, and Margaret and John had picked him up in Margaret's car and were driving him to the rectory. He spoke to them of his two brothers and their children. He was as proud of his nephews and nieces as he would have been if they had been his own children. Being with this old priest while at the same time confronting their abuse by a fellow member of the priesthood was weird, Margaret thought to herself. Simon's love for God and for people was palpable. You could not be in his presence without feeling that Simon himself gave you an incredibly good reason to believe in God. He was so gentle and compassionate and deeply spiritual. Not piously spiritual in that characteristic clerical fashion but in a genuine, earthy sort of a way. Margaret had read of godly men of ancient times who spent countless hours alone with God in some place of solitude, but to her, Simon was a person who experienced the presence of God while at the same time being completely present with people. *And yet*, she thought, *there is a deep sadness in this man.* A sadness that spoke of years of pain and struggle, as if something exceedingly precious to him had been placed beyond his reach by something or someone much more powerful than he was.

It was almost as if Simon had read her thoughts. "When I was a student preparing for the priesthood," he said, "my one prayer was that I might always reflect the love of God to the people of my parish. After I was ordained, I even dared to dream that one day I might become a bishop. I commenced my ministry in a city church as a curate and quickly became suspicious that the priest in charge of the parish was sexually abusing children. To my shame, at first I did nothing, until after a time it became too much for me to bear. To cut a long story short, I spoke to him about it, and within a couple of hours, I was summoned by the bishop. He rebuked me harshly for accusing my superior as I had and told me to go back to my room and pack my bags. I was to be removed from the parish. As it turned out, I was sent to a parish in northern New South Wales. I served in outback country churches all my life. Don't get me wrong. I loved the people in those country towns, and I loved the lifestyle. But I always knew that I was being punished for being a priest with a conscience. Despite the great reports given by those who witnessed my ministry, I was never spoken to about being elevated to any other role within the church. I was for a time bitter about that but then realized that if I had been approached to become a bishop, I would have declined anyway. My deep sadness was that my one feeble attempt to expose sexual abuse in the church had failed, and I had been silenced. But since I have met you both and Vince, I have decided that as long as God gives me breath, I am going to speak out and make as much trouble for anyone covering up abuse as I can."

"What happened to the priest that you confronted?" Margaret asked.

"He eventually became a bishop for some years but died a decade ago from cancer."

"Did you ever personally receive other complaints?"

"No! None! Being in the country, I was isolated from all other Catholics, other than those in my own parish. I am afraid I buried myself in love and care for those who I ministered to. I went through droughts and other tragedies with these families. I baptized their children, married their young men and women, and buried loved ones who died. I worked on their cattle stations when they were shorthanded, I broke in their horses, and I taught the children who did not live on cattle stations to ride. It was a good life, and I am incredibly grateful." Simon went silent then and sat with a half smile on his peaceful face.

When they arrived at the rectory, the housekeeper fussed over Simon, making sure he was comfortable in the large lounge chair and plying him with coffee and chocolate cake. Vince, wearing an open-necked shirt and jeans, welcomed them warmly, and when the four of them were seated, he said, "Father Simon, when I spoke to you last week and we organized this visit, I confessed that I had an ulterior motive." The old priest nodded and smiled. "John, Margaret, and I are all in a similar place. We have lived all our adult lives carrying the guilt and self-loathing that is, for many, the consequence of having been childhood sexual abuse victims. I know I am supposed to say survivors, but at the time, we were victims, and our victimization has damaged all of us. Each in our own way, we have confronted the shame we have felt and made a choice to move the blame for our abuse to where it belongs. However, we have all now become painfully aware that in a strange sort of way, our guilt insulated us from our anger. We want you to talk to us about how we can prevent our anger at our abuser from destroying us."

Vince looked at John, who said, "That is true, Father. As you know, I have the example of my mother. Even though I hurt her hugely, she was able to forgive me before she died. I want to know how she did that."

"And you, Margaret?" Simon asked.

"Yes, Father, I also am caught in the same web. Although, to be truthful, in my case I have learned that it is not anger that is my real problem, but it is fear. I suspect, however, that learning how to forgive myself and others may be especially important."

Father Simon drained his coffee and began to speak quietly. "I will be very frank with you. Forgiving McKean for abusing you, forgiving your parents or other responsible people for not protecting you, and forgiving yourself for the hurt and pain you have brought upon yourself and others by the way you have responded to the abuse is the only way for you to be ultimately free. Now, before you tell me how unfair it is that people who have been abused have to forgive their abuser before they can be free again, let me tell you that it is not McKean that will benefit from your forgiveness—it is you. I believe, John, that you once said that for all these years, you have been in a prison of guilt and shame, and McKean has been the jailer. And now you have transferred to a prison of anger and rage, and McKean is still the jailer. John, that is not the truth. Yes, you have been in a jail of guilt and shame, but you have always had the key, and you have always been free to leave. The same is true of your new jail. McKean is not the jailer; you are. You have the key. You are free to leave your prison. The door through which you are free to walk is called forgiveness."

It was Margaret who spoke first, and as she spoke, Vince and John nodded in agreement.

"But is it not true that by grooming us, and then molesting us, and then accusing us of evil, McKean is responsible for the guilt and the shame we have carried, and as a result, it is appropriate for us to be angry and to demand justice?"

"Yes, Margaret, it is true that McKean has caused you immeasurable harm, and he deserves to be punished. It is also true that your anger is appropriate. You are in no way responsible for what he did to you. You owe him nothing. What I am saying is the actions performed against you and the words he used to silence you were his. They were evil and inexcusable, but you know that while the actions and words stopped, the painful impact of the abuse has continued. Why is that? Why has it seemed like he is the ever-present abuser? I will tell you why. Your guilt and shame, or if you like, your emotional response to his words and actions, continued to damage you long after the abuse ceased. That is because the feelings of guilt and shame and anger were not his. The actions and words were his. The feelings are yours. Each of you have told me that you have come to understand that the feelings of shame and guilt you feel about having been abused are not appropriate. You are recognizing it as false guilt. That is good. You don't have to forgive McKean to resolve your false guilt. Instead, you do the opposite. You shift the blame back to him. Margaret, you have spoken before of a wild beast caged up inside of you. Up till recently, you were afraid to name him. You are still afraid that should you cease to hate yourself, you would lose emotional control. John, you have spoken of carrying real guilt as a result of having deliberately harmed others and yourself. Real guilt is a little more difficult to deal with than false guilt. You can't shift the blame for something you are responsible for onto someone else."

"I once argued with my counselor that the guilt I struggled with was not a feeling but a fact," John said.

"If you drive through a red light and hit and kill a pedestrian, you are guilty, whether you feel it or not," Simon replied." Your guilt is a fact. You have committed a crime. You have taken a life. You have robbed a family of a loved one. For all those things, you are guilty. You deserve to be punished. Only one thing would stop you from going to jail. In the unlikely case of when he or she hands down the verdict of guilty and the sentence of ten years' imprisonment, the judge says, 'I have an unblemished driving history, but I have chosen to accept responsibility for this man's actions and will serve his prison sentence for him.'"

The others laughed.

"That would be good," said Margaret, "but as you say, not highly likely."

"I am a priest because somebody did that for me," Simon said.

"You're joking!"

"No, Margaret, I am not joking. No one in this room knows anything about my past. But in my university days, I was an immoral man and used consenting men and women to gratify my own sexual needs. I drank heavily and was perilously close to becoming an alcoholic. I was an atheist and believed in nothing at all. One day, I did run a red light. I was drunk and angry. I wanted to die. I drove through a red light and crashed my car into a massive truck. I did not injure or kill anybody, thank God, but I suffered horrific internal and external injuries. I was in the hospital for an awfully long time and underwent many surgeries and much therapy. Nobody ever came to visit me. Nobody cared. I had no friends, and my family had disowned me long ago.

"One afternoon, after I had been in the hospital for more than a month, I woke from one of my operations to find an old man sitting by my bed. He told me that his name was Phil and that his son, Mac, a parish priest, had been admitted to the hospital at about the same time as me. The vehicle he had been driving had collided head-on with a car that had been driven by an unlicensed driver under the influence of the drug ICE. His son, like me, had had many operations but had ultimately succumbed to his injuries and died. Phil told me that during the days that he had been visiting Mac and sitting by his bedside in the intensive care unit, he had seen me in the next bed and knew that no one ever came by. I told him my name was Simon and I didn't feel like talking. He said that was okay, he would just sit with me a while. Two hours later when I woke again, he was still there. He told me that while I was asleep, two policemen came by to serve a notice that advised me that I was to be charged with a number of serious offenses relating to my accident.

"Every day that I was in intensive care, Phil came by. When I was moved on to the general ward, he still came, and when I ultimately went into rehab, he never missed a day. I had to learn to walk all over again, and every time there was even the slightest improvement, he would celebrate it with me. I had never met anyone like Phil. When I asked him what he did while I was asleep and he was sitting by my bed, he gave me a one-word answer, 'Praying.' I learned to trust Phil and shared my whole sordid story with him. He was with me the day the legal aid solicitor came by to talk about the upcoming court case. The solicitor told me that I was to be charged with culpable driving and driving while under the influence of alcohol, exceeding the speed limit, and running a red light. He told me that I should plead guilty to all those charges and that I should have someone with me who could give the judge a particularly good reason why I should not go to jail. If I got a good judge, I might just get a hefty fine and lose my driver's license for a long time. If I was unable to pay the fine, I would probably go to jail. Phil told the solicitor that he would speak for me at the court.

"I was still in rehab when my case went to court. Phil picked me up and drove me to the courthouse and pushed my wheelchair into the building. Because I pleaded guilty, I simply needed to be sentenced. The prosecutor asked for a jail sentence, as I would be unlikely to be able to pay whatever fine was imposed. Then Phil was called. It was the first time I had heard his surname. 'Would Mr. Phil Hansen please take the stand.'

"I could not believe my ears. The truck I had slammed into was a Hansen's Transport truck. I was stunned as I listened to him speak. He said that at the time of my accident, he had received the news that one of his trucks had been hit by a car being driven by a drunk driver. Almost immediately after he hung up the phone, it rang again. This time he was told that his son had been critically injured when his car had been involved with another being driven by a drug-affected driver. 'My son, Your Honor, ultimately died of his injuries. His loss has been extremely painful. However, in these past few months, I have met and spent time with Simon, who I subsequently learned had crashed into one of my trucks. I have been very impressed by this young man and have come today to tell you that I am ready and able to pay his fine, and I am also offering him the opportunity to come and live with me. I have been very lonely these months, Your Honor, and it would be a great blessing for me to have him in my home.' So, the judge imposed a hefty fine, and Phil paid it, and in due course, I went to live in his house."

Vince's mouth was hanging open. He could not get his head around the old man's story. He had always presumed that Simon had grown up in a middle-class Catholic home with the support of devout parents. "Wow!" he finally said. "How did you make the transition from a crippled, atheistic drunkard to a parish priest?"

"Well, when you have been loved by a man like Phil and benefitted from his kindness and generosity, you want to know what causes a man to be like that. I found that it was his relationship with God, and in time, I grew to have a relationship with God too."

"Have you ever wondered what prompted him to care for you the way he did?" asked John.

"Well, I certainly did at the time. Many years later as he was dying, he told me that six months before Mac's accident, his wife had died of cancer. Mac was all he had left in the world. He also told me that all the time that he was sitting by Mac's bed, praying that he would be healed, he believed that I was the driver who had caused his son's accident. When Mac died, although Phil's heart was broken, he felt that he should reach out to me. He told me that he had so much love to give and no one to give it to. So, he came and sat by my bed. It was only when the police came to the ward while I was asleep that he realized that I had not been the driver of the car that collided with Mac. That driver had also died a few days after the accident but in a different hospital. What I do know about Phil Hansen is that his concept of being a Christian was that he should be as much like his heavenly Father as he possibly could. So, for Phil, if his Father unconditionally loved the man who killed his son, he had to do the same. If his Father had completely forgiven him for all the sin in his own life, then he must do the same to those who have sinned against him.

"The power and influence of Phil's life was incredible, and yet he never went to university and never preached a sermon. He based his whole life on doing in every situation what he believed Jesus would have done. He could have been a wealthy man, but instead he poured all his money into helping others. Soon after I went to live in his house, he retired from managing the trucking business but continued to own it. Instead of going to the office every day, he worked from an office in his house. Without exaggeration, I can tell you that there was an endless stream of needy people beating a path to his door, and he helped them all."

"You said that your family had disowned you," said Vince.

"Yes, that's right. At the time I met Phil, I was very bitter toward my parents and siblings. But I could not go on being bitter in the presence of a man like Phil, and I did forgive them, and over time I have been reconciled to them all, except my mother, who, like your mother, John, died before the prodigal returned home. That is why I am telling you the story. I am not just encouraging you to forgive McKean because I am a priest and that is what priests do. What I saw in Phil was simply a reflection of what I later learned about God. He saw his Son Jesus killed on a cross and accepted His suffering and death as the basis on which He would extend forgiveness to the whole world. How could I go through life without seeking to reflect such great love and unlimited grace to the world in which I live."

The four people in that room at that moment could find nothing more to say. Simon sat lost in his musings about Phil, seeing his face, hearing his voice, and wondering at his compassion and generosity. Vince was pondering a love and forgiveness that meant that if the young man in the bed next to Mac's had been the driver who killed Mac, then it would have been him living in Phil's house and eating Phil's food. John was thinking about his mother searching for him until the day she died, wanting him to know that she had forgiven him. Margaret was wondering whether the love and forgiveness that Simon spoke about was more powerful than the self-hatred and fear she tried so hard to suppress.

It was Margaret who broke the silence. "Simon, could you please tell me how I could ever forgive myself for the things I have done to myself and to other people? The fear that has taken over my life since my abuse has almost always expressed itself in anger and violence. Because of that anger, I have hurt so many of the people who have reached out to me."

Simon sat with his head bowed and his hands folded on the table in front of him. Slowly he raised his head, and very softly, he said, "No, Margaret, I cannot give you the answer to your question. I can tell you that it is immanently possible for you to forgive yourself. I can support you in whatever process you choose, but I can't tell you how to do it. Ultimately, every person finds their own way. But this is what I can tell you. No one begins the journey of self-forgiveness unless they want to forgive themselves more than they want anything else. And no one who wants to forgive themselves more than anything else they want in the world will fail to do so.

It is only in the willingness to suspend all self-loathing and self-punishment that self-forgiveness occurs."

"I wish I knew how to do that."

"Margaret, just imagine I brought a young teenage girl and stood her in front of you. She has her whole life before her, full of potential and wonderful opportunities. And what if I told you that this girl, who has been sexually abused by a predator, was about to waste her whole life because she hated herself and did not want to live. What would you want to say to her?"

"I would want to put my arms around her and hold her."

"What would you expect her to do?"

"Push me away."

"What would you do then?"

"I would ask her why she hated herself so much."

"What would you expect to her to say?"

"She would probably say that she felt dirty and broken. She might say that nobody could ever love her because of what she had done and who she had become. She might show me the cuts on her wrist and tell me that cutting herself was her only relief from the pain. She would tell me that she hated her body, that she was envious of other girls, and that she feared and hated men. I think that she would tell me that she was afraid of living and afraid of dying."

"Then what?"

"I would probably say, 'So you feel like a helpless victim then?'"

"How do you think she might answer?"

"She might say something like 'No! No! I am not a victim. I am the evil person who made all this happen.'" Margaret's voice rose to fever pitch as she spoke these words. Turning her chair so that she faced away from the others, she buried her head in her hands and howled. This was no controlled weeping or even heartfelt sobs. This was at the same time the howl of a wounded animal and the wail of hopelessness and despair. This was the release of twenty years of the sharpest pain and the deepest grief. This was the breaking open of the cage that had imprisoned the tiger called fear and self-hatred. And, thought Simon, this was the test. Would the beast she feared turn on her and tear her apart, or would it slink away and leave her, knowing that she was neither a perpetrator nor a victim but a survivor in every good sense of the word?

The men in the room quietly wept with Margaret as she endured this time of torturous release. For John and Vince, they were tears of empathy and compassion, but for Simon, they were tears of joy and relief. This old saint instinctively knew what would follow this volcanic outpouring, and he simply sat and waited. The wailing and howling subsided slowly, and for a time, Margaret sat sobbing, gasping for breath and blowing her nose. John and Vince both reached out and placed their hands on her shoulders. For quite a long time, she wept quietly, and when at last she stopped, Simon said, "Margaret, hug the little girl and tell her that she is loved and that she is not broken."

The only sound in the room was the sound of Margaret breathing deeply and occasionally a whispered, "You are loved. You are not broken."

When Margaret eventually turned her chair and faced the others, she smiled shyly and said, "I must look a mess." Simon returned her smile but wisely did not attempt to engage her in conversation. He addressed them all as a group.

"I think we have all had enough for today. Why don't we have a cup of tea, and then Margaret and John can take me home. Goodness gracious, I have been away so long that Matron will think you have kidnapped me."

20
FREEDOM

The Rectory

The following week, they met again. On this occasion, Vince had collected Simon from the aged care center. Usually they were upbeat and jovial in each other's presence, but today they both traveled in silence.

Father Simon spoke first. "These are dark times, Vince. Last week, an American cardinal was laicized by the pope because of abuse charges, and many others have been found guilty of the same crime. It is not a dark time because guilty men are being held to account but because these events demonstrate what maybe many of us in the church have believed. Whenever, in past years, a parish priest or a brother or a nun was accused of the sexual abuse of children in their care, there was always someone higher up the pecking order who had committed the same crime and could be counted on to make sure that there were no consequences for the pedophile's criminal behavior. I am grieving deeply today, Vince."

"I understand, Father Simon, but I must say that my overriding emotion is anger. When McKean abused me, he was protected by the senior priest of the parish who knew that if the matter was taken further up the chain, that person would protect him. That protection or denial would continue right up to the archbishop and, as we learned recently from reports from Chile, right up to the pope. You told us last week about Phil, who sat beside you in the intensive care unit, even though at the time he believed that you were responsible for the death of his son. You told us that in doing so, he reflected God's love for humankind. We all know sexually abusing a child is the antithesis of reflecting God's love, but it is just as unloving when someone in a position of power puts the reputation of an institution and the rights of its employees above the safety and the rights of children. Of course, we all hope that innocent men are not found guilty, but the truth is, Father, I have spent my whole life believing that I was failed by my parents, the church, the government, and the police. The only hope I have left on a human plane is that the justice system will *not* fail me. And if pedophiles in the church or anywhere else cannot be convicted on the evidence of the victims alone, then there is no justice. Abuse victims have been called liars and treated like criminals far too long. We must pray, Father, that this is the beginning of a new day.

"I am sure in my heart that the real issue in the church is clericalism. When I was ordained, I understood that my ordination gives the ordained person a sacred power in the name and authority of Christ and through the Holy Spirit, to serve the people of God. My main roles were to be preaching, celebrating the sacraments, and leading others in building up the community of the church. Because of your influence on my life as a mentor, Simon, I learned that if I was to be a faithful shepherd to the people of the parish, I needed to remember that my real role was to serve them *under* the authority of Christ and not *with* the authority of Christ. You taught me to learn submission to the grace and mercy of Christ, so that I would become a reflector of his love and forgiveness. You showed me by your teaching and example that although the sacrament of holy orders says that a man is spiritually changed by ordination, in reality, he remains in every sense of the word a man, a sinner saved by grace, and that the only spiritual transformation spoken about in the Bible is that affected in the heart of the child of God by the Holy Spirit. My God-given vocation is not to submit to my bishop and then through my bishop to Christ but to submit first to Christ and then to my bishop, when and only when his orders are a true reflection of the heart of Christ."

"You are right, of course, Vince, even though what you are saying is heresy to many of our brothers. That sort of thinking is what had me banished to the bush, although it was indeed a blessing in disguise. I think that, without a doubt, the church must be reborn. This can only happen if we return to the Gospels. We must shun the idea that a worldwide, hierarchical institution like the Catholic Church, or for that matter any of the mainstream Protestant denominations, can reflect the limitless love of God through its priests and its people without also doing much harm through its struggle to retain its doctrinal uniqueness and its power and to protect its enormous assets.

"The reflection of God's love happens best when people live in open, loving, forgiving, and accepting communities. We do not need rules other than the law of love." Simon chuckled. "You know, Vince, the most authentic church I was ever a part of was a tiny little community church on the fringe of my parish in far northern New South Wales. The people who came to church on Sunday were the same people who played cricket and tennis together on Saturdays or watched football together on the television in each other's homes or played pool in the pub on Friday. Most of them were not Catholics, but every fortnight when I traveled more than seventy kilometers to their little town, they all came to church. I never wore vestments, and we adhered to no liturgy. We sang hymns and spiritual songs and even some Australian folk songs. Most Sundays, we met under a large tree near the church building, and everybody brought a picnic basket. We ate and sang and prayed and laughed and cried together. Their version of Mass or Communion was to share one of their sandwiches with their neighbor and to share a drink of cordial or beer with another. We never forgot to thank God for his love. These folks knew that the God who sent the rain that resulted in a good season was the same God who sustained them in a drought. I believe, Vince, that that little community had more in common with the Gospels than any great cathedral I have ever been in. I figure that if a priest had ever abused a child in that church, there would have been a trial, and the next day a hanging, and on the third day, there would have been a funeral, and on the fourth day, they would have had a party for the child, just to show them how much they were loved and appreciated." The two men were laughing heartily as they pulled up in front of the rectory.

"Since our time together last week," Margaret began, after they had been served tea and coffee, "I have done two things that I would like to share with you. I had my fourth session with Marie, my counselor. I told her about John and Vince and I meeting with you, Simon, and by the way, she said she would love the opportunity to be part of a gathering like this. Of course, I told her about my own experience in the group. It was one of the few times I had really felt safe in a group, and, Father Simon, your gentle challenging of me was so good and so timely. When I started bawling like I did, there was nothing I could do to stop it. I am sure Vince and John know that there is so much about sexual abuse that makes the act of revisiting it a terrifying prospect. I have done so much over the years to avoid doing that. However, last week, the dam broke. On one hand, the pain was overwhelming, but on the other I knew that the healing process had begun. I told Marie, and I want to tell you three guys, that I have totally forgiven myself. As you said, Simon, I realized that I wanted to forgive myself more than anything else, and as you led me through the image of the young girl who hated herself because she had been abused, I wanted so much to make it right for her. Then I realized that that young girl was me and that loving and accepting myself was what I needed to do. There are many things that I have done that I am ashamed of, and I will tell you what they are in a moment, but last week, Simon, here in this room, I cuddled the little girl within me. I know that I am still fragile and will continue to battle my mental health issues, but each day, I feel like I am taking more control of my life, and I have this sense of peace that I have never had before. It's like I am not ruled by fear as I was before.

"The second thing I did was to write my victim impact statement, and I was wondering if I could read it today."

"Of course, you can, Margaret," Vince said. "But before you do, I want to tell you what a privilege it was for me to see you working through your situation last week and to tell you that today there is a new glow about you that I am sure is an indication of the relief you feel."

"Yes, you are right, Vince. There has never been a time in my life that I have felt as light and as disencumbered as I feel now. Writing my victim impact statement has also helped enormously, as you, John, said it would. Anyway, this is what I have written."

> My name is Margaret. I am thirty-three years old, and I was abused by Justin McKean when I was thirteen. I affirm that what he has described in his statement relating to the abuse that he perpetrated on me is a true account of what happened. The impact of the abuse was almost immediate. I was overwhelmed by self-hatred. I withdrew from my friends and my family, as can be attested to you by my grandmother, who was my legal guardian, and by my teachers. I began to self-harm, a crime against myself that I have continued to commit till very recently. I developed an eating disorder at fourteen, and I made my first serious suicide attempt when I was fifteen. When I was admitted to the psychiatric ward, I was diagnosed as suffering with borderline personality disorder, and after I was discharged, I continued to engage in several bizarre behaviors. I started gambling, something I had never done before. I was introduced to drugs and quickly became drug dependent. I started shoplifting to support my habit, and I began also to steal money from my grandmother. I suffered frequent and sudden mood swings. I was afraid of everything. Then when I was seventeen, I broke into a pharmacy with another girl and stole money and drugs. We were arrested, and I spent time in a youth detention center. On my discharge from there, I continued to be drug dependent and for a time used prostitution to finance

my need for drugs. I was again admitted to the psychiatric ward, and from then till now have been hospitalized at least once a year for periods ranging from a few days to more than three months, and I was incarcerated in a women's prison on two occasions. Most of the long-term hospitalizations have followed suicide attempts. I have never been employed, and I have never been in a relationship. The psychiatric reports that I submit with this statement verify that psychiatrists believe that my sudden transition from a happy, sociable thirteen-year-old to an angry, paranoid, and isolated teenager relates to the abuse I suffered at the hands of Justin McKean. I have only recently ceased blaming myself for the abuse and have accepted responsibility for my own destructive and sometimes criminal behaviors. I no longer excuse my destructive behaviors on the grounds that I have been abused. However, the opinion of all the medical professionals who have been involved in my care is that the abuse was a significant factor in both my psychological and relational difficulties, which have undeniably affected my life since I was thirteen.

For some time, there was silence. It was John who responded first. He smiled at Margaret and said, "Thank you, Margaret. What do you think is next for you?"

"I think I need to go to court and read my own statement. I must look this man in the eye and affirm that I am not a broken human being and that I am a real survivor. Then I need to concentrate on building a strong intimacy circle. After years of social isolation, I desperately need to feel that I am a part of a community. I cannot thank you guys enough for embracing and loving me. And there is, of course, the situation that exists between my grandmother and me. I ruined that relationship, and Grandma was forced to take out a restraining order against me. I am, as far as I know, still not allowed within a certain distance of her house, and I am forbidden to approach her anywhere else. Marie has offered to meet with her, and if she agrees, to mediate a meeting between us. I am extremely nervous about that, but it is something I would very much like to do."

Vince turned toward Simon, who all this time had simply sat looking at Margaret like a proud and grateful parent. "I think we are all on the same page now, Simon, and I wonder if it isn't time for you to help us explore what is next."

"I am happy to do that, Vince, if the others are happy to proceed that way." Margaret and John nodded their agreement. Simon continued, "You will remember that both Marie and I have said a few times that there are a number of important tasks that we need to undertake as we progress toward healing. The first, as you will remember, was to shift the blame for the abuse to where it belongs, and you have all done that. The second was to accept responsibility for the way we have responded and maybe are still responding to the abuse. You have, I believe, all done that too, although it is good to remember that that step is not only a choice we make but an ongoing process. The third is of course an ongoing one also. It is about forgiving ourselves and seeking the forgiveness of others for the hurt we have inflicted on ourselves and on them. In some respects, this is the most difficult step because it involves seeking to reverse automatic ways of thinking and behaving that are rooted in our painful emotions. For instance, the act of isolating ourselves from others is not a healthy or even natural behavior. Instead, it comes out of several false beliefs. One of those, as you, Margaret, have demonstrated, is the belief that you are not worthy of other peoples' acceptance or company. Another may be that it is dangerous to let people get close to you because you will get hurt, and yet another may be that if people get close to you, they will reject you because of your abuse. John has spoken about walking out on his family because he was angry at their lack of understanding about how he felt, and yet he had never told them how he felt; he just expected them to know. Vince, you have told us that you have never sought close relationships with others and that your primary drive is to placate God, who is angry at you because of what McKean did to you.

"So, whether we are talking about isolating ourselves from others, or self-harming, or developing drug and alcohol dependencies, we are talking about destructive behaviors that, in the case of each person in this room, have been preceded by a choice that has been influenced by your painful emotions. To feel angry, or fearful, or guilty, or bereaved are all valid, painful emotions. It is when they are internalized and repressed that they result in painful and negative thinking that leads to wrong choices, which in turn result in destructive behaviors."

John interrupted the old priest. "I am sorry, Simon," he said, "but I need some clarification. Are you saying that attempting to take my own life, for example, was not simply the result of me being deeply depressed, as the doctor said, but was a direct result of the painful emotions producing negative thinking, promoting faulty decision-making that then resulted in the destructive behavior?"

"That is correct, John. The emotional pain, be it anger or fear or hopelessness, that a wounded person carries does not in itself lead to a person taking his or her life. What it does do is lead a person to think negative thoughts about him- or herself and life in general, and then the bad choices, which might seem to be the only option at the time, follow. If we see destructive behavior as the result of painful emotions, then we can absolve ourselves from all responsibility for it, and therefore, change and growth become improbable if not impossible. Both our good and bad behavior are the result of choices we make. Our decision to take responsibility for the wrong choices we made in the past precedes our ability to make good and right choices in the future. For instance, if a man or woman is feeling angry because of a hurtful event, and the choice he or she makes is to repress or internalize the anger, it is possible that that choice in some cases may then result in other conditions, such as depression and anxiety. On the other hand, if instead of internalizing anger, that person finds a healthy way of dealing with it, he or she may avoid becoming depressed and anxious."

"So, Simon," said Vince, attempting a sardonic smile, "if somebody verbally attacks me unjustly, and I become angry, but I make a choice not to internalize my anger, what are my options?"

"That is a particularly good question, Vince," Simon said with a mischievous smile, "especially for a priest who is trying very hard to appear to be saintly and pastoral even in the face of injustice. There are two alternatives to repression, which of course is really a denial of what you are feeling. The first is suppression. This allows you to feel angry and own your anger but choose to keep it under control until you can make a considered and thoughtful response. So, if the unjust attack occurs at the door of the church on a Sunday morning, with all the congregation present, suppression might be the most suitable approach. Suppression is different from repression in that it is not a denial of the angry emotion but the conscious and deliberate choice to own it and to deal with it, but not now. The second option to repression is expression. There are both healthy and unhealthy ways of expressing anger. The unhealthy way is to throw caution aside and verbally or physically attack the person, or maybe to go silent and withdraw. The healthy way is to either respond in a humble or loving way or to realize that you need time to cool down and choose to take a backward step and come back to it later. This is using suppression to help ensure that when you do express your anger, you do it in the most helpful way for both you and the person you are angry at."

"Yes, I guess that's right," Vince said thoughtfully. "I remember a Baptist pastor, who is a friend of mine, saying that he had learned that if someone was attacking him verbally, it was helpful to believe that it was that person who, at that moment, had the problem, not him. The problem was not his until he allowed himself to adopt a position of offense or defense. He said that helped him to listen without interruption so that he fully understood what the other person's problem was, and then if it needed to be pursued, or if he needed to apologize for something, he would ask for some time to think about it, with the promise that he would come back to him or her with a response. He said that sometimes if he just listened, so that his attacker unburdened him- or herself, the issue would just seem to dissolve. I have been trying to practice the same thing with varying degrees of success."

"So, Father Simon," Margaret said, "you are saying that we have a choice to make between three options. We can go on repressing our anger, as we have all done for most of our adult lives, or we can suppress our anger and deal with it at some other time, or we can express our anger in either a negative or positive way. That helps me to understand my own journey so much better. For most of my life, I have denied—or as you say, repressed—my anger. Deeply internalized it. As a result, I have suffered physical, psychological, spiritual, and emotional damage. Last week, I began for the first time to express my anger. That was what the howling and the swearing was all about. I think now that that was all positive. Then during the week, I wrote my victim impact statement and shed some more tears over that. I think there is some anger still being suppressed, and I am believing that when McKean is sentenced, I will find a way of expressing it."

"That's good, Margaret. However, your anger is not like an infected finger. With an infected finger, you drain off the pus until it is all gone, and the finger heals. In one sense, you have indeed done that emotionally regarding your painful past. But your anger is and always will be an automatic emotional response to threat. That is the way we have been made. Many things will happen that will trigger a fearful response in you that may leave you feeling angry. Among these will be, for instance, reports of other incidents of abuse. You will hear of a child being abused by a religious figure that they should have been able to trust, and your anger will rise quickly and hotly and will demand to be repressed, suppressed, or expressed. Your initial response may be to repress it, but because you have learned how destructive it is to do that, hopefully you will express it instead."

"I know I have said this before, Simon," John said, "but I have to revisit it. For my mother to go on living after I broke her heart and for her to ultimately die in peace, she had to do more than just express her anger and her grief. She had to forgive me. I am desperate to know what forgiveness is and if it is possible for me to forgive McKean in the same way that my mum forgave me."

"Yes, it is possible, John. However, our time is gone, and this old man needs his nap before dinner. We will talk about it next week. By the way, Margaret, if John and Vince agree, I would be more than happy for Marie to join us next week."

21
OPPOSITION

An Office in the Archdiocese of Melbourne

It was the second time that his auxiliary bishop had asked Vince to attend his office. The first, a few weeks ago, had followed the church service where Vince spoke about institutional child sexual abuse and named McKean as his abuser. On that visit, the thought had been that a backlash from McKean supporters might make it untenable for Vince to continue as the parish priest. The bishop had told Vince that he planned to transfer him to another parish and suggested that in the period leading up to McKean's sentencing, he should take long service leave. Vince had agreed, on the condition that John, Tim, and he could address a congregational meeting with the bishop present. In fact, there had been no backlash, and indeed the congregation had increased in number. Subsequent events in the wider Catholic Church, including the guilty verdict against senior Catholic clergymen all over the world, had begun to occupy the minds of the people, and many expressed their admiration and support of their priest who had the courage to speak up regarding his own childhood abuse. There had been no further talk of a transfer or a congregational meeting. As Vince rang the doorbell, he felt thankful that what might have been a stressful situation had seemingly come to nothing. The bishop welcomed him warmly, and soon they were seated in a large and formal office. The bishop was a kindly man, of medium build and slightly thinning silver hair, who had on a previous occasion asked Vince not to address him formally as Your Excellency but simply as Paul.

"Thanks, Vince, for coming at such short notice. I hear that your parish is going particularly well. Your recent parish records show a significant increase in attendance at both the early and late-morning masses. Your oversight of the school and your support of the principal and staff has been greatly appreciated by them. My reason for asking for this appointment is that my attention has been drawn to the sermons you have preached lately, and I thought that you and I might discuss what seems to be some measure of departure from what one might expect from their parish priest. As you are aware, your sermons are put up on the church website, and I have taken the liberty of listening to the last two."

"That is good," said Vince. "I would appreciate your feedback and input from your long experience as a pastor."

"Vince, three weeks ago, you preached on the parable of the prodigal son. Do you remember that?"

"Yes, I do, Paul."

"I thought your treatment of the context and setting of the story and the emphasis on a lost son coming home was excellent. You said that the traditional view was that he was tired of the limitations and expectations of living with his father, and out of that discontentment, he made the outrageous demand that his father give him his share of the inheritance, which was tantamount to saying, 'I wish you were dead.' I had no disagreement with that. You explained that he may have felt that life on the farm was not for him, or he may have been abused by his brother or by a servant, and perhaps he was angry or hurt. Or he may have felt that his father was too demanding. You pointed out that it was a drastic step to ask for his whole inheritance, and in the modern world, we would call it cutting all ties to his father. You said that he clearly had no intention of returning to the family. You also said Jesus made it clear that he only returned when he had no money, no future, and nowhere else to go. In his desperation, he was prepared to work on the farm as a servant and receive a servant's wage. He confessed that he had sinned against the father but did not ask for or expect forgiveness, nor did the father say in so many words, 'I forgive you.' Up till that time, I had no quarrel with your sermon.

"You then went on to talk about God's prodigals and the church's prodigals, saying emphatically that when a child of God leaves their local church, it must not always be assumed that he or she is severing their relationship with God. You said that many people who have been sexually or spiritually abused by leaders in the Catholic Church are walking away from an institution they once trusted, but they are not necessarily walking away from Christ and his universal church. I have called you in here to ask you to explain what you mean."

"For me, it is quite simple, Paul," Vince replied. "I believe that I am a loyal member and faithful priest of the Roman Catholic Church. However, to be faithful to the scriptures, I need to see Catholicism as a part of Christ's church in the same way as Anglicanism, Presbyterianism, and Lutheranism are. I acknowledge, as I did in my sermon, that as institutions, they are as flawed as we are. Our being children of God does not depend on belonging to one of these or any of a myriad of other religious institutions; it depends completely on the grace of God and our willingness to become one of a great multitude of believers called the church. The Roman Catholic Church has been my spiritual home since I was born, as it has been for many generations in our family. My father walked away from the church because of my abuse as a child by a priest. His only connection with God was through the Catholic Church, and the only revelation he had of Christ was what he received every Sunday, from the very priest who covered up my abuse and protected my abuser. It followed that when he left the church in his anger and confusion, and later took his own life, he believed that God had let him down, because the only God he knew was the Roman Catholic Church.

"On the other hand," Vince continued, "even though I was abused, I chose not to leave the church but rather to stay and become a priest, even though I did it initially in order to placate the God who I believed I had sinned against. My theology was the same as my father's. We both confused the church with God. The sad thing, Paul, is that I went through my complete training to be a priest believing that the only place one could find God was in the life and liturgies of the Roman Catholic Church. It has taken recent encounters with a retired priest, an agnostic alcoholic, and a former prostitute to help me understand this is not so. The latter two are prodigals returning home because they had no resources, no hope, and nowhere else to go. They did not come home to the church, although they are attending Mass in my parish, but they came back to a heavenly Father who is celebrating their return.

"Paul, I am encouraged by your interest in my sermons, and as you rightly suggest, there has been a shift both in my theology and my ecclesiology. It is a work in progress, but I cannot any longer embrace a theology that supports the idea that a person can only come to God through his or her priest or the Roman Catholic Church, or for that matter any other denomination. All of us come to the Father through his Son, Jesus Christ. Nor do I believe that it is appropriate for Christian people to be taught that their priests and bishops are exclusively the representation of Christ in the world and are therefore above and removed from 'ordinary people.' All of us, ordained priests and the people of the parish, are equal in the sight of God because we are all created in God's image, redeemed by the same Christ, and indwelt and gifted by the same Holy Spirit. If such beliefs mean that I have departed from Roman Catholic teaching, I would be both surprised and disappointed."

When they parted later that morning, Paul shook Vince's hand, saying, "Be careful, Vince. There are enemies of the church who want to set priests against each other. We do not need a split in the church over ecclesiology."

Vince replied, "But, Paul, it may be that God is leading the church into a time of renewal by causing us to challenge some of our traditional dogma and practices."

As he rode the tram back to his church office, Vince wondered whether his willingness to examine everything he believed would strengthen his sense of call to the priesthood—or convince him that he was mistaken.

22

A DEFINITION

The Rectory

It was Marie who drove Father Simon to Vince's house. She had been pleased when Margaret had rung her and asked her to become part of the group meeting with Simon each week, and she had volunteered to collect him from the aged care facility where he lived. It had been three weeks since she had first visited him and told him her story, and she had seen him twice since then. He had challenged her during those visits to shift the blame for the death of her family on to the drunk driver who had taken them from her. It had been hard for her to make this adjustment because she knew that if she could not hide behind her guilt, she would have to confront her anger. She had been afraid to do that and had resisted Simon's encouragement to do so. Now she was anxious to speak to him alone before they reached Vince's house.

"Father, something very strange happened to me after my last visit to your home. I was in my office, and I had a phone call from a prison chaplain who cares for inmates of a prison for women in Melbourne. She rang me with a request from the woman who was driving the car that collided with my husband's car. She is serving a six-year sentence there and has also been undergoing treatment for her drug addiction. The chaplain told me that the woman, whose name is Kaye, has come to faith and wants to tell me how sorry she is for her part in the death of my husband and two daughters. Father, I cannot explain how I felt. At first, there was this icy calm, and I told the chaplain that I would need to think about it and that I would call her back. But when I hung up the phone, I began to tremble uncontrollably. Then I began to cry. At that moment, my receptionist arrived at the counseling center, and she said that she could hear me screaming at the top of my voice, 'How could she?' repeatedly. When I calmed down a little, I told my receptionist that this woman, Kaye, was trying to take the blame for the death of my loved ones. I told her that she was trying to take away my guilt. I know now, Father Simon, that I was being completely irrational, but at the time, I felt that if she took away my guilt, then I would not be able to survive. My receptionist was wonderful. She cared for my needs that morning, but more importantly, she helped me understand that the blame for the accident was not mine, and that this was the moment where I had to let it go. Father, I have let it go, and the relief is enormous."

"Will you visit Kaye?"

"Probably. It is a daunting thought, but yes, I think I will."

"What if she asks you for forgiveness?"

"Father, I know this sounds strange coming from a counselor, but I am not sure that I understand how to do that yet."

"Well, today we are talking about forgiveness, Marie, so your timing is impeccable."

They drove on, each lost in their own thoughts. When they pulled up in front of the rectory, Simon said, "You are on the same page as the others since your experience of letting go of your guilt, Marie, so today's conversation will be as applicable to you as it will be to them."

John, Vince, and Margaret welcomed Marie and Simon. Margaret said playfully, "I am glad you are here. I was getting a bit fed up with being the lone female in the group."

"That's why I have come, Margaret. I'm all for gender equality."

"So am I," said John. "That's why I am waiting for Margaret to serve the tea."

"That's not equality, John; that is role stereotyping."

"On the contrary, Margaret. I am practicing gift recognition. We men are excellent when it comes to solving the world's problems, but we are not gifted when it comes to pouring the tea. On the other hand—"

"Stop right there, John. You are already in a lot of trouble." Vince laughed.

When they were all seated together in the lounge room, Simon said, "Last week, we finished our session saying that this week we would answer John's question about what forgiveness looks like. Because so much of our conversation has been around the need to forgive ourselves for the wrong choices we have made and the hurt we have caused others, it seems that a good place to start today is to address the question, If I forgive myself, what will that look like? Is that okay with everyone?"

They all nodded, and John said, "I would personally like to start with a definition of forgiveness. I am sure Marie that you have been asked for that fairly often."

"Yes, I have, John. I usually begin my answer by saying what forgiveness isn't. Forgiveness is not minimizing or condoning the event that hurt us in the first place. Nor is forgiveness the same as forgetting, and most importantly, I tell people that forgiving another person does not mean that we are obligated to reconcile with them if to do so means to continue in a relationship that is toxic and harmful. And lastly, forgiveness of a person we have resentment or bitterness toward is a concession to ourselves more than to them. I usually tell people the kindest thing that they can do for themselves is to forgive those who have hurt them. However, I am looking forward to Father Simon telling us how to put legs on that definition."

"That's very helpful," said Vince. "One of the roadblocks I come up against when I think about forgiving McKean is the thought that it is an act of kindness to the man who damaged so much of my life. When I realize, however, that whatever it means to him that I have forgiven him, the primary and most important consequence is that I have acted therapeutically toward myself. That makes forgiveness a much more palatable and plausible thing to do. So, Marie, let me have a go at a definition of forgiveness. *I forgive another when I no longer want them to suffer for what they have done to me, so negating the need to remain resentful and bitter."*

"That is good," Simon said, "because it assumes correctly that our bitterness and resentment are our principal responses to our hurt and that the primary reason for forgiving another is to free ourselves from the destructive effects of those painful and unnecessary emotions. I also like the use of the words *no longer want,* because that suggests that forgiveness requires a shift from *I want* to *I no longer want.* This is what makes forgiveness both a difficult and a radical thing to do."

"Yes, you are right, Simon." This time it was Margaret. "My experience has been that whenever someone suggests I should forgive McKean my reality is that I don't want to. My sense of justice says that he does not deserve forgiveness. But you are saying that my wanting to forgive him is not based on what he deserves, but instead, it is based on what I need to do for myself."

"My sister, Clare, sent me a card last week with a Bible verse on it," John said. "Apparently the apostle Paul was writing to Christians in Ephesus, and he told them *to forgive one another as God in Christ has forgiven them.* What does that mean, Simon?"

"Well, John, it is sometimes difficult to define forgiveness without a model and a modus operandi. The people Paul was writing to knew that Jesus had willingly died on a cross, affording to God the opportunity of forgiving humankind, on the basis that Jesus paid the price for humanity's sin. So, Paul is saying that in the same way that God forgave your sin (through the death and resurrection of Christ), you should forgive others. He is saying that Christ not only died for the sins we have committed but also for the sins that have been committed against us by someone else. Paul is giving them a model (this is how God forgave you) and a modus operandi (this is how you must do it)."

"And," added Vince, "the encouraging but unspoken element of this was that God did not forgive us because we deserved it. It is interesting that there are three things that we are told to do as God has done. First, Jesus told us to love one another as he has loved us. Then through Paul, God said we should forgive others as God in

Christ has forgiven us, and Paul again tells us to accept one another as Christ accepts us. Given that God loves, forgives, and accepts us unconditionally, then his direction to us as His children is that we should do the same. If the Christian community on earth practiced only those three things, it is easy to imagine that most of the world's injustice, poverty, and violence would disappear."

"Margaret," John said, "what do you think?"

"I feel like I have had the most amazing revelation today. You all know that for years I hated myself with such virulent hatred that I have suffered complex psychiatric and physical illnesses for most of my life. Two weeks ago, I was able to release that self-loathing and shame and embrace the truth that I was not responsible for my abuse. I know now that I was able to do it because I had reached a place where I wanted to do it more than anything else in the world. Today I have heard in this discussion that I can forgive myself if I no longer want to punish myself. And that is true. I do not want to punish myself anymore. I have done that far too long. I want to love and nurture myself. I don't want to go to court next week and tell McKean that I hate him. I want to tell him that I now love myself so much that I want to let go all my bitterness and resentment. I have never been a real believer, but, Vince and Simon, you have demonstrated to me that there is a loving God in the universe and that he has forgiven me for everything that I have ever done to myself and others, and because of that, I am able to love and forgive myself."

"I guess I am in a similar place to Margaret," Marie said. "I have the opportunity if I wish to take it, to meet face-to-face with the woman who took the lives of my husband and two daughters. Before today's session, I was not sure that is what I want to do. But I am ready. I want to forgive her so that I can move on. I want to do it for me. I do not have to decide whether she deserves forgiveness. I am a daughter of God, and he loves, forgives, and accepts me unconditionally, and that means that I am lovable, acceptable, and forgivable and capable of loving, forgiving, and accepting others. I am so glad you invited me today. It has changed my life."

"Well, we should stop. All this happiness is too much for this old man," Simon said with a tired smile. "Monday is the day that McKean will be sentenced. John, Vince, and Margaret will be reading their victim impact statements, and all being well, I will be there also."

"I would love to come too, if that's okay," said Marie.

"Of course, it is okay. In the meantime, harness your horses to the chariot, young lady, and drive me to my illustrious palace, please."

23
TRIAL

The sentencing of Justin McKean occurred six months after he appeared before Justice Mason Milburn in the county court and entered a guilty plea. On that occasion, the prosecution had submitted a confession written and signed, in the presence of his bishop, by McKean, in which he gave the names of people he claimed to have abused. His confession included the number of times he had abused each one and the exact nature of each assault. Each of the victims named in the confession had, in subsequent police interviews, affirmed that the information was true in every case. At that court appearance, Justice Milburn had remanded Father Justin McKean until a future date when he would appear again for sentencing. Justice Milburn had invited survivors to submit victim impact statements, which they all did, although only five planned to read them themselves. The other six would be read to the court by James Churchill.

It was a cold, damp morning, but the weather had not discouraged a large crowd from turning up. Margaret, Tim, John, and Vince arrived, accompanied by Marie and Simon and their solicitor, James Churchill, who ushered them past members of the press and those waiting to get in to the security officer at the head of the queue. A few words from James to the security officer, and they were ushered into the second front row. When Justice Milburn entered the room, they all stood and remained standing until told they could sit.

The prosecution, a smartly dressed young woman, took the stand. "Your Honor," she began, "on the fifteenth of May 2019, Father Justin McKean, after presenting at the Ballarat Police Station with a written and signed confession, was arrested and charged with eleven cases of grooming children with intent of performing sexual acts with and on them, twenty counts of committing an indecent act with a child, and eight counts of sexual penetration of a child under sixteen, all of which occurred between 1985 and 1995. Each of the facts in the confession have been affirmed by the alleged victims. There have been no further charges, and an exhaustive police investigation of Father McKean's activities, before the abuses began and after they allegedly ceased, has not turned up any evidence of further criminal behavior. However, in light of the seriousness of the abuses confessed to by Father Justin McKean and confirmed by each of the eleven survivors, the prosecution recommends that the maximum penalty be applied in this case."

She continued for some time, reinforcing the prosecution's demand for the maximum sentence, and when she had completed her submission, Justice Milburn addressed the court. "The prisoner has chosen to represent himself and will address the court following the submission of the eleven victim impact statements. Suffice for me to say that the prisoner has made a full confession of his criminal behaviors, so accurate in fact that I have been advised that none of the alleged victims have as much as altered even the tiniest detail. In a written statement to the court, the prisoner acknowledges that his crimes must incur punishment. However, he has requested that I take three matters into consideration. They are as follows. One. All the evidence obtained by the legal team representing the alleged victims confirms that his behavior in the past twenty-four years has been exemplary. Two. That in turning himself into the police, he demonstrated remorse for his crimes and has continued to do so. And three. Since his arrest and imprisonment, while waiting for his sentencing, he has been subject to horrific verbal and physical abuse. He has requested that I consider these three issues before I decide on a suitable sentence."

Justice Milburn cleared his throat and in a firm voice said, "Before I pronounce the sentence, I may impose on the prisoner, are there any victim impact statements to be read?"

James rose to his feet quickly. "My name is James Churchill, Your Honor. I represent all those who were named in Justin McKean's confession and who have subsequently been interviewed by the police, confirming that the details in the confession were an accurate record of what occurred in every case. Each of these people have prepared victim impact statements, which have been submitted to both counsel for the prosecution and to the defendant. Five of these will be read this morning by the survivors themselves. The other six will be read by me. I seek leave, Your Honor, to make some introductory comments before they read their statements."

"Leave granted, Mr. Churchill."

"Thank you, Your Honor. Each of the eleven people, all of whom are present in court this morning, were children attending three different Catholic churches where Justin McKean served as parish priest in the ten-year period when these offenses occurred. The offenses occurred, Your Honor, between 1985 and 1995, and at the time they were abused, their ages ranged from ten to thirteen years. In my discussions with them, they acknowledged that hundreds of religious and government institutions failed to adequately protect children from sexual abuse, and the Roman Catholic Church, at that time, was one of them. They also acknowledged that when cases of sexual abuse were reported to these institutions, few if any dealt with the reports and the perpetrators in an appropriate manner. Today, while their statements will detail the direct impact of the crime of child sexual abuse on their own lives, it is important to remember that much of their suffering has been a result of not being appropriately protected and, following their abuse, not being believed and taken seriously."

"Thank you, Mr. Churchill. This morning, each of the five people presenting their victim statement will read from a statutory declaration. No additional comments will be allowed. The same will be true of those that will be read by Mr. Churchill. The prisoner has waived his right to cross-examine either those who speak today or those who have issued written statutory declarations only. When it is your turn to read from your statutory declaration, I ask that you state your name first and that you speak directly into the microphone provided. Mr. Alan Jennings, you are first. Please step forward."

During James's introduction, Vince watched Justin McKean, who sat in the dock, avoiding eye contact and staring steadfastly into a space in front of him. There was a great deal of hostility in the room toward the prisoner, but Vince found himself feeling sorry for this pitiful man. As Alan Jennings stepped forward, Vince could see that he was extremely nervous. He had only met Alan once before at James Churchill's office. He was a big man with red, curly hair and a luxurious red beard flecked with gray. As he faced the crowded courtroom, he smiled fleetingly at someone behind Vince, probably his wife. When he spoke, his voice was softer and a tone or two higher than might be expected from a big man. "Your Honor, my name is Alan Jennings. I am thirty-two years old and live with my wife in Malvern, a suburb of Melbourne. I was groomed and sexually molested by Justin McKean, from the age of eleven, and then raped by him when I was thirteen years of age. He was my parents' parish priest. Following the occasion when I was raped by Justin McKean, my behavior at home and at school rapidly deteriorated, as has been attested to by my mother in a letter accompanying this statement. I went from being a normal thirteen-year-old boy to an antisocial, withdrawn, and angry child. I rejected my parents, disobeyed my teachers, and became violent in the schoolyard. Feelings of anger, shame, and fear were almost continually with me. At fourteen, I was suspended from school, and when the suspension was lifted, I refused to return. Instead I would stay in bed till midmorning every day, and then when I rose, I would leave the house and stay away, often till the early hours of the next morning. At sixteen, I was introduced to illicit drugs and soon afterward left home altogether. I began shoplifting and at seventeen was arrested for my part in an armed robbery. I was sent to a youth detention center where I was to stay for nine months. However, my behavior was so bad that I kept getting charged for affray and causing grievous bodily harm to both fellow inmates and center staff. Each appearance in court resulted in my sentence being increased, so as well as the nine months in the youth detention center that I was originally sentenced to, I spent another three years in an adult prison.

"After my eventual release, I joined a men's anger-management course and gained employment for the first time in my life. A year later, I met and married my first wife. I treated her very badly and was ultimately charged with physically abusing her, and because of my past record, I was sent back to jail. There I met a Catholic chaplain to whom, for the first time, I told my story of abuse. He became the one person who understood my anger and the first person who encouraged me to report my abuse to the authorities. I refused, as I could not see that anything good could come of that. After my release, he introduced me to a psychologist, who has helped me enormously. I am no longer an uncontrollably angry man. I am happily married to my second wife and a member of our local Catholic church. The psychologist's report submitted with this statement asserts that the aggressive, antisocial behavior I exhibited throughout my teenage and young adult life was a direct consequence of having been sexually abused as a child by Justin McKean. That, Your Honor, is my victim impact statement."

"Thank you, Mr. Jennings," the judge said. "You may be seated."

For the next ninety minutes, the court listened as Tim, Margaret, John, and Vince all read their statements. When Vince had completed presenting his statement, Justice Milburn directed James Churchill to read the other six statements. Each of them was deeply moving, and at times, even the experienced and case-hardened James Churchill struggled to hold back his tears. When the presentation of the victim impact statements concluded, Justice Milburn again addressed the court.

"I appreciate the input I have received today from both my learned colleagues and the written and spoken victim impact statements. As I said earlier, the prisoner has waived his right to ask questions of those who have written and presented their reports and instead has asked permission to address the court. I have granted the requested permission. However, the court has been in session already for two hours, and as it is now midday, I am going to propose a recess. We will reconvene in two hours."

The family and friends of the survivors surrounded each of their loved ones as they left the court, congratulating them on the victim impact statements they had written, and most of them moved off to have lunch in nearby restaurants. Tim, Marie, John, Simon, Margaret, and Vince walked to the Quest on William Street, a hotel a short distance from the court. Everybody was in great spirits and chatted eagerly about the proceedings, except Simon. When their lunch had been served, Vince turned to him and smilingly commented that his friend was unusually nonverbal.

Simon apologized and quietly said, "I am sorry, Vince, but I am feeling completely overwhelmed by what we have heard this morning. Eleven painful and heart-wrenching stories from eleven people, all of them different individuals, and yet each of the stories were strikingly similar. Each of them came from loving families and were, before meeting and being abused by McKean, happy and well-adjusted children living normal lives. After their abuse, each of them became withdrawn, angry children whose behaviors both at school and home were radically changed. All of them ended up dealing with their pain in inappropriate and self-destructive ways, and most of them are still prisoners of guilt and shame. I guess I am just finding it difficult to cope with hearing all those stories together on one morning."

"I understand, Simon," commented Marie. "I found it difficult too, and I am used to hearing painful stories. For me, the most depressing factor was that except for you guys and Alan Jennings, the survivors of McKean's abusive behavior are still living without hope. It is possible that there are thousands of people out there who do not know that they can be free of the debilitating effects of childhood sexual abuse."

"That is true, Marie," Vince said, "and without you and Simon, we would not know that such freedom is possible either. I, for one, will be forever grateful to God for both of you, and indeed for you, John and Tim and Margaret, for all being a fellowship of healing where we have been able to weep and laugh our way to a new way of seeing our lives and our future."

When later they entered the court together, each of them felt confident that whatever McKean said in his address to the court, and regardless of the severity or otherwise of the sentence handed down by Justice Milburn, the healing pathway that they were on was totally independent of those things. What they had discovered together would continue to equip them to make healthy choices in the future.

Justice Milburn, when the court had been called to order, invited Father McKean to address the court. There was silence in the room, but Vince could still feel the hostility with which McKean was being confronted when he rose to speak. Every person in that court had experienced unspeakable pain because of what this man had done, and his action in addressing the court seemed to be an undeserved concession to a man who deserved nothing but the harshest punishment. He now spoke in a firm voice.

"Your Honor, like you, I have listened intently to the information presented by these men and women with whom I had sexual contact when they were children, and I am sorry that each of them has traveled such a painful road. However, I wish to say that I am charged with having molested eleven children, not with having ruined the lives of eleven adults. I respectfully submit that whatever the cause of their emotional instability, their mental illnesses, and in some cases their criminal history, they must accept personal responsibility for their individual behaviors and choices. I take responsibility for the crimes that I committed against eleven children but respectfully ask that, as you consider the sentence you hand down, you base your decision only on my behavior over twenty years ago and not on the tales of woe that we have listened to today."

To say that there was an uproar in the court would be to make the understatement of the century. Men and women, many of them shedding angry tears, abused McKean continuously as court security rushed to protect him from bodily harm. The clerk called loudly for order to be restored in the court, but his voice was drowned out by the shouting. Justice Milburn was taken completely by surprise. What he was expecting to be a humble apology from McKean had instead been a plea for mercy on the basis that he was not responsible for the pain he had been listening to for two hours. Some of those who had written victim impact statements were sobbing loudly. Others sat in silent disbelief at what they had just heard. McKean simply took his seat, and Vince noted that he was probably the most composed person in the court. When order was finally regained, Justice Milburn spoke directly to McKean, ordering him to stand up while he was being addressed.

"Father McKean, your remarks are completely out of order and are among the most offensive I have heard inside or outside a courtroom. I will not take anything you have said into account in sentencing you, other than to note that you are completely unremorseful. I consider what you have said today as just another act of abuse against those who, by your own admission, you abused more than twenty years ago.

"I am sure, Father McKean, that you and everyone here will appreciate the purpose today is not to determine your guilt but to decide on a suitable sentence. The issue at stake here is not that you are a priest of the Roman Catholic Church or of any other church. You, as the Royal Commission on Institutional Response to Child Sexual Abuse has shown, could well have been an employee in one of hundreds of institutions where children have been and still may be vulnerable. No, the issue is that you are a pedophile, convicted on your own confession of having sexually abused eleven children. I do not agree that your claim that you have not offended for twenty-four years and that you have voluntarily surrendered yourself to the police are reasons for a lesser sentence. By your own admission, your reason for doing so was that your bishop, having been informed of two cases of child sexual abuse, which involved you as the sole perpetrator, gave you an ultimatum. Your only two options were to hand yourself in with a full confession of your crimes against eleven defenseless and vulnerable children or to have the matter reported to the police and endure a trial. I was tempted to think that surrendering to the police as you did and making a full and extremely accurate confession was an act of contrition, but having heard what you have just said, and realizing that you have no concept of the damage your actions have caused, I suspect that confessing to your crimes was done only to minimize the consequences for yourself.

"In pronouncing your sentence today, I need to reflect on three things, but first we need to remind ourselves of your background and the nature of the charges. You were raised in a happy and well-adjusted home in country Victoria and acquitted yourself well both academically and in your chosen sport of cricket. When you were fifteen, you informed your parents, both of whom are here today, that you had a calling to the priesthood. You pursued your studies to that end, and you were ordained in 1985 at the age of twenty-five. During the next ten years, you abused eleven children and have pleaded guilty to eleven charges of grooming, twenty charges of committing an indecent act with a child, and eight charges of sexual penetration of a child under sixteen.

"Each of your eleven victims have made victim impact statements. We have heard of people whose lives have been shattered, leading to such things as alcoholism, drug addiction, mental illness, prostitution, criminal activity, domestic violence, imprisonment, and an inability to establish and maintain meaningful relationships. A cynic such as yourself, Father McKean, might be tempted to believe that it is convenient if you can blame a childhood experience for all the bad choices you make in life. However, each of these eleven survivors have psychologist's reports that say that there was no evidence in their childhood of dysfunction or maladjustment. It is clear to me that not only is childhood molestation and rape a horrific trauma on its own, but years of living with the belief that they are responsible for what happened, and that you are a good person who they have somehow corrupted, is mental torture of the very worst and most evil kind. Some of these children, Father McKean, lived with this secret and this shame until you confessed to their abuse. They were too afraid to tell anybody because of the threats you made to them.

"In deciding on the sentence I am going to impose on you, I have taken, as I said earlier, three matters into consideration, none of which are in your favor. The first matter is your careful grooming of each child. You deliberately chose each child, and they became your target. You were kind to them, and they learned to trust you. Some were shy children who lacked confidence when it came to their peers, but you demonstrated love, acceptance, and encouragement, positioning yourself between them and their families and their friends. The second matter was the molestation and rape of these children. That was the goal you patiently and calculatingly worked toward. Much of your initial touching of them and your cajoling them to touch you was done in the context of them believing that you loved them; however, seven of the eleven survivors recounted that when you raped them, you were harsh and cruel. One man remarked, as he recalled your rape of him when he was thirteen, 'It hurt physically, but what hurt and frightened me more was when he yelled at me, blaming me for what happened. Most nights, I see his angry face in my nightmares.' The third thing I am considering is that when you were confronted some years ago by the father of one of the boys, you lied and denied it. This is bad enough, but even worse, you on at least one occasion, when hearing of one of your victims' bad teenage behavior, told his mother that it was probably the result of bad parenting. You have lived for twenty-four years knowing that your victims and their families have been suffering severely, and you have done nothing. Some of those we have heard from have spoken of a time when they sought for and received help from qualified counselors and kindly priests, while others still live in a world of tears and pain.

"If I took each person's situation into account and sentenced you separately for the crimes committed against each one, the sentence would exceed sixty-six years. There would be many who would think that was fully justified. They will probably consider any sentence I impose as too lenient. Others would argue that you have already suffered significant punishment in that never again will you be able to practice as a priest, and those who think like that will find any sentence I impose on you too harsh. Father McKean, will you please step forward. With consideration of the powers vested in my position as a justice of the county court of Victoria, I hereby sentence you to twenty-five years' imprisonment, with a nonparole period of nineteen years. Your name will be also added to Australia's Sex Offender Registry, on which you will remain for the rest of your life."

The sentence handed down by Justice Milburn was met with applause from the crowded courtroom. As Margaret was leaving the court, she was approached by a smartly dressed woman of a similar age to herself, and Margaret was captivated by a deep calm and peace that seemed to visibly surround this stranger. "Paula Jennings is my name," she said. "My husband, Alan, presented one of the victim impacts statements. I have written you a hasty note," she said as she handed Margaret an envelope. "My contact details are enclosed. I am hoping that we may be able to catch up soon." And then she was gone.

John, Tim, Vince, Margaret, Marie, and Simon sat in the bistro of the hotel. They all expressed their approval of the custodial sentence. It was John who first ventured into the discussion on how the whole proceedings had left them feeling.

"I think I came here expecting that at the end of the day, I would have an empty, hollow feeling. I thought that justice would be done and that I would be happy about that, but I felt that the overwhelming feeling would be that nothing had changed. We are still survivors living with the pain of what McKean did to us, and he is still a pitiful excuse for humanity, except now he is living in a stinking jail with the shame of his conviction, instead of living in a comfortable rectory, surrounded by adoring parishioners. But instead, what I am feeling is that something has changed. It is like a door has been slammed shut on over twenty years of being half-dead and half-alive. I am free now to make healthy choices about the rest of my life. I have new friends to whom I will always be grateful, I have been reunited with my family, I have a new job and can afford to rent a decent unit, and I am making real progress learning how to forgive myself for the hurt I have caused others. A few months ago, none of this would have been possible, and none of these changes are a direct result of McKean being jailed."

"I feel much the same," said Margaret. "There was a time when I thought that no sentence would be sufficient to atone for the wrongs that McKean committed against me and others. But today, I had the overwhelming feeling that, at last, one of the institutions that we have trusted as a community has not, like the others, failed us. The institutions of the family, school, church, and the police have all failed to protect and nurture me, but today, the justice system has functioned as we should expect it to."

Later that evening, Margaret opened the envelope that the woman at the court had handed her. The contents of the short note obviously written during the court session came to her at first as a huge shock. The note said:

> Dear Margaret, you do not know me personally, but you may remember me as that foul-mouthed teenager who many years ago harangued you on Facebook. I deeply regret my actions then, and I hope that one day I can apologize to you face-to-face. Like you and Alan and your other three brave friends who told their story, I too have a story to tell. After seeing you in court today and realizing who you were, I felt that you, more than any other person I know, are the person to whom I would like to tell my story. Enclosed, please find my contact details. I look forward to meeting you soon. Yours Sincerely, Paula.

Margaret sat on her bed for a long time. That evil little girl of her nightmares had found her at last. Except that now they were both adult women. While the thought of spending time with Paula was a daunting prospect, Margaret had to admit that she was probably better equipped to deal with such a meeting than at any other time in her life.

24
KAYE

A Victoria Women's Prison in Melbourne, Victoria

It had been arranged that Marie would meet the Rev. Carol Mustafa, the prison chaplain, in the Boon Beans Coffee Shop. Carol had explained that it would be good to spend an hour together before they went to the correctional center at the normal time for visitors. She had arranged for Marie to be on Kaye's visitors list for the day, and the center had made a small room available for their meeting. Carol, a tall Sudanese woman in her thirties, welcomed Marie with a warm smile and a spontaneous hug. "I am so pleased that you could come," she said. "I suspect that it must have been an exceedingly difficult decision."

"Well, it was at first. To tell the truth, I was angry that you had approached me with that proposition. Since my husband and two daughters died, I have taken the blame for their deaths, and the idea that Kaye was about to rob me of that by taking the blame herself was unthinkable. In the end, it was your phone call that brought me to the realization that for me to carry the blame was simply an irrational way to avoid facing my grief. Since then, a group of incredibly special new friends have helped me to the point that I was able to accept yours and Kaye's invitation."

"That's great, Marie. Sometime I would like to hear more of that story. Maybe after you see Kaye, we can come back here for a while before you drive home."

"I would like that."

"Maybe I should just tell you a little about my relationship with Kaye. You would know that after the accident, she was charged with several serious offenses, including the manslaughter of your family. She pleaded guilty and ended up here on remand, awaiting sentencing. She was ultimately jailed for twelve years, with a six-year nonparole period, and returned here to Phyllis Frost. She was, among other things, addicted to illicit drugs and was high the night of the accident. She has been deeply remorseful, although she had not mentioned the idea of meeting you until a few weeks ago. I was called to see her one evening, and she was deeply distressed. It turns out that she had been reading a Bible she had found in the prison library. She wanted to know whether God could forgive her for the way she had lived and for what she had done. Well, to cut a long story short, she prayed. Her prayer was a litany of the wrongs she had done to a long list of people, and then she asked God to forgive her. I assured her, as her pastor, that God had forgiven her. For a day or two after that, the relief and gratitude she felt was obvious to everybody. Then one day, when I caught up with her, she was overcome with remorse again. She said that she had been thinking about you and wondering how you could bear the pain of losing your husband and daughters in the way that you did. She said she did not expect you to forgive her and would never ask you to, but she said she needed to tell you that she was completely to blame for your loss, and to tell you that she was sorry. That is when I decided to approach you. I told her last week that you were coming. I think she is pleased but very afraid."

When they arrived at the prison, there was a queue of visitors waiting to be processed. Carol and Marie went directly to the head of the queue, and a prison officer greeted them warmly and ushered them into the center with no formalities other than the normal security checks and asking Marie to put her name in the visitor's book. Another officer appeared, obviously a friend of Carol's. They embraced, and then Carol introduced Marie. "June is the officer who is designated to look after me," she said with a smile. "She organizes all my appointments with inmates and is responsible for my safety." June shook Marie's hand very firmly.

"I am incredibly pleased to meet you, Marie. I have a friend, Margaret, who speaks of you very highly. We met here a few years ago, and she has kept in touch ever since. She has had a tough time, but when we last spoke on the phone, she sounded like a different woman. I can't wait to catch up and hear more of her story."

"You are right, June. Some great things are happening for Margaret, but all the credit is hers for having the courage to face her demons." They had reached the consulting room. It was a surprisingly bright and welcoming room, Marie thought, not what she would have expected in a prison.

June said briskly but pleasantly, "I will go and get Kaye. You are welcome to stay here with Kaye as long as you need, and when the interview is finished, just press the buzzer, and I will come and usher you out."

As she left the room, Carol smiled encouragingly at Marie and said, "I will meet you back at the exit. I will be praying for you, Marie."

When June returned, she was accompanied by a blonde woman in her late thirties or early forties. Her otherwise attractive face showed the signs of a hard life, and her forehead was creased with worry lines. She wore prison garb, and where her three-quarter sleeves ended, a couple of tattoos were visible.

"Kaye, I would like you to meet Marie," June said simply. "I will leave you girls together." When June had left, the two women sat on opposite sides of the small table. Kaye was clearly extremely nervous.

"When I asked whether you could visit me, it sounded like a good idea at the time, but now I am not sure."

"I think it was a good idea for both of us, Kaye. At first, I was reluctant, but some good things have been happening in my life lately, and I realize that us meeting today will be a significant part of the journey I am on. I am deeply impressed that you have expressed a desire to speak to me."

"Thank you, Marie. I guess I wanted you to hear this from

me and not secondhand from Carol. I was fully responsible for the accident that killed your husband and your daughters. For a long time, I blamed the drugs, the weather, the road, and even your husband, but none of those things contributed to what happened. That accident would have happened in broad daylight, on the driest day. It happened because I was driving under the influence of the drug ICE. I was angry, suicidal, and even homicidal. I did not care what happened to me or anybody else. Your family was just unlucky that they were the ones on the road that night. Even though I am the mother of two little girls who I never see, I cannot begin to imagine what it has been like for you to have all your family stolen from you like that. I wanted to tell you personally that I am deeply sorry that my actions have caused you so much terrible pain and loss."

For the past couple of days, Marie had wondered what her reaction would be when Kaye owned the responsibility for the accident that killed her family. She had not counted on Kaye being so forthcoming as to admit that, though she was charged with three counts of manslaughter, she had in fact on that night intended to kill herself and anybody else who got in the way. A wave of nausea flowed over her, and for a moment, she felt on the edge of fainting. She breathed deeply and tried to remind herself that if Kaye was going to express her sorrow at what she did that night, then it had to be the whole truth, no matter how painful it would be for both of them. She found herself going into survival mode, and instead of responding like a devastated wife and mother, she dropped into the role of a counselor. Kaye had stopped talking and was looking at the floor.

Marie said, "Tell me a little about yourself, Kaye. How did your life hit rock bottom?"

"I will tell you about myself as long as you understand that nothing I say is an excuse for me killing your husband and children."

"I promise not to let you make any excuses."

"My life has been on a downward spiral since I was thirteen years of age. I lived in a country town, and I was a member of the choir in an Anglican church and was befriended by the associate minister.

Dad had left my mother just after I was born, so I had grown up without a male presence in my life. This man, who was in his thirties, showed an interest in me, and I guess I liked the attention. We used to have choir practice on a Thursday after school, and then he would drive me and my two friends home. One evening after he had dropped them off, he drove to a park and told me that he loved me. I wasn't sure what to do with that, but when he put his arms around me and started kissing me, I became very afraid. I broke free and somehow got out of the car, and I ran as fast as I could. I had only covered about two hundred meters when another car pulled up beside me. It was two boys who I thought were friends of my older brother. I was so relieved that they had come by I just jumped in the car, but instead of taking me to my house, they drove in the opposite direction to some bushland a few miles from the town. I was beaten and assaulted by these boys, and when they had finished, they drove me back to the edge of town and pushed me out of the car. By the time I had walked home, it was very late, and Mum had already rung the police and reported that I was missing. I told the police about the two men, and they were picked up and charged. However, I did not tell anyone about the pastor because, rightly or wrongly, I have always thought that no one would believe me anyway.

"After that evening, and the subsequent police interviews and court cases, I was wracked with shame. Even the police blamed me for the assault. They said if I had not been wandering around in the park so late in the day, it would never have happened. From then, my life went from bad to worse. By the time I was fifteen, I had left home and was homeless. I was introduced to drugs when I was sixteen and almost instantly developed a heroin addiction, which later led to me taking ICE. At eighteen, I got pregnant and gave birth to twin girls. My mother told me that I could come back home and live with her and that she would help me raise the girls. My drug addiction was too powerful, however, and my mother could see that I was a danger to my children and that, because of the drugs, I really had no interest in being their mother. I stole money from her and caused her a great deal of heartache. She eventually kicked me out and took out an intervention order to prevent me from ever going back. That was six years ago. My little girls are seven now and probably don't know that I exist.

"The night of the accident, nearly three years ago, I had just heard through a friend that my mother, who I knew had married some bloke with a couple of kids, had left Victoria. I had no idea where they had gone. I was heartbroken and angry that I would never see my daughters grow up. I was on my own in my unit and got well and truly stoned on ICE and alcohol. I went mad. I wrecked the furniture and broke a window. I went next door and found the neighbor's car with the key still in the ignition. I stole it, and the rest of the story you know."

The two women sat in silence. Despite the palpable emotion in the room, neither of them wept or spoke. Marie was stunned that this stranger whose journey had so powerfully intersected with her own suffered the same overwhelming grief as she did. She had come expecting to feel angry at this woman who had ended the lives of her family, but what she was feeling was a deep empathy with Kaye. They were sisters in grief, both broken by circumstances beyond their control. Both women stood at the same time and found themselves in each other's arms. Then the sobbing began, and for an exceedingly long time, there was a mutual outpouring of grief. They were still in each other's embrace when Marie asked, "What are your little girls names?"

Kaye answered without lifting her head from Marie's shoulder, "Brittany and Bianca." They stood together a little longer and then stepped apart, still holding each other's hands. Neither of them would ever forget this moment for the rest of their lives.

Marie said, "My twins' names were Fiona and Grace. They were seven, too, at the time of the accident."

They sat down again, and Marie said, "You have not asked me to forgive you, but I want you to know that I do. I do not forgive you because of your story, because nothing that you have told me is an excuse for what you did to me. I decided a couple of weeks ago that I did not want to be defined by my loss, nor did I want to be dictated to by bitterness and anger. I learned from a godly old priest that I could forgive you because of what Jesus has done for both of us. Carol told me that you asked God to forgive you for all the things you had done to hurt others. Can I ask how that made you feel?"

Kaye thought for a moment. She looked at Marie. Her eyes were still full of tears, but she wore a peaceful smile. "I felt like I do now. Loved and forgiven. For the first time in my life, after I prayed, I knew that His love and forgiveness enabled me to see myself as a good person who could make a difference for others. I suppose the other feeling was hope. Hope that I could one day forgive myself, and instead of functioning out of my painful emotions as I have in the past, I will start making good choices out of knowing that I am lovable and forgivable."

"You have already started making good choices. What do you think your next one will be?"

"Well, ultimately, I choose to be a good mother and get my children back. But I know that before that can happen, I need to make a choice to kick my drug habit. That's the choice I make today."

"Well, Kaye, I also want to make a choice. I choose, if you would allow it, to be your buddy and to support you in all the choices you make."

"That would be fantastic, Marie. I can hardly believe that you would do that for me, but it would be absolutely wonderful to have you as my friend."

"Maybe," Marie said as she pushed the buzzer, "we can both make these choices for the sake of two little girls, and in memory of two others."

When June entered the room a few minutes later, the two women were sharing a farewell embrace, with Marie promising to be back in two weeks. When they reached the exit, Carol was waiting, and together they drove back to the Boon Bean Coffee Shop. When they had ordered their coffee, Marie said, "Thank you, Carol, for organizing today. This has been the most amazing and most exhausting day of my life. Kaye's courage and honesty moved me beyond words. I have promised her that I will be a regular visitor."

"That's great, Marie. I am very pleased about that."

"Carol, I can't ever get Vic, Fiona, and Grace back. But she can one day be a wonderful mother to Bianca and Brittany, and I want to help her do that."

"Days like today, Marie, make everything I do in this sad and miserable place seem worthwhile."

"Well, Carol, with your happy disposition and mammoth smile, you seem to me to be the right person in the right place. How did you come to be a chaplain here?"

"When I was ten years old, in the year 2000, I was living with my parents in southern Sudan. We were a Christian family, and like millions of Sudanese, we were caught up in a brutal civil war. We escaped our homeland that year and fled to Uganda. We lived there for five years in a huge refugee camp. In 2005, a peace agreement was signed, and many Sudanese families moved back to southern Sudan, but our family was offered the opportunity to come to Australia. While I was in the refugee camp in Uganda, I did get to attend a school. Most days, the classes were conducted under a tree. When we arrived in Australia, we lived in a suburb of Melbourne, and I attended the local high school. I was a long way behind the Australian fifteen-year-old kids, but I worked hard, finally gaining a place in university when I was nineteen. In 2013, I graduated with a degree in psychology and then went to a theological college and graduated with a degree in theology in 2017, at twenty-seven years of age. Then last year, I was approached by a friend who worked in the justice system, and he told me that Corrections Victoria was seeking a suitably qualified person with a refugee background to work as a chaplain in this center. I applied and commenced working here halfway through last year. When I began here, I was assisting a senior, very experienced chaplain, and I was concentrating on working with mainly African refugees who had been incarcerated. However, early this year, the senior chaplain became ill and had to resign, so now I am the only one here. It is very demanding and terribly busy, but I love the job and feel very privileged to have it. I guess living in a refugee camp for five years was rather good preparation for a role in the prison system." Carol finished with an engaging smile.

"That's a great story, Carol. I know Kaye is grateful that you are here."

As Marie drove home, her thoughts went through the amazing list of events that had led her to and prepared her for today, and she thanked God for a godly old man named Simon who was probably, at this very moment, sleeping in his chair on the veranda of the aged care center where he was a resident.

25
RECONCILIATION

The day after her unforgettable meeting with Kaye, Marie had a scheduled appointment in her counseling rooms with a lady named Sally, who was Margaret's grandmother. Although Margaret had lost contact with most of her family, she knew how to contact an uncle. She phoned and explained to him that she had turned her life around and that she would love to be able to tell her grandmother this but was unable to do so because of the restraining order that was still in force. She told him that Marie was willing to mediate a conversation between her grandmother and herself. She asked her uncle whether he would talk to her grandmother Sally and suggest to her that if she was open to such a meeting, she could call Marie and set up an appointment. Within a day, Sally had rung Marie, and two days later, she had arranged for the restraining order to be lifted. Marie had, after talking to Margaret, arranged for Sally to arrive thirty minutes before the scheduled mediation.

Sally, like Margaret, was tall and slim. In her early seventies, she was smartly but not expensively dressed, and when she arrived at the counseling room, the receptionist could see that she was very nervous. Marie felt comfortable with this obviously anxious but outwardly friendly woman and explained to her as they sat down facing each other that they had half an hour to talk before Margaret arrived. Sally was obviously pleased about that and immediately asked Marie to fill her in with Margaret's story. It appeared that she had almost no knowledge of what had been happening in her granddaughter's life in the past twenty years. Marie told Sally that it was Margaret's story to tell but that she could tell her why she was sure that this was the right time for them to be reunited. Margaret had identified that she had been driven by intense self-hatred and now attributed much of her mental illness, her substance addictions, and her antisocial behavior to her unwillingness to blame her abuser for her abuse. She had now accepted responsibility for the destructive behaviors that had their root in the painful emotions that she had internalized. Working with a counselor, and meeting with a caring group of people, and presenting her victim impact statement in court had all been factors in Margaret's desire to attempt to heal relationships with people she still cared about but no longer interacted with. Sally was deeply moved by the thought that the abuse Margaret had suffered as a child still caused her so much pain, and she sat for a long time with her head bowed. Marie knew that she was weeping for the granddaughter she had not seen for almost twenty years, and perhaps also for her own pain as a grandmother who had lived her own life while her granddaughter had plumbed the depths of mental illness and despair.

The chime of the doorbell announced Margaret's arrival. They could hear the receptionist welcome her and ask her to wait while she let Marie know that she had arrived. Marie rose, and when the door opened, she beckoned Margaret to enter the counseling room. Sally also stood, her face still wet with tears. The two women appraised each other before Sally moved toward her granddaughter. In a moment, they were in each other's arms, both seeming to laugh and cry at the same time. Marie took her chair and waited until they had disengaged themselves and sat together on the couch.

"Thank you, Gran, for agreeing to come," began Margaret. "I have treated you so badly that I would not have been surprised if you had refused to be in the same room as me."

"I have waited a long time for this day, Margaret. I knew when I heard that Father McKean had made a confession, your name would be among those he admitted to abusing. I came to the court last week and stood in the big crowd outside on the street. I saw you leave the court with your friends, and I so wanted to run up and congratulate you for having the courage to be there and read your victim impact statement. I was not sure you would have wanted me there, so I decided not to speak to you then. And I recognized Father Simon. I was a young girl when he was the priest at our church. I was brokenhearted when the church sent him away to the bush. And here he was supporting my granddaughter."

"Simon coming into my life has been the most wonderful thing that has ever happened to me, Gran."

"I am sure it is, dear. During the Royal Commission and the pain of seeing priests and nuns, among others, exposed as abusers, the one thing that sustained my faith in the church was my memories of Father Simon. He was such a loving and caring man that, as a child, I used to imagine that Jesus would have been just like him. There was a rumor that persisted for many years that the bishop had sent him away because he challenged the senior priest in our parish about the sexual abuse of children. My father, your great-grandfather, used to say that Simon was banished because he was a priest with a conscience."

"Maybe it was a time when nobody really understood how to respond to information relating to the sexual abuse of children, especially in the church."

"But not exclusively in the church. Your grandfather and I did not know how to deal with it either. Or, if we did, we did not have the courage to do what we should have done. We failed you, Margaret, and I am deeply sorry." Sally and Margaret were holding hands on the couch. Now they hugged each other again.

"It's okay, Gran. I am sure that my behavior at home and at school didn't make it easy for you and Grandfather to know what was going on for me. Since I left home, I have been in prison once, in mental hospitals often, and in between, I have done some terrible things to myself and others. I have not asked you here today so that I could ask you to forgive me. I would understand if you couldn't do that. I asked you here to tell you that I am sorry that I hurt you and Grandfather so much."

"And I have come to tell you that I am sorry that I have not been beside you all these painful years of your life. Of course I forgive you, and I hope that we can make the rest of our journey together."

"I want that more than I can say," Margaret said with a sob in her voice.

Grandmother and granddaughter hugged again, and Marie chose that moment to leave them to talk together. Out in the reception area, she sank down wearily on the couch, put her head back, closed her eyes, and stretched out her legs in front of her. Sighing, she said softly,

"Nancy, I am so tired I could cry."

Nancy stopped what she was doing and came to sit beside Marie. "I have been thinking that you desperately need a break. When you told me that you plan, on top of everything else you do, to visit Kaye every fortnight, I was concerned. Not only has your schedule been very full of late, but you have been on an emotional roller coaster yourself. I have watched you closely, Marie, and have decided that you have pushed yourself to the edge, emotionally and physically. My son and daughter-in-law have a beautiful cottage by the sea at Ocean Grove, and I am sure they would be thrilled if you used it for a week or two."

"Nancy, I would love that, and I do feel I need it, but what about my clients?"

"I have checked your diary for next two weeks, and all your appointments are regular fortnightly sessions. I am sure that if they miss a session, it will not be too influential. I am happy to ring them and explain that you will not be in the office next week."

Marie smiled. She loved Nancy, and her motherly concern for her was no surprise. She reached out and laid her hand on Nancy's and said, "I accept. If it suits your son and daughter-in-law, I will go down on Saturday."

At that moment, Margaret and her grandmother stepped out of the counseling room. Marie stood, delighted to see the two women standing hand in hand. They were glowing. With a smile, Sally said, "Thank you, Marie, for helping us come together. It has been wonderful. We have a lot of catching up to do."

Margaret smiled warmly at her grandmother. Then turning to Marie, she said, "When we came out of court on Monday morning, a lady handed me an envelope and said that she hoped we could catch up. It turns out that she is the wife of Alan Jennings, who was the first person to read his impact statement. But here is the amazing thing: she claims to be the girl who harangued me with threatening Facebook posts when I was sixteen."

Marie saw the puzzled look on Sally's face. She quickly explained. "The girl who stalked Margaret on social media claimed to have been the daughter of the other woman who died in the incident where your daughter took her life."

"Do you believe her?"

"I certainly did at the time. But I guess I will know more after I see her tomorrow."

"It's strange. That little girl was two at the time, and I thought I heard she died two years later. I must be mixing that up with someone else. Her name was Paula, I think."

"That's the name of the person who gave me the note. Well, tomorrow will tell. Come on, Grandma. Let's go get a coffee, and then I will run you home."

26
ANNA

As she was leaving the court after McKean's sentencing, Margaret had been approached by a woman who introduced herself as Paula Jennings. Her husband had been one of the people who had read his victim impact statement to the court. Paula had handed Margaret a note that said she had been the teenager who harassed Margaret on Facebook twenty years before. In the note, Paula asked if Margaret would meet her. After some amount of struggle with the idea, she had agreed.

They had arranged to meet in Cisco's World of Coffee in Prahran. Margaret arrived early and was checking her emails on her phone when Paula arrived. Margaret stood and extended her hand, which Paula took. Once again, Margaret was captured by the serenity and peace that seemed to emanate from Paula.

"Thank you for meeting me," Paula said, smiling. "I really do appreciate it."

"That's okay," Margaret replied. "Can I order you a coffee? I am having a skinny latte."

"I will have the same, thanks." When they sat down together, Paula said, "As I said in my note, I am the girl who harangued you all those years ago on Facebook. I only stopped when I was admitted to a psychiatric hospital on my sixteenth birthday. I was depressed and had begun to self-harm." Margaret noticed for the first time a nervous tick that appeared occasionally near Paula's left eye.

"At the time I began to troll you, I was terribly angry, but that does not excuse my behavior. I wanted to tell you that I am sorry.

You didn't deserve that. It was a stupid, senseless, and hurtful thing to do."

"Thank you, Paula. I guess I don't understand what it is like to know that your mother was killed by an irresponsible drug addict, but I do know what it is like to grow up without a mum."

"There is something else I need to tell you. Something that makes what I did to you even more inexcusable. You see, I am not the daughter of the woman who was killed by your mother. And my name isn't Paula. It's Anna."

"Whoa! Slow down, Anna, or whoever you are. It's a bit too much to take in."

"Sorry, Margaret. I am sure it is very confusing. Let me start at the beginning. The woman who was killed in the flat that night was my aunty Janet. Her daughter, Paula, and you were in the bedroom asleep. She was about eighteen months old when she came to live with us. I was four years old. Paula was an extremely sick girl even before her mother's death, and she needed twenty-four-hour care. My father did not want my mother to take Paula on, but she felt this sense of obligation.

"My father once told me that from the day Paula arrived, it was as if he and I did not exist. My mother was totally obsessed with Paula and focused only on her needs. I was immediately enrolled in a childcare center, and my father would drop me off early on his way to work and pick me up on the way home. I know that by the time I was five, I was withdrawn and very, very lonely. When I started school, my father would get me up and drive me to a friend's place, and I would have breakfast there, and then her mother would take her and me to school. My father would pick me up on the way home from work. When I was seven, Paula died. My mother became deeply depressed. She would be asleep when I left for school and still in her dressing gown when I got home. She never spoke, and on the weekends, she never got out of bed.

"On my eighth birthday, they took my mum to a hospital, and I never saw her again. After about a year, my dad and I moved into my friend's house, and my dad married her mum. When I was fourteen and so depressed that I had missed heaps of school, I heard that my mother had died. I know now that she was in a psychiatric hospital and that she committed suicide. By this time, the other emotion I had become aware of, apart from sadness, was hate. I hated Aunty Jane for getting killed. I hated your mother for killing her. I hated Paula for taking my mum away from me. I hated my mum for rejecting me and replacing me with Paula. I hated my dad for marrying my friend's mother, and I hated my stepmother because she tried to act like she was my mother, and she wasn't. Then one day, I can't remember how it happened, I found you on Facebook, and the rest of the story you know."

"Well, at least I now know why you started to attack me on Facebook, but I know that there is a lot more to your story. I have the time if you want to tell it to me."

"Okay! Thanks. The next four years are a bit of a blur really. I think my anger dissipated or just morphed into depression. I guess, from the statement you made in court, you know all about that. My time was split between stints in hospitals and long, boring days at home on my own. One day when I was nineteen, it suddenly occurred to me that I was invisible. There I was, with all this misery, and people just carried on with their lives as if I wasn't there. No one else's life was affected daily by the fact that Aunty Jane died or that Paula died or that my mother died. No one cared that I sat alone all day, longing for someone to put their arms around me and tell me that I was loved. I was a waste of space. I was an unnecessary impediment on my family. It was crystal clear to me. There was one good and decent thing I could do, and that was to remove myself from the earth. I got up from in front of the television and walked out the door. I did not take my phone or my purse. I was wearing a simple cotton dress and slippers. I waited at the bus stop near our front gate. What happened next, I only know because a neighbor saw it all unfold. A bus stopped, and other people waiting at the bus stop boarded it. I didn't. When the bus moved off, I stepped on to the street behind it, into the path of a passing car.

"To my great disappointment, I did not die that day. I was

admitted to the hospital with a broken arm and leg and head injuries. I was so angry that I was alive that I refused to cooperate with the medical staff, and I treated everybody who tried to help me horribly. Then one day, this tall, young man in his middle twenties came to see me. He introduced himself as Alan and told me that he was the driver of the car that I stepped in front of. He said he could not swerve to avoid me because of the traffic. He had braked as hard as he could but had not been able to stop in time."

"What did you say to him?"

"I told him he need not have worried. I really wanted to die, and he said that he didn't believe that. He told me that he saw the look on my face just before the car hit me, and that look said, 'Help me,' not 'Kill me.' He said that he had not been able to get that look out of his mind. He had thought of me every day. He came to the hospital several times to see me, and the staff told him that I was not receiving visitors. But, he said, he knew he had to see me, so this time he just came in without asking anyone if he could. I was dumbfounded that he cared enough to come. I guess I wondered what he wanted, but he told me that he did not want anything. He just wanted to help me through my recovery, and one day he would tell me why he knew this was what he had to do."

"What happened then?"

"Well, he came every day after that, and when I was discharged, he would come to my house and take me out in the car and push my wheelchair around the park. We told each other our stories, and I guess, to cut a long story short, we fell in love and married ten years ago."

"What a fantastic story, Anna. What about your depression? Where are you with that now?"

"Well, you know a little of Alan's story. By the time I met him, he had done a lot of work with his counselor, and I guess he in a way became my therapist. He helped me understand that my depression was largely the result of unresolved anger and grief. We began to go to a local church, and the priest helped me to forgive the people I was angry at." She smiled. "Thank you for listening to me, Margaret."

"Not at all, Anna. I feel so privileged that you have shared your story with me." Margaret told Anna about the meetings that she and others had been having with Father Simon and shared that at their next meeting, they were going to talk about forgiveness.

"It would be fantastic," she said, "if you could come and tell us what you learned from your pastor."

"I would love to come, if you are sure that the others won't mind me gate crashing your group."

"They won't mind," Margaret said, standing up. "And by the way, I do of course forgive you for the Facebook posts. Looking at you now and seeing how happy and peaceful you are, I just can't imagine you writing them." The two women embraced each other. Anna paid for the coffee, and they left the shop together.

27
THE GIFT

The Rectory, Melbourne

Father Simon was in good form as he and Marie arrived at the rectory. Vince welcomed them and led them into the lounge room, where John and Margaret were talking to the two new members of the group. John had invited Tim, and Anna had come at the invitation of Margaret. There was much joviality and laughter as they all helped themselves to coffee or tea and one of the delicious muffins that Anna had brought to share. Simon called for attention. His eyes were twinkling with amusement.

"I have a question to ask Vince," he announced.

Vince, surprised, turned to face the old priest. "Okay, fire away. Ask me anything you want to, as long as it does not involve football or cricket." The others laughed. Simon was a sports buff, and he loved to stir Vince about his lack of sporting knowledge.

"No! Not this time. My question relates to something in which you have unquestionable expertise. What is the secret of a good sermon?"

This time it was Vince's turn to laugh. He mockingly bowed, saying, "You, Your Gracious Eminence, have much more experience in sermon crafting than I. Tell us the answer."

Simon chuckled. "A good sermon has an introduction and a conclusion. The closer they are to each other, the better the sermon."

"Are you alluding to my long sermon last week?" asked Vince, trying to sound offended.

"No, my boy. Far be it from me to rebuke my parish priest." Laughing, they sat themselves down in a circle. Vince welcomed Tim and at the same time congratulated him on his presentation at the county court. Margaret welcomed Anna, explaining briefly, to the intense interest of the others, how their two lives had intersected.

Marie, obviously still very excited about her meeting with Carol and Kaye at the Phyllis Frost Women's Prison, commenced the conversation by saying, "I told you all that I was planning to meet Kaye, who is serving six years in prison for the manslaughter of Vic, my husband, and our twin girls. It was one of the most amazing days of my life. First, I met Carol, the chaplain. She herself is quite a remarkable person who, with her family, lived for five years in a refugee camp in Uganda after fleeing from southern Sudan. Carol explained to me that Kaye had a spiritual encounter during which she asked God to forgive her for all the pain she had caused many people throughout her life, including me. Following that experience, she felt a great need to tell me how sorry she was. Boy, does she have a story! Well, part of that story is that she has twin daughters who are the same age now as my daughters were when they died." Marie paused as a gasp of empathic surprise came from the group. "Amazing, isn't it. They are being cared for by her mother, who apparently has whisked them off somewhere without Kaye's knowledge or permission. She hasn't seen her girls since her imprisonment, and now that she has had this amazing turnaround in her life, her goals are to beat her drug addiction and get her daughters back.

"The most wonderful thing about my meeting with Kaye is that even though she did not ask for my forgiveness, I knew that I needed to give it to her anyway. I told her that I could not forgive her just because she had had a lousy life, but I could forgive her because what I wanted more than anything in the world was to live a life without bitterness. Simon, I was able to share with her what you said last time we met here."

"And what was that Marie?"

"That when it came to forgiveness, God had given us both a model and a modus operandi. The model was that God forgave us because Jesus Christ had been our substitute and paid the price for our sin. Therefore, the modus operandi for us is to set ourselves free by forgiving in the very same way those who have hurt us. As you can imagine, we hugged and cried a lot. I promised her that I will support her for the rest of her term of imprisonment and help her beat her addiction and get her kids back."

"Thank you, Marie," Vince said. "I was praying very diligently for you that day. What a wonderful story of healing yours is turning out to be. Does anybody have any questions for Marie?"

"I do," said Anna very softly. Her eyes were full of tears, and her face wore a look of deep compassion. "This woman Kaye gets high and kills your husband and twin daughters, Marie, and now you are going to invest the next few years of your life helping her get her twins back. You have lost everything you had because of her anger and irresponsibility, and she will regain all that she has lost because of your compassion. Are you sure that this is what you want to do? Are you even sure this is the right thing to do?"

"That is a particularly good question, Anna. But it is more than a question. To me, it's a summation of the very premise on which I can forgive Kaye. Let me respond to what you said by telling you what I have learned from Father Simon. God lost everything he held dear because of our sin, and we will regain all that we have lost because of his compassion. What he has done gives me the opportunity to do the same."

Nobody spoke for a very long time. Each person was lost in the profundity of what Marie had just said. Then Margaret, first looking at Vincent and then letting her gaze sweep the whole group, said, "It might be a good time to tell you some of what has happened to me since we last met. With Marie's help, I met with my grandmother Sally, who I had not seen for nearly twenty years. She raised me from about the age of five, when my mother, who was a drug addict, killed herself after causing the death of another woman in a fight. By the time I was sixteen, she had to take out a restraining order on me because of my behavior toward her and my grandfather. Marie told her that I turned my life around and said that if she was prepared to do so, I would like to meet with her. We met in Marie's office. I told her that I was sorry that I had treated her and my grandfather so badly. I told her also that I was not asking for her forgiveness or even for her to risk reconciling with me. I have labeled myself as a victim all these years, but in relation to my grandmother, I was the perpetrator, and I had no right to expect anything from her.

"The first thing she told me, Simon, was that you had been her childhood hero and that memories of your love and your faithfulness had sustained her faith in the church throughout the painful revelations of the Royal Commission on Institutional Response to Child Sexual Abuse. The second thing she told me was that she had forgiven me, and when I was ready, I could, if I wished, go home and live with her. I am telling you this story because I, like Kaye, have experienced what it is to be forgiven. I know, Simon, that you said when we forgive someone for the hurt they have caused us, it is we who get the benefit. I know what you mean. But I feel I want to say that to be forgiven is the most undeserved blessing you will receive, and for me, it has been life-changing. I know that I don't deserve my grandmother's forgiveness, and I am deeply humbled by it. I will never take it for granted, nor will I knowingly violate her trust again. She has given me a second chance, and I am incredibly grateful."

"That is not all," Anna said. "The very day after Margaret was forgiven by her grandmother, she and I met. I initiated the meeting because I wanted to tell her I was sorry for verbally attacking her when we were both teenagers every week for two years on Facebook. I know that it caused her great pain, but just as her grandmother had forgiven her, so she was more than willing to forgive me."

"That reminds me of a story that Jesus told," said Father Simon. "He told about a man who owed his employer the equivalent of millions of dollars. Knowing that the man could never pay back the huge debt, the appropriate action would be for his master to throw him in jail, sell his wife and children, and take the proceeds. It would pay back at least something of what he owed. Instead, the master had compassion on him and forgave him the debt. You would expect, would you not, that the man would be grateful. In Jesus's story, however, this man goes out of his master's presence and almost immediately meets a man who owes him a much smaller but still significant amount of money. Instead of doing what his master has done to him, he has the man thrown into jail until the debt is paid. Jesus finished his story by saying, 'So that's what my heavenly Father will do to you if you refuse to forgive your brothers and sisters from your heart.' That's what we have heard today. Margaret has sinned against her grandmother, and Anna has sinned against Margaret. Margaret's grandma forgives Margaret, and then Margaret is able to forgive Anna."

"That's right, Simon." It was John who spoke. "And Margaret's grandma learned about forgiveness, when she was just a girl, from a faithful young priest who was banished to the bush for being a priest with a conscience."

Tim had been silent throughout the discussion, but now he cleared his throat and began haltingly, "I am not very good at explaining myself in words, but I do have something I want to say today. My situation is a little different from the rest of you in that, as a teenager, I displayed the symptoms of schizophrenia. I had my first psychotic episode at thirteen, and by the time I was eighteen, I was regularly experiencing eight of the ten most common symptoms of schizophrenia. Childhood schizophrenia is not common, and it is generally thought that the onset occurs when there is a combination of factors, especially a genetic propensity and a traumatic and intrusive childhood experience. From a medical perspective, there is no cure, and the earlier the condition appears, the more severe its effects in adulthood are likely to be. My adoptive family has been fantastic, and their support and the medications that I am on mean that I cope surprisingly well but not well enough to hold down a full-time job or begin and maintain a long-term relationship. For long periods of time, I can feel somewhat detached from the sort of emotions I hear you speak about, like grief, guilt, and anger. But then, if I experience a psychotic episode and these emotions rise to the surface, it is then that I struggle most with guilt and anger. And then, to make things a little more complicated, in the months following a psychotic episode,

I am subject to severe mood swings that make me difficult to live with, and it feels like I am on an emotional roller coaster. This group of people has been amazing to me, and I am very grateful for your acceptance."

Anna had been listening intently. She now spoke directly to Tim. "I understand what you said about employment, Tim, but how do you occupy yourself each day?"

"I do photography, drawing, and painting," Tim said with a shy, almost embarrassed smile.

"I would love to see some of your work."

"I have some photos of it on my camera. I will show you later."

"No!" said Simon. "Show us all now. I think we would all like to see it."

Tim opened his camera, and the others gathered around him. For the next five minutes, they watched spellbound as Tim scrolled through a collection of photos, pastel drawings, and water and oil paintings.

"They are magnificent, Tim," Anna said. "What do you do with them?"

"Nothing at all, much to my mother's disgust. In fact, you are the only people outside of the family to have seen them. They are all stacked in a storage cupboard in my mother's house."

"Oh no! What a waste! Do you know what my husband, Alan, does? He works in the art gallery mainly organizing exhibitions of the work of artists. He would go crazy over these. Would you like to send these photos to him?"

"I could, I guess. Do you really think they are good enough?"

"They are magnificent," Marie said. "Tim, this is your gift, and as I looked at your drawings and paintings, it was as if you were touching the peaks of joy and the depths of despair often in the same work. Your paintings come from a unique place, and what you see as a disability is also the ability to see things as the rest of us cannot see them. But it is not a gift that should end up in the cupboard."

"If your husband is impressed by what he sees, Anna," Vincent said, "I would be more than happy to donate the use of our church hall for an exhibition of Tim's works."

"Sounds great," said Tim. "I feel nervous about letting the world judge my art, but if you think that it is a good thing, I trust you all and will give it a go. Anyway, I have brought a painting to show you. I did it after our visit to court, and I thought that if I showed it to you, it might explain how I am feeling about what has been happening."

Tim went out to the hallway and brought in a painting wrapped in brown paper. It was large, about a meter square. When he unwrapped it, he held it up for them to see. There were gasps of amazement and admiration and then silence as each person allowed the painting to affect them. In the middle of the painting, a boy knelt alone. Two groups of people, one to his right and one to his left, had their backs to him and were walking away from him. His arms were stretched upward and were elongated to symbolize that he had been reaching upward for a long time and with great desperation. Above the kneeling boy was the most magnificent depiction of the crucifixion of Christ. Gathered around the cross was a crowd of men, women, and children. Some were in the clothes of the rich, some wore army uniforms, and many were obviously poor and represented people on the edge of society. Some of the people were standing, shouting and shaking their fists at Jesus, while others knelt, stretching out their hands toward him. Above the crucifixion scene was another scene. In contrast to all the frenetic action of the rest of the painting, this was an idyllic scene of peace. There were beautiful trees, an enchanting stream, and people lovingly connecting with one another. The three different scenes in the painting were brilliantly connected by the way the artist had used his colors and his brushstrokes. To the eye of the observer, it was not three different scenes, but the story of a man caught in the pain of rejection, traveling through unbelievable loneliness and suffering toward the experience of unconditional love and forgiveness. There was not a dry eye in the room. Even Tim, who was standing behind the painting, had tears flowing down his face, moved deeply by the responses coming from those who gazed at his painting. Margaret was gently weeping. The painting seemed to express so many feelings she knew well, and in that moment, she was speechless. Then, with a sob in her voice, she said quietly "I feel like I am standing in a magnificent cathedral and that this painting is its centerpiece."

"Tim, do you have a number of paintings like this one that tell your story?" John asked. There was a note of excitement in his voice.

"Good question, John. I think I know where you're going with that," said Vince.

"Yes, John, I have a series of smaller paintings, ten of them in fact, which I have painted over ten years. The series begins with a choir of children singing in a beautiful church. It captures the beauty of the church and the devotion and joy of the choir. But away from the choir, there is a boy sitting cross-legged on the floor with his head in his hands. Behind him is a door, and you can just see the leg of a man disappearing out the door. The next one is a schoolyard and a boy standing on his own as the other children play. Between him and the other children is a little girl in shabby clothes, reaching out a hand to him. The third one involves the boy alone in his room, with his dreams. The fourth, fifth, and sixth ones are centered around the theme of psychiatric illness and institutions. The seventh, eighth, and ninth are scenes of ordinary life. One is a family gathering, another is a visit to the country, and the third is set in a shopping center. Each scene is depicted through the eyes of an observer who views it all from the outside. The last one I have not quite finished. It depicts a hospital, a courthouse, a prison, and an empty park bench on which lies an old overcoat. The man and a group of friends walk arm in arm down a warm and inviting road. Why do you ask, John?"

"What I am envisaging, Tim, is a Festival of Healing and Restoration. It would feature an exhibition of your art and maybe other creative things that we or other survivors might be able to contribute. The main feature would be called The Walk, or something like that. It would be part of the exhibition and would be set up so that when you got to the end, there would be a coffee and chat area, with this painting in the most central place.

"You've got it John," said Vince. "That's a magnificent idea. I would love to work on that with everybody here, and, Alan, and make it a citywide event."

Margaret said, "A little bird told me that among us is a person who has written a series of songs along a similar theme to Tim's series of paintings. And not only has this person written the songs, but this person also sings these songs and plays a German-made zither at the same time."

"This festival is getting bigger and better all the time," said Simon with a huge grin.

"I better own up," said Anna. "As a matter of fact, although I have written several songs, both Alan and I are singers, and we both play the zither and the guitar, which, as musical instruments go, are cousins. The zither does not have a neck like a guitar does and can have up to fifty strings. Mine was made in Germany by my great-grandfather and was passed down to my grandmother, then to my mother, and after her death, when I was old enough, it came to me."

Margaret could not contain the joy she felt or the smile that lit up her face.

"I suggest that Tim and Anna and Vince should do some groundwork on the festival, and the rest of us will help where we can. Simon, I think you have got something more to say today."

"Thanks, Margaret. It has been a wonderful day, and to round it off, I would like to take up something Tim said earlier. Tim, you started talking about yourself by saying that your situation is a little different than that of the rest of us because you suffered with schizophrenia. I would like to say that, on the contrary, you are very much like the rest of us. It is true that you have a mental illness, but so have Margaret and John and Anna. It is true that you depend on medication to some extent, and that is also true of every person in this room except me. It is true that you carry on your heart the indelible scars of emotional wounding; so does everybody else here today, including me. No, we are all very much in the same boat as each other, and we share that boat with thousands like us. Where you might have been different from some of us is that until today, you had not realized that with your great pain, there has come an amazing gift. Gifts often come to us wrapped in pain. Until today, you thought that the best thing you could do for the world was lock yourself up in your mother's house and wait for your next psychotic episode and your next stint in the hospital. You also thought that your gift was not worthy to be shared with the world, so you locked it in the cupboard. It has been what you thought about yourself and your mental illness and your gift that makes you feel different to us.

"Today, I have watched this group of people who, as representatives of thousands of others you are yet to meet, invite you to come out of your *orbis terrarum dolores* and enter the real world of *gaudium inter doldrum*."

Vince laughed. "Okay, our ancient and illustrious Latin scholar will now, for all our benefit, translate."

Smiling, Simon went on, "*Orbis terrarum dolores* means a world of pain. At some time or other, we have all lived in that world. Maybe, Tim, you have lived in that world until today. But there is another world that true survivors enter by faith in a God who loves us unconditionally. It is the world of gaudium inter dolores, which means joy amid pain. It is not possible to live in a world without pain. Why, even the greatest gifts of life, such as love and trust, in their very nature carry the real possibility of loss and grief. No, there is no life without pain. But Jesus taught us that there is a wonderful world that by its very nature fosters love and nurtures creativity. It is called the world of joy amid pain. Today, Tim, I have seen a new light in your eyes as your friends have introduced you to what may well lie ahead of you in your gaudium inter dolores."

It had been a good session, and as Vince returned to the rectory after taking Father Simon home, he was making plans. Yes, there was some work to be done on the healing festival, but there was something he needed to do first. It had been on his mind for several days, and now he knew for certain that the time had come for a visit to Justin McKean.

28

THE CONFRONTATION

Hopkins Correctional Center, Ararat

One of Vince's friends, Maurice Mason, was the pastoral care practitioner at the Hopkins Correction Center and was helpful in arranging for Vince to visit Justin McKean. As he pulled up in the carpark, he wondered what sort of welcome he would receive from the disgraced priest. McKean had agreed to put his name on the prisoners' visiting list, and today Vince would be one of hundreds of visitors who would pass through security into the large room where prisoners met their visitors. When Vince saw Justin in court, it was the first time the men had seen each other in twenty years. Justin had not changed much. Certainly, he was older, but the blond hair still showed no signs of graying, and the startling blue eyes were the same. Would it be awkward? Would McKean be defensive? Would Vince become angry and aggressive? Vince looked around him. There were prisoners sitting at tables with their visitors. Some of them had gone to the canteen with their visitors, where the latter were purchasing sausage rolls and chips to share. When Justin McKean entered the room, he spotted Vince and crossed the room to his table. As he arrived, he put out his hand, and the young priest stood, and they greeted each other. As they took their seats, Justin studied Vince for a moment and then said, "I must admit that I was surprised to hear you had requested the opportunity to visit me. It has been a very long time since we both met." Vince realized that McKean's voice had not changed.

"This all might be a little easier," he said, "if we talk over a coffee and something to eat. What will you have? It's my shout."

"The pies are good, and the cappuccinos are passable."

When Vince returned with the pies and coffee, Justin began to eat with gusto.

"The food is a bit light in here," he said, "so having a meat pie is a treat."

"Justin, as you heard at the court, a group of people, including myself, have been meeting together with an old retired priest, Father Simon. These sessions have been immensely helpful, but recently during one of them, I became certain that I needed to visit you. As the first boy that you groomed and abused, I wanted to know so many things about what started you on a journey that left eleven people devastated."

"It is true, Vince, that you were the first, but that is no reflection on you. I had fantasized about sex with children since I was fifteen. I guess you were the first opportunity. I found myself in a parish where the priest, to whom your father turned for help, also groomed children for sex, and because of that, he turned his back on my extracurricular activities, including my relationship with you. I am pleased to see that it did you no harm. I suspect that most people who are complaining about being abused are looking for a payout, and the harm they are claiming is in most cases bogus."

Vince felt the anger rising in him. He really wanted to murder this supercilious, unrepentant man. But he knew he needed more information. "Why did you hand yourself into the police if you do not think that you have harmed anybody?"

"Because, Vince, I was afraid for my life. Many years ago, Tim Purnell's father beat me up very badly after his son complained about me. I was sent to another diocese after I recovered, and for the last twenty-five years, everything has gone well. However, last year, this Tim was in a psychiatric hospital, and he told an inmate about what I had allegedly done to him. The guy Tim spoke to knew me and, driven by his schizophrenia, began to stalk me. I would come home and find my house broken into and threatening notes left in every room. Then one day, when I was driving my car, the brakes failed, and I almost killed myself. The police told me after an investigation that the car had been tampered with. A few days after my discharge from the hospital, your bishop came and told me that you and another man had accused me of sexual abuse. I knew that it was only a matter of time before this mentally deranged lunatic was going to kill me, so I handed myself in. I wrote a confession with the hope that it would cause the judge to give me a lighter sentence. No, Vince, if you came here expecting to hear a heartfelt confession from some pathetic criminal, then you will be disappointed. I am not a criminal; I have not hurt anybody. You all liked what I did to you at the time, but now that some of you have developed mental or relational issues, you all look for something or someone to blame. Well, you can go back and tell your friends that I am not here for what you have alleged I have done. I am here because it's the safest place for me right now."

The rage that rose in Vince at that moment was indescribable, and later he was to describe it as homicidal. Then a calm came from deep inside his being, and he spoke confidently and firmly. "Before you end this interview, Justin, let me say what I came here to say. I have not come to see you in order to forgive you. My friends and I have forgiven you already. We don't need an apology from you. Any apology from you would be meaningless. And even if you were repentant for the hurt you have caused us, your repentance would still be meaningless. We need only to know that if we are ever going to live free of the shame and fear that your vile actions instilled in us, then we must forgive you as Jesus has forgiven us. You said earlier that you have done no one any harm. Of course, if you want to believe that, then I can't make you do otherwise.

"But let me tell you that, of those eleven people, three have spent a total of five years in prison, we have all been addicted to either illicit drugs or prescription medicine, and four of us have spent a total of eight years in psychiatric hospitals. None of us have had a meaningful relationship up till recently, either with other people or with God. As for me, my whole life up till the last few months has been lived trying to placate an angry God who was bent on punishing me for causing you to morally fall. That is what you told me and all your victims at the time you abused us. We are not after money. Through the ministry of a priest old enough to be your father, we have found something more precious than money. We have found healing and transformation through faith in Jesus Christ, who died for our sins and for yours. For the record, I do not believe that you handed yourself into the police because you were afraid for your life. When you knew that John and I had summoned the courage to go public about you, you handed yourself in to avoid as much shame as possible. Just like you are doing now, by denying that you hurt anybody. Listen, Justin, until you can face up to your own rottenness, you will never find peace."

Justin rose abruptly. His face was twisted with hate and red with anger. He made as if to walk away and then stopped and turned, taking two menacing steps toward Vince. His voice could be heard throughout the visiting lounge. "How dare you come in here whining about your miserable life and accusing me for somehow wrecking it. Like the others, you got what you wanted and what you deserved. I am not responsible for the eleven shipwrecks that you have become. Now get out and never come back."

The two men stood facing each other, and an eerie silence fell on all the prisoners and their visitors. An old man, probably in his seventies, stepped forward and walked to within a few feet of where the men were standing. "I know you, Vince. I was the senior priest in the church you attended as a boy and where Justin was a trainee priest. I rebuked your father when he reported your abuse, and I arranged Justin's transfer to another parish. Vince, this man is not big enough to own the evil he has done, but insofar as my behavior contributed to your abuse, I am sorry. Almost every man in this prison has been involved in some sort of sexual crime, and in that sense, you could say we are bad men. Some of us, however, like you, have had a transformational experience. I could never expect my victims to forgive me, but I can only pray that, like you, they will find healing. God bless you, Vince. I bet you are an awesome priest."

Justin turned and strode out of the room, and gradually, the visitors and the prisoners returned to their conversations. Two prison warders crossed the room to Vince and offered to usher him out. The man who had spoken stopped them. "Officer," he said to the eldest of them. "May I have a quiet word with this young man?" The officer nodded but did not move away from Vince.

"I am afraid I heard almost all your conversation. I know Father Simon too. We young priests used to call him disparagingly 'the priest with a conscience.' I am glad that he has lived long enough to be vindicated. God bless you for your courage. I will pray for you and your friends."

The older officer chuckled and said to Vince, "This old codger is Michael O'Shea. Whatever he has done in the past, he is a great man now. He gets out in a few days. He has been here longer than me." Vince smiled as he shook the hand of the old man who had come to his rescue.

"Well, when you do, Michael, please get in touch with me."

As he reached the exit door, Maurice, the pastoral care practitioner, caught up with him. He spoke apologetically. "I am sorry, Vince, that your visit ended up the way it did. If Michael had not stepped in, I would have. McKean was more aggressive toward you than I had expected."

"On the contrary, Maurice. I had no expectation that it would go well. I can't get over meeting Michael O'Shea though. It is amazing. He was our parish priest when I was a boy. I still have a letter written by Michael to my father in response to my father alleging that McKean, who was under his supervision, had molested me. He told my father that because of the inexperience of the young priest and the comparative unreliability of a child's evidence, he would be treating the matter as minor. But in deference to the fact that my father and mother were faithful members, he would transfer McKean to another parish."

"You're joking! Vince, are you really saying that Justin McKean sexually abused you when you were just a boy and that what we witnessed today was a childhood victim fronting his abuser as an adult?"

"Yes, that is exactly what I am saying, and Michael sheltered him from the consequences of his actions, because apparently he was also involved sexually with a child at that time. I was vaguely aware that he had been charged and jailed, but I hadn't given much thought to the possibility that I might meet him today. The other amazing thing is that he is about to be released. What will happen to him, Maurice?"

"I don't exactly know yet. The authorities have a couple of options. They could transfer him straight from here to a place near here that was built to house released perpetrators who are not seen as suitable to be released into the wider community. It has no security fences, but it is staffed by armed guards. They can leave their house and go into town, but only accompanied by a guard. They are all required to wear an ankle bracelet so that if they escape, they can be easily tracked and captured. The other option is that he can be released into society, wearing an ankle bracelet and subject to all sorts of restrictions and curfews. The final option is that he is simply released into society with strict parole requirements but comparatively free to go where he likes."

"What option are they likely to choose for Michael?"

"Well, Vince, Michael has been a model prisoner. When he first came here, I understand that he underwent both medical treatment and psychotherapy for depression and anxiety. During this period of his life, he met a man, Joe, who—like you—was a survivor of childhood sexual abuse. He was a farmer, and through his church, he gained permission to come in here and conduct church services. He was so highly regarded by the authorities that they encouraged him to be a sort of unofficial chaplain. Anyway, Michael and Joe became great friends and used to study the Bible together. Apparently, the other guys used to joke about the 'mick and his Protestant mate.' After a short time, Michael experienced a total transformation. As part of this, he wrote a letter to each of the three boys he had molested, explaining that while he could never ask them to forgive him, he wanted them to know that he now fully accepted responsibility for what he did to them as children and the impact that it had on them and their families. He told them that it was he, not them, who was guilty before God.

"Some years ago, Joe suddenly died of a heart attack. Michael took over the Bible studies, and in the past five or six years, there have been so many guys wanting to attend that he now runs five sessions a week. He does not allow the men to call him Father, and some of the guys have told me that his studies are brilliantly nondenominational. Another friend of his has compiled his studies into booklet form and is also helping him write a book about his journey. I understand that this man, who is of similar age to Michael, has provided a granny flat in his backyard for Michael, if the authorities approve. Given his record and his reputation in here, I am almost sure that is what will happen. The amazing thing about Michael is that he has absolutely no expectation that those he abused and those who were abused by priests under his supervision should forgive him. I asked him once whether he had ever forgiven himself. Do you know, Vince, what he said?"

"No. But I suspect it was something profound."

"He said no man had the right to forgive himself for abusing a child, unless he was willing for the rest of his life to receive from those he had wounded, unbridled anger and disgust. If he was willing to do that, then he must understand that self-forgiveness is only possible because Jesus Christ had made the ultimate sacrifice and that, based on that sacrifice, God had forgiven him, making it possible to forgive himself. He told me that he had forgiven himself, but he knew that in the minds of others, he was lower than a sewer rat. He said that he deserved to be thought of that way and would never obligate anyone to change their mind about him. He told me that one day he would die, and he would face Jesus and expected him to say, 'Michael, you have sinned a great sin, and many remain on earth, suffering because of your deeds. But I have heard your cry of repentance, and I want you to know that I have died for your sins, as repulsive as they are, and I have died for the pain and the hurt carried by your victims. My love is without limit but not without cost. I, too, have experienced the human condition with its betrayal, its misuse of power, its grief, and its pain. It was necessary that I did, so that my death and resurrection would be for all people.'"

As Vince was driving home, he called John on his hands-free phone. He told him that he had just visited Justin McKean and asked him if they could meet. They agreed to meet at the rectory and have dinner together. After he hung up, Vince thought about how upbeat John had been lately, especially since they had begun to organize the Festival of Healing. Despite settling into his new job and commencing his university studies, he spent many hours with Margaret, Tim, Marie, Simon, and Anna, putting the festival together and advertising it throughout the city. Vince prayed that what he was about to share with him concerning his prison visit would not derail him in any way.

As they ate their dinner, they chatted about John's work and the preparations for the festival.

"I have never felt as energized as I do right now. I am really chuffed to see what this festival means to Tim as he prepares his exhibition. Anna and Allan have bought into it very enthusiastically and have been a terrific help. We are getting great coverage in the media as well, so I am pleased."

"That's great, John. I hope what I share with you won't ruin your enthusiasm. I felt very strongly that I should confront Justin not just as a victim but also as one priest to another. My visit was organized by a friend of mine. Maurice is the pastoral worker in the prison, and he was not optimistic about the visit and was surprised when Justin agreed, as I was. I met Justin in the visiting lounge, and unbeknown to me, the man who was entertaining guests on the table across the aisle from us was Michael O'Shea. He was the priest in charge of the parish that I attended when McKean abused me. He covered for McKean and told my father that it was a minor matter."

"Yes, I remember you telling me that the first time we met here in this very room. I think you told me that he was also abusing children."

"Yes, that is right. Anyway, he was sitting in the noisy room just across the aisle, but apparently he could hear our whole conversation."

"So, what did McKean have to say?"

"Well, basically, he does not accept that he has done any of us harm. He thinks that all our various psychological and emotional struggles have no relation to what he sees as our sexual interactions with him. I tell you, John, to say that made me angry is an understatement. I felt that if I could kill him and get away with it, I would. Well, I gave him what I thought about it all, and he finally stood up to leave and very angrily told me never to come back. At that moment, Michael O'Shea stood up and approached us. He told us he knew us both, and of course McKean would have known that he was in the prison. I hardly recognized him. He would be in his seventies now. He told me in McKean's presence that McKean was not a big enough man to own the responsibility for our abuse but that he personally wanted to apologize to me for his part in the abuse that I and others had suffered."

Vince went on to tell John all that Maurice had told him about Michael. He spoke about his transformation, his ministry, and his imminent release. John was amazed at this turn of events and, to Vince's relief, was not fazed by McKean's lack of contrition. He simply said, "I really did not expect him to be repentant, so I am not surprised. But I can't help but think that you were meant to be there to meet Michael O'Shea. What is his future?"

"Well, as I said before, he has turned his life around and has been writing a book on the evils of child sexual abuse and its prevalence in the Catholic Church. A man he met through his Bible-teaching activities in the prison, and who is the coauthor of the book, offered him the opportunity to live in a granny flat on his property after his release next week. Whether that becomes a reality or not depends on whether the authorities see him as low risk and suitable to be released into the community. Maurice is confident, giving Michael's reputation and behavior in the prison, that that is what will happen. I have told Michael to contact me on his release. I am hoping that he might visit our group sometime. It would be fascinating to hear him tell his story, don't you think, John?"

"It would indeed, Vince. By the way, have you caught up with the latest news from the Vatican on the first law relating to the reporting of sexual abuse and cover-ups in the Catholic Church worldwide?"

"No. What has the pontiff said?"

"Well, basically that the first law obligates all officials in the Roman Catholic Church to report cases of clergy sexual abuse and attempts to cover it up to their superiors. The first law also requires that they cooperate with civic authorities but stops short of requiring church authorities to report abuse allegations to the police."

"I guess it's a start. But I cannot imagine that survivors and advocates will be happy about the first law. They would think, and I would agree, that it is imperative that the law requires that all child sexual abuse by clergy should be mandatorily reported to police as well as to church authorities."

"Let's hope that is what comes next."

29
A TIME TO HEAL.

A Parish Hall in Melbourne

A large crowd had been growing outside the hall since eight o'clock on this Saturday morning, even though the advertised opening time was nine o'clock. Vince, John, Marie, Margaret, Tim, and Simon, as well as others they had recruited, had worked long hours over several weeks to put the Festival of Healing together. The media had given them great coverage, volunteers had handed out leaflets in the city, and clergy had spoken about the upcoming festival in their churches. The tenor of the advertising was that this festival was for those who had been sexually molested as children and those who loved and supported them. They were being invited to view artwork produced by survivors, attend a recovery workshop of their choosing, and personally meet with and talk to other survivors. There would also be opportunity to attend any one of the three healing services that would take place during the day.

On the church grounds, there were food vans and tables and chairs where people could talk and eat, and it was here that the early arrivals were already sampling the food and interacting with one another. In this area, later in the day, crowds would be able to listen to musicians, poets, and storytellers. Inside, the main hall was set up as an art exhibition where survivors of sexual abuse had the opportunity to view paintings and drawings produced by other survivors. Each of the paintings had the name of the artist attached to it, and a price tag if it was for sale. Above the door leading into the second hall was a beautifully painted sign that simply said, "Those who wish to continue their journey of healing are invited to enter The Walk."

At nine o'clock, the doors opened, and the waiting crowd filed into the hall. One of the first people who began perusing the works of art that were beautifully displayed along both walls of the hall was an elderly man. He was tall, and over his stooped frame, he wore a gray overcoat. Perched on his head was a tweed hat. He spoke to no one but simply stood for a long time in front of each painting. From their place on the wall, numbers of powerful images presented themselves to this silent man. In the very first painting, a boy sat alone at the foot of a great tree, while other children nearby were playing a game of football. He was fondling the ears of his dog, and a large tear was in the act of rolling down his cheek. Beyond the playing children, but within sight of the weeping boy, was the village church.

The second painting was a stark contrast to the first. It portrayed a scene of chaos and desolation. It was clearly winter, as the trees bowed by the wind had lost their leaves. The neglected house with its broken windows was surrounded by a dilapidated and broken fence. Three people, a man, a woman, and a boy, were the central piece of the painting. Each of them was walking away from the house, with their backs to one another. It was clear to the man looking at the painting that, for each one, living near the other in the context of such devastating pain and shame was no longer possible. Surrendering to what seemed to them was the inevitable, they were walking away from one another.

The old man turned away from the painting and, crossing the room, stood in front of the doorway with its beautiful sign that invited him to take The Walk. As he stepped inside, he realized that the room had been converted into a tunnel. On the left side of the full length of the tunnel were ten beautifully presented paintings, and on the right side of the tunnel, a light had been placed opposite each painting, illuminating it so that it seemed startlingly alive. The ten paintings told the story of a boy who grew from childhood to manhood, as you moved from one painting to the next. He was always on his own, even though many of the scenes were of ordinary occasions like family gatherings—except in the last one. This powerful painting depicted three buildings. The first was a hospital, the second was a prison, and the third one was a courthouse. In front of the buildings was an unoccupied park bench on which lay an old overcoat. In the foreground of the painting, the boy, now a man, walked arm in arm with three friends along a warm and inviting pathway.

The man in the gray coat and tweed hat spent a long time in the tunnel. At each painting, he paused and stood, seeing beyond the images on the canvas into the heart and mind of the artist. The isolation, the hopelessness, the anger and despair depicted in the paintings brought tears to his eyes, and each tear was accompanied by almost unbearable emotional pain. As he stepped out of the tunnel, he was confronted by the largest of all the paintings. So powerful was its impact on him that he found it almost impossible to breathe. A boy, the same boy who had been the subject of the ten smaller paintings, knelt in the center of the painting. To his right and his left were people with their backs to him. The boy was reaching upward. Above the boy was a magnificent representation of the crucifixion of Jesus, and above that an idyllic scene of peace and serenity. So overwhelmed was the man in the gray coat that he instinctively removed his tweed hat and knelt before the painting. Completely oblivious of the people around him and broken beyond words, he sobbed loudly and long. At some point in his emotional outpouring, he became aware of someone standing beside him with his hand on his shoulder. Struggling to his feet, he realized that the man beside him was Vince. The two men embraced, and Vince said softly, "Hello, Michael. Come with me to my office, and I will get you a coffee." The two men walked from the room together. In his office, Vince poured two cups of coffee and set them on the table between them.

"I am so glad that you came, Michael. I would not have judged you harshly if you hadn't. Thank you also for bringing your friend with you. He told me that a condition of you being released into society is that he accompanies you whenever you go out. He is in the garden right now, drinking coffee and listening to some poetry written by an abuse survivor. You have obviously been deeply affected by what you have seen so far."

"Yes, Vince. I have been affected beyond words. During my fifteen years of imprisonment for child sexual abuse, many things happened to me, not the least of which was my encounter with a farmer who used to come into the prison and conduct church services. He confronted me with the real horror of what my victims had suffered and what they would be still suffering. I became deeply depressed and attempted several times to kill myself. He visited me every week, and although he never allowed me to trivialize what I had done, he helped me to accept God's forgiveness for my sin against these boys. In the months that followed, I wrote to each of the boys that I had abused. I did not ask them to forgive me. I do not have a right to ask for that. Instead, I told them that I was completely responsible for what had happened, and regardless of anything I said to them at the time, they were not to blame themselves. I got a couple of responses that quite frankly expressed the hope that I would rot in prison, and of course, that is what I deserve.

"I did, however, get three responses thanking me for accepting responsibility for my abusive actions, because being able to shift the guilt from themselves to me was a great relief. One of these responses made the strong point that accepting responsibility for my actions all these years later did not in any way negate the seriousness of what I did to him. This was the only letter I replied to, affirming that what he had said was true and reaffirming that I was not seeking forgiveness or acceptance, but rather I was hoping that my confession would help him to cease blaming himself for the abuse. To my surprise, I received a reply, asking if I would be happy to attempt to explain why I, as someone he as a child had trusted, had used that trust to sexually abuse him."

"Did you attempt to do that?"

"Yes, I did."

"Would you please try and explain it to me?"

"If you have time, I would be happy to tell you what I shared with him."

"Yes, I have the time."

"Well, I told him that in my attempt to explain what I did, I needed first to tell him what I believed and felt at the time of my offending, and after that, what I know and believe now. I also asked him to remember that nothing I would say in reply to his question was meant to be a rationalization of my behavior, nor was it meant to be a justification for what I did. In fact, I now know that the sexual abuse of any child is an act of the utmost evil, with immeasurable negative consequences, regardless of whether the abuser is a trusted person with unquestioned authority, or a family member, or a stranger.

"From the time I was about sixteen, I was aware that I was sexually attracted to prepubescent children. All my sexual fantasies related to children, and for several years, I confessed these and other sexual thoughts as venial sins. However, when I became a trainee priest, my fantasies became opportunities. I fancied that children were attracted to me because I loved them and that ultimately my sexual involvement with them was the natural outcome of my love for them and their love for me. I was aware that other adults saw such behavior as evil, but I could not, at the time, understand why.

"I now know that I engaged in the most blatant type of self-deceit in order to satisfy my sexual desires. That self-deceit led to my deliberately deceiving the children who became my victims and deceiving the adults who trusted me as their priest. I also understand that one of the sick buzzes I got out of molesting a child was a euphoric feeling of power and control. What I did, I did in secret and in defiance of those who thought they had authority over me. I was aware of other colleagues who did the same, and I admired them as people who took grave risks in doing something that they did not believe was wrong.

"I now know the truth. I was nothing more than a predator who deliberately lied to myself in order to satisfy both my unholy desires and my lust for power and control over those I saw as weak and defenseless. I refuse now to excuse my behavior on the basis that my brain was wired in such a way that I found children sexually attractive, or that being a red-blooded male, I was the victim of a system that demanded celibacy. I was a predator, and I am convinced that there is no punishment devised by man that is severe enough for one such as me. I have in my latter years discovered that, while nothing can change the irreparable damage I have inflicted on others, I am, as undeserving as I may be, like all humankind, a recipient of God's mercy. Whatever that may mean in relation to my future, what it means in my present is that I have committed the rest of my life to making, if possible, the pathway of victims of child sexual abuse a little easier."

Vince, as a priest, had sat through many confessions in his time, but none of them had moved him personally, as this one had done. He struggled with what he should do. Should he pronounce some sort of absolution, as he might after one of his parishioners made their regular confession, or should he simply join his voice to those who had expressed the hope that this disgraced priest should rot in jail. What he eventually did was something entirely different from either of these options.

"Michael, although the church has given me the authority to give you absolution for your sins, I have instead decided to leave that matter to you and to God for four reasons. First, I am not sure that I can sincerely speak the sacred words of absolution to you yet, as my wounds still loom too large. Second, you have not asked for forgiveness. Third, you are more deeply aware of your sinfulness that any person I have ever met, and finally, you are also more aware of the depth of God's unlimited mercy than I have ever been, at least up till this moment. Instead, I want to respond as one of those children who was abused by a colleague of yours and who, after his crime, was protected from the consequences of his actions by you.

"Just like you have said, I, like other victims, have spent my whole life carrying the blame of my abuse as heavily as if the sin was mine, not Justin McKean's or yours but mine alone. For many survivors like me, this self-blame turned into self-hatred and often expressed itself in unbridled and destructive anger. However, for me, it became unbearable shame and crippling guilt. I still have your letter to my father, in which you described his complaint against McKean as 'minor because of the inexperience of the priest and the unreliability of a child's testimony.' I now understand that, on your part, this was the sort of blatant cover-up that was occurring in institutions all over the world, not just in the Catholic Church. Anyway, as a result of what McKean told me and as a result of your letter, I was so convinced that I had sinned against McKean and against God that I entered the priesthood in a desperate attempt to placate a God who was, I assumed, angry at me. In recent days, I have met with some fellow survivors of McKean's reign of terror, and together with Father Simon's guidance, we have learned two wonderful truths that none of us had understood before.

"We learned first that by shifting the blame for our abuse from ourselves to our abuser, we could release ourselves from shame. That was life-changing for all of us. The second thing that we learned was that when we did shift the blame to where it belonged, we were enabled to feel the legitimate, internalized emotions we carried, which in my case was anger. We found that we could not only get in touch with these painful emotions, but now we could decide what to do with them. We could deeply repress them so that they became as destructive as our shame, or we could forgive our abuser. At first, the idea of forgiving someone who did not deserve to be forgiven was both unfair and impossible. Personally, it seemed to me that to be asked to forgive McKean was like being revictimized.

"Eventually, Father Simon helped us to understand that God, in his mercy, had allowed Jesus to carry the whole offense of the whole world to the cross, and that on the basis of what Jesus had done, all sins committed by us and against us were forgivable. No person who has ever lived in the past, or lives now, or will live in the future, deserves God's forgiveness, and therefore, the only rational thing to do with undeserved forgiveness is for us to extend it to other undeserving people. The relief that I experienced when I forgave Justin McKean, as God has forgiven me, is indescribable. But even more importantly, for the first time in my life, I understood something of the unlimited mercy of God. Michael, I hate with a passion what you and Justin did to me, and I will do all in my power to make sure that in the future, innocent children will be safe; nevertheless, I acknowledge that in experiencing the unlimited mercy of God, we, you and I, are undeserving brothers, sons of a sovereign God, and recipients of his never-ending grace."

Michael O'Shea could not speak. He could not even move. He had not spoken to a priest for fifteen years, and never in his wildest dreams had he imagined that when he did, he would hear what he had just heard. It was not just the honesty and frankness with which Vince had described his own sexual brokenness but the theological and spiritual integrity that was on display when Vince spoke of the destructiveness and deceitfulness of sin, so abhorrent in the eyes of God on one hand, and the mercy of God, so limitless and so unconditional on the other. Michael was also struck by something else—something that he had not before experienced in the institutional church. Something he had never expected to experience this side of heaven. That something was a generosity of spirit that saw beyond his abject sinfulness and called him a brother.

The two men rose from their chairs and embraced each other. Vince glanced at his watch.

"In fifteen minutes, I will be leading a special healing service as part of our Festival of Healing. You are very welcome to attend. In the meantime, two special friends of mine, Allan and Anna, will be playing and singing in the garden space. I will walk out with you, and you can formally introduce me to your friend."

They walked together, and as they approached a table where an elderly man sat alone, he rose to greet them. "Vince, this is Arthur."

The two men greeted each other, and Michael said, "Arthur and I have been friends since I met him in prison. He was visiting his son, and we got to talking. Since then, we have been writing a book together. The wonderful thing is that Arthur has offered me the opportunity to rent the granny flat in his backyard. He is also, in the eyes of the authorities, my guardian."

"I am certainly glad to meet you, Arthur. I was just saying to Michael that you are about to hear something special. The couple who just came on stage are about to play and sing. Enjoy. I have some things to attend to."

Allan and Anna had indeed come to the platform. Anna had her zither, and Allan was carrying his guitar. Anna introduced them and said that they were going to sing three of their own compositions. The crowd of about two hundred fell silent as the couple began to play. The music was hauntingly beautiful, and even before a word had been sung, the tears were flowing down Michael's face. As Anna began to sing, the words of each verse she sung were a description of a broken life, and the chorus when she was joined by Allan's voice, which harmonized beautifully with her own, was about the healing that was available for those who needed it most. For fifteen minutes, the two hundred people sitting in the garden were captivated by Anna and Allan, and although few of them would have known the couple's individual stories, it was clearly evident to all that their songs and their music came from a very deep and emotional place.

When the music finished, most of the two hundred people filed into the church for the first of three special healing services that would be celebrated that day. Scores of people continued to arrive at the festival and joined with many others viewing the exhibition in the hall or attending a recovery workshop. The church was packed as Vince came to the front and stood by the lectern. Some of his regular congregation noticed that he had not robed for the service but wore a black suit and clerical collar. He smiled warmly as he began to speak.

"Before we commence the service, I have two things to say by way of an introduction. The first is that many of you who are attending this service are not communicant members of this congregation. Some of you are members of other parishes, some of you are Roman Catholics but no longer attend church, and some of you are non-Catholics. You are all very welcome. Because of the ecumenical nature of this service, I have invited the Rev. John McArthur from the local Uniting church, the Rev. Peter Jones, vicar of the local Anglican church, and Pastor Colin Martin from the Baptist church to participate in this service. The second thing I need to say is that the theme of this service is healing, and appropriate readings and prayers will be offered, and two very familiar hymns will be sung. We will also be blessed by Allan Jennings, a survivor of childhood sexual abuse, and his wife, Anna, who will sing a beautiful song, especially written by them for today's service."

Vince sat down, and a very tall, thin man with neat, long black hair and a freshly trimmed beard stepped to the microphone. He lurched rather than walked, and as he faced the congregation, it was clear that he had suffered a severe head trauma at some time in his life. He was obviously nervous.

"My name is Tim Purnell. A long time ago, I was a choir boy in this very church. I am a survivor of childhood sexual abuse and a survivor of a self-afflicted gunshot to the head. Most of the paintings in the exhibition are mine, and if you have seen them, you know my story. I am grateful that in the last few weeks I have stopped blaming myself for my abuse. I have also stopped blaming God. Today I want to invite you to stand and join me as I lead you in singing the well-known hymn, 'Amazing Grace.'"

Michael O'Shea, standing in the very back row, was once again moved to tears, first by the sound of Tim's glorious tenor voice and second by the sound of more than two hundred people singing in unison. When he remembered that many of these people had been wounded by the church or another institution, and many of them had felt abandoned and betrayed by a God that should have loved and protected them, the heartfelt singing of a hymn that focused on God's unlimited love and grace seemed anomalous. Then he looked again at Tim, and he understood. Everybody in that church knew that Tim was that happy little boy in the first painting. They knew also that the other paintings had illustrated the depths of his suffering—a suffering that could not have been conveyed in words. But they also knew that he was the man in the last painting, walking away from the hospital and the prison and the park bench into a life of new hope and new joy. The people were singing for Tim. They were in that moment partakers in the joy of his unfolding transformation. He was reaching them through his discovery that in his brokenness, he had found his precious gifts for art and music, and they were responding by harmonizing with him and making something beautiful happen together. Michael was startled when, as the hymn finished, the congregation broke into spontaneous applause. Were they applauding Tim? Or themselves? Or God? or maybe all three? Whatever the reason for the applause, it seemed completely appropriate.

The Rev. John McArthur stepped forward and, opening the New Living Translation on the lectern, began to read from Psalm 23. As he read, the words appeared on the screen that had been placed in the sanctuary.

> The Lord is my Shepherd; I have all that I need. He
> lets me rest in green meadows;
> He leads me beside peaceful streams. He renews my
> strength.
> He guides me along right paths, bringing honor to
> His name.
> Even when I walk through the darkest valley, I will
> not be afraid, for you are close beside me.
> Your rod and your staff protect and comfort me.
> You prepare a feast for me in the presence of my enemies.
> You honor me by anointing my head with oil. My
> cup overflows with blessings.
> Surely your goodness and unfailing love will pursue
> me all the days of my life,
> And I will live in the House of the Lord forever."

It was John who spoke next. Since he had begun counseling with Marie and Simon, and due no doubt to drinking a lot less and eating good food, he had slimmed down and now cut a handsome figure as he stepped up to the lectern. He had looked forward to this opportunity to share part of his journey with the people who attended the Festival of Healing, but now that the time had come, he, like Tim, felt incredibly nervous. "Like many of you here today, I have lived for many years under the burden of guilt. I believed that I was responsible for the abuse I suffered when I was a boy. That guilt and shame led me into a life of addiction and mental illness. I saw no way out of this shame except by suicide. Then I met my psychologist. From her, I have learned many things, but I simply want to share one of them with you. I learned that there was no healing possible for me until I made the choice to move the blame for my abuse from myself to my abuser. The self-hatred and condemnation that I lived with was the result of believing that I was responsible for the actions of my abuser. I not only hated myself but also my family, who, out of anger, I had rejected. And of course God. I hated him with a passion. He had not been my Good Shepherd. He had done what no good shepherd would ever have done. He abandoned me. At least that is what I thought until a few weeks ago. As a boy, I had loved and trusted a bad priest who had used me to satisfy his own sexual needs. My counselor helped me shift the blame for my abuse to where it really belonged. Then I met a good priest, Father Vince, and through him, another, Father Simon, and through these three people, who I now firmly believe God brought into my life, I have reconnected with my estranged sister and the Good Shepherd.

"My mother loved and trusted the Good Shepherd. Watching me walk down the road of self-destruction was the valley of the shadow for her. But she never ceased to believe that her Shepherd was good, and that he would bring me back. She believed that up till the day she died. I thought that I could never forgive myself for causing her so much pain and for not being there while she was dying. When I learned that she had forgiven me for causing her suffering, I was determined not to rest until I found out how she could do that. I have learned that she believed that Jesus Christ died for the sin of the whole world and freely forgave us in order that we might find freedom by forgiving ourselves and others. Now I believe that too, and through faith in my Redeemer, I have forgiven my abuser for what he did to me, and I have forgiven myself for what, in my pain, I have done to others. I have only begun my journey of healing. I am in the early days of breaking free of my addictions and building new relationships, but I am confident because wherever this journey takes me, I now have the company of the Good Shepherd."

John sat down. There was a moment of the most all-pervasive silence that you can imagine. Then someone began to applaud, and then another, until the whole congregation had joined in this spontaneous and joyous acclamation, empathic to what John had shared. Claire and Sam sat quietly in the back seat, wiping away the tears of joy and relief. Allan and Anna now stepped up to the microphone with their instruments. Alan introduced them and identified himself as a sexual abuse survivor. "We are going to sing you a song that we have written ourselves. Since beginning our own walk of faith a couple of years ago, writing songs has become important to us." They began to play, and Michael would say later that he wasn't sure what he heard first, the words of the song or the soft, gentle weeping that seemed to come from all points of the hall.

> In our brokenness we came, Lord Jesus,
> And in love, you warmly received us.
> We brought with us our pain, Lord Jesus,
> And you did not send us away.
>
> Your love is enough! Your love is enough!
> Your love our broken hearts have healed
> Our lives with lasting peace are sealed.
> Your love is more than enough!
> We brought our shame and sadness, Lord Jesus Christ:
> Our anger, fear, and loss.
> For all this pain, you suffered, Lord,
> Taking it with you to the cross.
>
> Your love is enough! Your love is enough!
> Your love has healed our broken hearts.

Your love has banished all our shame.
We now have joy in Jesus name.
Your love is more than enough
You taught us how to love again, Lord Jesus,
How to trust others and forgive.
You are our loving healer, Lord Jesus;
Now we are not afraid to live.

Your love is enough! Your love is enough!
Your love has healed our broken hearts.
Your love has given us lasting peace.
Your love is more than enough!

As Alan and Anna finished their song, there was no need for applause. The power of the words was not only in the song but in the story of the singers, and the atmosphere in that church at that moment could only be described as one of reverent awe.

The Rev. Peter Jones from the local Anglican church was the next to take his place at the lectern. He immediately began to read from Matthew 6 in the New Living Translation.

Your Father knows exactly what you need before you ask Him. Pray like this.
Our Father in heaven, may your name be kept holy.
May your Kingdom come soon
May your will be done on earth as it is in Heaven.
Give us today the food we need.
Forgive us our sins, as we have forgiven those who sin against us.
And don't let us yield to temptation but rescue us from the evil one.
If you forgive those who sin against you, your heavenly Father will forgive you.
But if you refuse to forgive others your Father will not forgive your sins.

Father Vince Patrick stood as the reading finished and in a tone that conveyed that he understood the mood of the congregation he began his sermon based on the reading from Matthew.

"To put it very simply, Jesus was saying that when it comes to asking God for forgiveness, which is the most important thing any of us can do, we may as well save our breath if we in turn are not willing to forgive those who have hurt us. I must confess that what I am about to tell you, I did not understand myself until recently. When we live with guilt, that is the belief that we have sinned against God or other people, we are in a prison for which we alone have the key. That key is to humbly receive the unlimited and undeserved forgiveness of God. However, the reality is that most of us don't only live in a guilt prison, but we also live in an anger prison. We are in that prison because we have not forgiven those who have hurt us. The key that allows us to escape that prison is forgiving our enemies the same way God has forgiven us. You may say, 'Wait a minute, Father. That person is a bad person and does not deserve to be forgiven.' I am sure that is true, but God has already demonstrated, when he forgave you and me, that true forgiveness is never deserved.

"I understand that if we have been abused by someone we trusted, like a priest or a teacher or a family member, to be asked to forgive them is like being victimized all over again. But the truth is that our forgiveness of them is not primarily for them; it is for us. We are the ones who are in prison, and Jesus tells us that we can break out of that prison by forgiving our abuser in the same way that Jesus forgave us.

"This may be the first time you have ever heard forgiveness explained like this, and you might decide to reject the concept completely, even angrily. I am a priest, and I rejected this understanding of forgiveness for more than twenty years. But recently, Father Simon, who some of you know, challenged me by asking me what I wanted more than anything in the world. Was it to maintain my rage against the man who abused me or against the church that allowed it to happen, or was it to live the rest of my life free of the need to remain angry? I had a choice, and I chose to be free. You also have a choice, as difficult as that may sound. The forgiveness you offer may never benefit your abuser, but it will richly benefit you by releasing you from the exhausting task of maintaining your rage. I have asked Father Simon to lead us in a healing prayer. Will you please stand." As the congregation stood, Father Simon walked slowly forward to the lectern, supported by Margaret.

"Before I pray, I want to invite you to enter deeply into this experience. If you are in that place where you still carry the guilt for something someone did to you, I invite you to envisage yourself physically placing the blame for that painful event on the perpetrator. If you have already done that but are still burdened by the guilt of the hurt you may have afflicted on others, I invite you to reach out your hands as if to receive the gift of God's forgiveness.

"Let us pray. Our dear heavenly Father, many of my brothers and sisters here this morning are deeply broken. Some of them are not even sure that you exist because when they called out to you in the past, it seemed to them that you did not come. Some of them are reluctant to give up their anger because they are afraid that if they do, they will not survive. They believe that it is their anger that has sustained them in times of depression and defeat. My prayer is that today, men and women who were sexually abused as children will find the strength to take the guilt and shame they have carried as victims and place it on the shoulders of their abuser. Give them the courage and strength to do that. I pray also for those who carry guilt because they have, in their anger, hurt others. Help them receive your forgiveness. Help them to know that it is you who—by your love, forgiveness, and acceptance—makes them loveable, forgivable, and acceptable. And help them to know that through your undeserved forgiveness of them, they will be empowered by you to forgive others, so setting themselves free. In Jesus's name we pray. Amen."

As Margaret helped Father Simon back to his seat, Pastor Colin Martin of the local Baptist church stepped forward and announced that as the service ended, Alan and Anna were going to lead them in one of the greatest hymns of all time. With great enthusiasm and conviction, he said, "Charles Wesley wrote thousands of hymns, many of them while riding around England on his horse. This one was written immediately after his conversion and calls us first to admire the love Jesus demonstrated in dying for us. Then this hymn calls us to appreciate the greatness of his love and mercy, and finally to celebrate the freedom that Christ brings to those who trust him. This magnificent hymn begins with the words, 'And can it be that I should gain an interest in my Savior's blood? Died he for me who caused His pain; For me who him to death pursued. Amazing love how can it be that thou, my God, should die for me.' Let us stand and sing it together.

Vince had never heard any hymn sung like that one that morning. It was a fitting climax to what had been a very powerful occasion. People lingered after the service, seeming reluctant to leave the safe, healing atmosphere of the service.

As Father Simon left the church, he was approached by a tall man in a gray coat and tweed hat. He looked carefully at the man, and then an expression of recognition showed on his face.

"Well, good heavens! If it is not Father Michael O'Shea. What a surprise to see you here. You are very welcome, Father," he said as he stretched out his hand in greeting.

Michael took his hand in his. "Thank you, Father Simon, for your warm welcome. I hope you don't mind if I ask you not to call me Father. In most people's minds, I am what was referred to in the service as a bad priest. It is a title I deserve much more than Father. Now that I have come to know the limitless grace of God, I am most comfortable with being called Michael."

"Well, Michael, it shall be. Vince told me of course about running into you during his recent visit with Justin McKean. He was excited about meeting you, especially when he learned more about your journey from the pastoral care coordinator. I would be thrilled to have you visit me at my home. Would that be possible?"

"Of course, it would. My friend would be happy to drive me there. We are actually writing a book together, and given that you have been such a great help to the people who put the festival together, it would be an opportunity to ask you some questions about the pathway of healing that you helped them find."

When the Festival of Healing finally ended well into the night, more than four thousand people had viewed the exhibition, and just under two thousand had attended the special healing services. The team that had manned it all day was exhausted but delighted by the success of the venture and determined to make it an annual event.

30
NEW BEGINNINGS

Dame Phyliss Frost Centre, Ravenhall, Victoria

Carol, the chaplain at the Dame Phyllis Frost Centre, had organized for Marie and Margaret and one other to meet with Kaye at midday, but she had suggested that they meet her first at the Boon Beans Coffee Shop. The three women arrived at the coffee shop at ten, and Carol welcomed them warmly. Marie introduced the smiling chaplain to Margaret, and then to Carol's surprise and amazement, she said, "This is Val, Kaye's Mum."

"This is amazing. Marie. I knew that you were searching for Kaye's mum, but I can't believe you found her. Welcome, Val. I am sure glad that you are here."

"Carol, my plan is that Margaret and I go and visit Kaye and gently break the news that Val is here and willing to meet her. We were hoping that if Kaye agrees to see her mum, we could call you, and you could bring Val to the meeting room."

"That's fine, Marie. I have arranged for you to use the same room as other times. We will all go into the center together, but while you and Margaret go to the meeting room, I will take Val to my office, and we can wait there. If and when I get your call, I will take Val to meet with you."

"Thanks, Carol. I just want to thank you for all that you are doing to help my daughter. Marie has told me that without you, Kaye would never have come to where she is now."

"I appreciate that, Val, but most of the credit must go to your gutsy daughter. The courage and determination she has shown in coming off drugs and reaching out to Marie and accepting the responsibility for killing Vic and the girls is nothing short of amazing. I must say though that I still cannot believe you are here. How did you do this, Marie?"

"Well, let's just say that Val being here is nothing short of a miracle. I give God all the credit, but I should also say that he worked through two good friends of mine. One of them was the policeman who attended the accident the night Vic and the girls died. The other was the doctor who looked after Kaye when she was admitted to the hospital. I know this is hard to believe, but I had known the policeman, Rod, and the doctor, Cath, for many years before the accident. So, when I needed to find Val, I turned to them."

The four ladies talked together over coffee, and before they rose to leave, Carol suggested that they pray together about the afternoon that lay ahead. On the drive to the prison, Val rode with Carol. She confided in the chaplain that she felt incredibly nervous about the possibility of meeting Kaye. "Don't get me wrong. I really want to do this. I have prayed that one day Kaye would get her life together and be reunited with my husband and I, but even more importantly with her children. There was no way that was going to happen while she was on ICE, but now, thank God and thanks to you, it is possible. Kaye always loved our house in Caulfield, and because we hoped that this day might come, we decided when we moved to Sydney that, to put distance between us and Kaye, we would rent it out rather than sell it. We kept it because we hoped that one day Kaye and the girls would live in it as a family. We even talked last week about us selling our house in Sydney and returning to Melbourne so we could buy a house that would be closer to Kaye and the kids." Val giggled nervously. "Listen to me, Carol. Talk about getting ahead of myself. She hasn't even agreed to meet me yet."

"I am sure she will, Val. I pray with her every couple of days, and I know that she wants reconciliation with you and the children more than anything in the world."

When Marie and Margaret entered the room where Marie always

met Kaye, she was already waiting. Marie introduced the two women and explained that Margaret had once been an inmate in the Dame Phyllis Frost Centre and that she had successfully kicked her drug habit and had been reconciled with her grandmother, who had raised her.

"I thought if you guys hit it off, Margaret could be a great support for you on your journey."

"Thanks, Margaret, for coming. Marie has told me all about you, and I believe that one of the officers here, June, is a friend of yours. I feel like I know you already and am looking forward to hearing your story."

"Thanks, Kaye. I am looking forward to traveling with you also."

Marie took a deep breath and said, "Kaye, you know that I have been looking for your mum."

"Yes, you told me last time when you were here that you had two friends helping you."

"That's right. Well, we found her and her husband and your children living in Sydney."

"Oh my goodness. Do you think that Mum will want to see me?"

"Do you think you are ready for that yet?"

"Yes, I am ready. If she wants to see me, it must mean that she is open to reconciliation. I so much want to tell her that I am deeply sorry for all that I have done to her. I know that I don't deserve her forgiveness, and even if she did not forgive me straightaway, I would understand. I am so desperate to see my girls."

Margaret reached out and took Kaye's hand in hers. "Kaye, I have been where you are right now. I needed to be reconciled with my grandmother, who raised me and who I hurt very deeply. I was anxious about it, but like you, I knew I wanted it to happen."

Kaye looked earnestly at her two friends. "Yes, I am anxious, but with all my heart I want it to happen as soon as possible."

"Would now be soon enough?"

"You are kidding me!"

"No. She is in Carol's office right now."

"I can't believe it. It's so wonderful. Scary but wonderful."

"Will I call Carol and ask her to bring her in?"

"Yes! Yes please." As Marie rang Carol on her mobile, Margaret asked Kaye whether she wanted to be alone when her mother arrived. Kaye said that she would feel more comfortable if they were there, at least from the start.

When Val walked into the room, the atmosphere was electric. Two women who had been estranged for seven years, with a history of unspeakable pain between them, stood appraising each other. For Kaye, her last memory of Val had been her standing, hands on hips, with an angry but determined look on her face, saying loudly, "If I have to live for a hundred years, I will make sure you never, never hurt these girls." For Val, her most recent memory of Kaye was of her going berserk in Val's house, picking up a chair and smashing the lounge window. The police had come, and she had watched as Kaye was taken away. Now Kaye saw no anger in Val's expression, just love and hope, and Val saw a calm, peaceful person, confident in who she had now become. After a moment of hesitation, they approached each other quickly with welcoming arms outstretched. The other two women glanced at each other and quietly left the room.

When at last Val and Kaye had disentangled themselves from their embrace, the older woman said, "I never gave up believing that this day would come, and there are two beautiful girls in Sydney who have never stopped believing it either. My husband, Bob, and I kept our house in Caulfield where you grew up because we dared to believe that one day you and the girls would live together there. I never stopped loving you, Kaye, even though I was determined never to let you hurt your children. The pain of choosing between you and protecting your children was almost unbearable, and without the hope that this day would come, I don't know how I would have survived."

Kaye sobbed quietly for a while and then said, "Mum, I love you so much for having the courage to do what you did. I am so very thankful that you protected my children, and I am so sorry that my behavior caused you to have to make such a horrendous choice. No mother should ever be forced to do that. I do not deserve another chance—"

"But you do, Kaye," her mother interrupted, taking her daughter's hands in hers. "What you have done has more than earned you the right to have your girls back. To face up to what you did the night that Vic died, and to reach out to God and then to Marie and then to me, these are not the actions of an addict or of a person filled with self-destructive hatred. You have always been the daughter I gave birth to and the daughter I have always loved, but I had to watch you being destroyed by the choices you were making. Now I have my daughter back. God has given you back to me. Yes, Kaye, you more than deserve to have your children back."

By the time Marie, Margaret, and Carol entered the little room, the two women had dried their tears and were seated on the couch, looking at photos of the girls. For some time, all the women talked excitedly about their plans, the most important of which was arranging for Kaye's girls to visit her on Mother's Day.

31
THE PERPETRATOR

The Rectory

When Vince personally invited the guests, who were now sitting in his lounge room, he did so with a considerable amount of apprehension. He had of course told each one who was on the guest list, and each of them were given the option of declining. They had all come, and now they sat in little clusters while at the same time partaking of the sumptuous afternoon tea prepared by his housekeeper.

When at last Vince called them to order, they took their seats and looked expectantly at him. He smiled. "While most of us are known to each other, that is not the case for all of us. So, I have decided to begin this afternoon's meeting by making formal introductions. The venerable but ancient cleric sitting on my right is Father Simon, without whom more than half of us would not be here. At a time when trust in the church and in priests is at an all-time low, Simon stands as a rocklike reminder that goodness and integrity are values that are still held and demonstrated by many within the church. He will speak to us later in the meeting. Next to him is Marie Forsythe. Marie is a psychologist whose compassion and wisdom are valued deeply by those of us in the group who know her well. In addition to being a therapist, she has been a fellow traveler on the road to healing. Beside her is Kaye, who has just this week been discharged from prison and reunited with her children after serving five years of imprisonment for her part in the car accident in which Marie's husband, Vic, and their two children died. Next to Kaye is Margaret, who as a child was abused by Father Justin McKean. Beside her is her grandmother Sally. Sally and Margaret have been reconciled recently after many years of estrangement. Next to Sally are Anna and Allan Jennings. Allan is also a survivor of child sexual abuse, and he and Anna played a huge part in our Festival of Healing a few months ago. Next to Allan are John and Tim. They, along with Margaret, both grew up in this parish and were sexually abused by McKean. As a result of Marie's counseling, John came to me and told me his story and gave me the courage to go to the bishop with both his and my stories of abuse. My visit to the bishop led to McKean being confronted and eventually handing himself into the police. Tim is the extraordinary artist whose work is now being recognized widely and whose paintings were a feature of the recent Festival of Healing. Next to John and Tim are John's sister, Claire, with whom John has been reconciled after many years, and her husband, Sam.

"Seated beside Sam is Michael O'Shea. Michael was the priest in the parish where McKean abused me. He was subsequently arrested and incarcerated for fifteen years for the sexual abuse of children. I met Michael when, some months ago, I went to Ararat to confront my abuser, and I was deeply moved by that encounter and subsequent conversations with him. I have asked him here today to tell us his story. He has asked that we do not address him as Father, as he knows that his behavior in the past disqualifies him from bearing such a title. Welcome, Michael."

All eyes turned to Michael, and to say that the entire group was enamored by his presence in the meeting would be far from the truth, but they respectfully waited for him to speak.

"I do not expect that I am a speaker you would choose to listen to, and I am aware that I am here at the invitation of Vince. So, let me say at the beginning, if anything I say in the next few minutes offends you, or if any statement I make sounds like a rationalization of my evil actions against children, please interrupt and challenge me.

"As Vince said, I served a prison sentence for abusing children and have been discharged on the assumption by the justice system that I have paid for my crimes. However, both you and I know that if I had spent the rest of my life in prison, it would not be recompense for my crimes. If I knew that going back to prison would bring healing to even one of the boys I abused, I would go back today.

"During my time in prison, and through the intervention of some very determined and outraged people, I came to understand the abject wickedness of my behavior. I have written to all the boys whose lives I have blighted and told them that it is I who alone is responsible for the abuse they suffered, not them. I told them that I would not presume to ask them for forgiveness, only that disregarding anything I have said to the contrary, they shift all the blame that they might have carried onto me, their intentional abuser.

"My abusive behavior cannot be explained away or justified in any respect. I now know that it is evil for any adult person, let alone one who is in a position of trust and power, to sexually abuse a child, and it shocks me to think that I have not always thought that. My time in prison has been transformational. First, I have understood the depth of wickedness to which I sank, and second, I learned about the unlimited mercy of God. He has given me the chance to become a voice for those who have been abused, and I have taken the first steps toward doing that by writing this book." Michael stopped talking and held up a book. On the front was a painting of a weeping boy sitting cross-legged on the floor. "The cover has been designed by Tim, and Vince has kindly written the foreword. My friend Arthur has helped with the layout and the editing. Arthur's son was also imprisoned for abusing children and some years ago took his own life. Hopefully, the book will be used to make institutions safe places for children and alert parents and other concerned adults to the cunning and methods used by those who would groom and entrap their children.

"The most transformational experience I had in prison was what I would describe as my first real personal encounter with Jesus Christ. I am sure that you will be surprised at that, as before I went to prison, I had been a priest for many years, but then again, so had Martin Luther before he understood the grace of God. Through this encounter, I learned how much God hates all sin but particularly sin against children. I began to see truths in the teachings of Jesus that I had never seen before. He especially blessed children. He praised the faith of children. He healed sick children and on one occasion raised a dead twelve-year-old girl to life. He warned his disciples not to hinder children, for to such belongs the kingdom of heaven. I was overcome with guilt. So great was my guilt that several times I attempted to end my life. Then an old farmer, who himself had been abused as a child, spoke to me about the undeserved but unconditional love of God and told me that if I repented of my sins, as foul as they were, God would be faithful to his promise and forgive my sin.

"At first, I would not accept it. It seemed to me that I had done so much irreparable damage to children God loved that forgiveness was unthinkable. It even seemed to me then to be so unjust and unfair that I, as a priest of the church, had abused innocent children, and now, in my long overdue guilt, I could find comfort in God's love and forgiveness. My friend showed me that my forgiveness did not come cheap. He helped me see that God laid aside his holiness and became a man and took the sin of the whole world on himself and then died on a cross.

"I do not expect or ask people to forgive me or to see me as anything but the lowlife I have proven myself to be. I deserve nothing but disdain and disgust, but if there is anything that I can do to make children in our institutions safe, or to help those who have been abused to find a measure of healing, that is how I want to spend the rest of my days. If you have any questions you would like to ask me, I would be happy to try and answer them."

For the next hour, the members of the group interacted with Michael, and by the end of the session, it was obvious that all of them had embraced the sincerity of this man. At the end of the hour, Vince asked Simon if he would finish up the afternoon with some thoughts. After a brief silence, Simon spoke.

"I have two things to say. All of us here in this room are on a therapeutic journey. We are moving from a point where our lives were diminished by the trauma of abuse toward another point, where we refuse to be diminished any longer. Through shifting the blame to where it belongs and forgiving both ourselves and others, we are experiencing an expansion of our lives. New hope, new relationships, and new possibilities are opening to us. What Michael's visit has done for us today is remind us that with recovery comes new responsibility. Michael has had the courage to admit that he has unique insight into the things that will put today's children in danger. He has the doubtful expertise of one who in years past practiced the deception and cunning designed to groom a child for sex. Now, because of the transformation that has occurred in his life, he wants to use that sinister knowledge to inspire other adults to do whatever it takes to keep children safe.

"This fight must be continued at every level of society, including the family itself. Those of you who were abused, on the other hand, have another field of expertise. You are the ones who were deceived and entrapped. You know from your perspective how it happened, and you also must be involved in the fight to keep today's children safe. All of you are discovering gifts that have come to you wrapped in pain. You must use these gifts to ensure that what has happened to you might not happen to others.

"The second thing I want to say is that Michael has reminded us today that evil flourishes where there is secrecy and unaccountability. Abusers create for themselves a world where only they, with their seared consciences, and their victims, with their projected guilt, exist. The tragedy of such a world is that the predators are free to continue their evil while their victims are conditioned to live their lives in shame-filled isolation. Each of you in this room has made a choice to move out of the self-centered isolation of the victim into the empowering world of the forgiver and the forgiven. Some of you, for the very first time in your adult lives, have experienced the redemptive experience of being loved by God and others. You must learn to embrace the safety of a community of friends as passionately as you, in your brokenness, craved isolation. The mountains that seem too high to climb and the rivers too dangerous to swim become surmountable when viewed from the perspective of being part of a loving, accepting community.

"We have discovered together that there is unlimited power to heal the human heart in the ever-present but indefinable love of God. He hates the evil that led to our brokenness, but he loves us so much that he will not leave us broken. He alone has the power to restore the hope and faith that others have sought to destroy. His plan is that those he has redeemed and restored will always be the reason why broken people will never be left without hope."

As Simon finished speaking, Vince rose from his chair and left the room. When he returned, he was carrying a bread roll and a silver chalice of wine. He went back to his chair and addressed the group. "This is a poignant moment. In this room, we represent the pain of the whole world. Between us, we have experienced grief, betrayal, mental illness, violence, sexual abuse, emotional isolation, poverty, homelessness, incarceration, and despair. Some of us have also caused enormous suffering to others who, because of our behaviors, have experienced physical and emotional violence, loss of relationships, and great sadness. We are those who have been sinned against by others, and we all know that we have sinned against others. It is appropriate then that we partake together of these symbols of God's unlimited love for us. The bread that Jesus said is his body and the wine that is his blood speak to us of his suffering and death, and the fact that we as a forgiven and redeemed people are gathered in this room speaks of his resurrection."

Simon quietly interrupted Vince. "Vince, this is a good thing that we are about to do, but I was wondering if I could do something first."

He nodded at Margaret, who rose from her chair and left the room. A few moments later, she returned with a dish of water and a towel. She placed them in front of Simon. Smiling at her, he said, "Margaret, help me to kneel on the floor." She did, and when he was settled, he looked around the group and said quietly, "When Jesus was about to leave this world, he was anxious that the disciples would always have a way of remembering the depth of his sacrificial love. As I thought about this group and the fact that in the natural progression of things, I will be the first to leave it, I felt that to wash your feet would not only be an appropriate way for me to say farewell but also a wonderful way to remind ourselves that we are, and always will, be the focus of God's love."

Michael stood up and, placing a chair in front of Simon, removed his shoes and socks. Simon took his feet and placed them in the dish. He then lifted them out again and wiped them with the towel. Anna wondered to herself which of the two men shed the most tears. One by one, each person sat in that chair, and the old priest washed their feet, until only Simon's feet were left unwashed. John and Tim helped him to his feet, sat him in the chair, and Margaret and Marie knelt in front of him and gently washed and wiped his feet.

Vince broke the bread, and going to each person, he offered them some, all the while repeating the words of Jesus, "This is my body, broken for you. Take, eat this in remembrance of me." When everybody had been served the bread, Vince took up the chalice and again went from one to the other. As he did so, he repeated the words of Jesus, "This cup is the new covenant in my blood."

When at last their time together was over, they went to their houses. Vince took Father Simon back to the aged care facility where he lived and helped him to his room. Simon thanked him as he sank into the chair by his bed. "It's been quite a day, my boy. Quite a day." His eyes were closed before Vince left the room.

32

CELEBRATION

Six weeks after the momentous meeting in the rectory when Michael addressed the group, they and several hundred others gathered in the Church of St. Francis for the funeral service of Father Simon. Three days earlier, as the nurses were helping him into bed, as they did each evening, he asked them whether it would be possible for him to speak to all the staff on duty that evening. A few minutes later, four nurses, two orderlies, the manager, and the matron stood around his bed. Simon reached out and took hold of the matron's hand. "I know this must seem very strange to you all, but I have asked you to come because I sense that it is time to thank you all for your care. Since coming here three years ago, I have known nothing but love and generosity. I am indeed a truly fortunate man, and I want you to know that I am grateful to each of you for your affection and patience. I also wanted to tell you that even though you may not all realize this, your loving servanthood is a beautiful reflection of Jesus. Thank you all for being Jesus to me. Soon I will be meeting him face-to-face, and I will be able to tell him that for three years I have been in the presence of people who are always showing people what he is like."

Even as he spoke the last sentence, his eyes were closing, and his voice trailed off as he drifted off to sleep. The next morning, when the nurse went to wake him for breakfast, the expression on his face was the same look of peace he had the night before, but sometime during the night, he had breathed his last breath.

Now, as Vince stepped up to deliver the eulogy, it seemed to him that every seat was occupied by people who, like himself, had tangible reasons for being profoundly thankful for the influence of this gentle, loving man. People like Sally who, when their faith in the church was threatened by the disclosure of the deeds of bad priests, were sustained and strengthened by memories of this kindly and godly priest who reflected the love of Christ for the poor and marginalized. And Margaret, her granddaughter, who trusted Simon to take her to that painful place in her life that she had so strenuously avoided, where instead of being overwhelmed by grief and sorrow, she found the unconditional love and mercy of God. And Marie, the psychologist who, while helping others, realized that she herself needed the wisdom and love of Father Simon in order to break the destructive power that self-condemnation had over her life. And agnostic John who saw in Simon a valid reason for believing in God and the church again. And the brilliant but severely damaged former choir boy Tim, whose hatred for priests and the Catholic Church knew no bounds until he experienced the unconditional love with which Simon embraced him. And he, Vince, to whom Simon had been a father, a mentor, a teacher, and a very dear friend. So many people. So many stories. So many reasons to heap praise on a departed saint, if one dared.

Simon had spoken to Vince about this day. "Vince," he said firmly, "from the time I first came to know Jesus as my Savior and friend, my prayer was that people would see something of Christ in the way I lived. If there has been any merit in my life, it has been that Christ lives in me as he lives in all believers. When I die, do not eulogize me. God must be given the glory. Those who come to my funeral must know that if Christ can live in one such as I, then he can do the same in them."

"Father Simon," Vince began, "was a damaged young man who went within inches of taking his own life. However, during those desperate days when his only regret was that he had failed to end it all, God reached out to him. The instrument that God used was a businessman whose own son, a parish priest, had died in a car accident. Recently widowed and now bereft of his only child, he told Simon that because of God's love for him, he had so much love to give and no one to give it to. He embraced Simon as his own son, spoke for him in court, paid his fine, traveled with him through many months of rehabilitation, and took him into his own home. Simon saw the authenticity of this man's life and decided to become a follower of Christ. Later when he joined the priesthood, he said that his one desire was that people would see his life as a reflection of the life of Christ. All of us who knew him during the rest of his life on this planet were affected by his love and integrity as a man of God.

"Many of us know that he spent almost his entire ministry as a priest in remote rural parishes, and while he was grateful to serve God anywhere, he and others knew that the original decision to move him a long way from Melbourne was made because he dared to expose the truth about child sexual abuse in the Catholic Church. He loved the people he served in Christ's name, and for nearly fifty years, he did so with great energy and compassion, and there are people here today who have traveled over five hundred kilometers to join us in giving thanks for his life, and in particular for his faithful ministry to them. On his retirement, he returned to Melbourne and became a tireless counselor and advocate for men and women who as children were sexually abused.

"He asked me not to make this eulogy about him but to share with you the three great truths that were foundation stones for his life and ministry. The first great truth upon which he built his life is the unconditional love of God. He was never in doubt that despite his youthful years of debauchery and violence, God loved him unconditionally and would never give up on him. Having experienced such undeserved and unlimited love in his own life, he understood that he had the ability and responsibility to love others in the same way that God loved him. And this he did. Always ready to listen to the stories of others, he never reacted judgmentally or critically but always responded with love and a generosity of spirit that gave people hope and left them feeling loved.

"The second foundational truth on which Father Simon built his life and character was the unconditional forgiveness offered him by God through the death and resurrection of Jesus Christ. He was never in doubt about this. One of his favorite statements about Jesus was 'But if we confess our sins to Him, he is faithful and just to forgive us our sins and to cleanse us from all wickedness' (1 John 1:9 NLT). Equally important to him, however, were Jesus's words, 'But when you are praying, first forgive anyone you are holding a grudge against, so that your Father in heaven will forgive your sins too' (Mark 11:25 NLT). Simon was once referred to cynically, by priests who covered up sexual abuse against children, as a priest with a conscience, and as a priest with a conscience, he suffered persecution by the church he loved and served. Yet he carried no resentment. He shared with me once that his one great disappointment was that 'my efforts as a young priest to protect children seemingly failed,' but he knew that he needed to accept his heavenly Father's forgiveness and move on for the sake of those he ministered to. When I and others went to him for help to deal with the anger and resentment we felt about being abused as children, he taught us how to forgive those who had wounded us and to forgive ourselves for wounding others out of our pain. He was not speaking to us as a priest but as a man who had experienced hurt and anger yet had discovered the power of forgiveness in his own life and was delighted to share it with us.

"The third great principle on which Father Simon built his life was the apostle Paul's command. 'Therefore, accept each other just as Christ has accepted you so that God will be given glory' (Romans 15:7 NLT). When, in the most desperate hour of his life, the man who became his benefactor accepted him unconditionally in the name of Christ, it transformed his whole life. As a priest, he turned no one away. He, like his Savior Jesus, healed the broken and dejected and gave new hope to those who had given up.

"Today, Father Simon would have me point you to Jesus, who alone can and does forgive us, giving us a new life and fresh hope. He would want me to tell you that he was who he was by virtue of the Christ who lived in him."

As people shared afternoon tea together in the parish hall, the atmosphere was one of great thankfulness for Father Simon's life and new hope for the future.

NOTES

All biblical quotes are taken from the New Living Translation of the Bible.

Page 5. "The Dreaded Question," a poem by Warren Cann, 2018.

Page 17. "I Know the Truth," a poem by Warren Cann.

Page 36. The apostle Paul on forgiveness, Ephesians 4:32.

Page 36. Jesus Christ on forgiveness, Luke 23:34.

Page 37. The apostle Peter on forgiveness, 1 Peter 3:18.

Page 124. Psalm of comfort, "The Lord is My Shepherd," Psalm 23:1–9.

Page 125. "Anna and Alan's Song," original written by Graeme Cann.

Page 138. The apostle John on forgiveness, 1 John 9.

Page 138. Jesus on forgiving others, Mark 11:25.

Page 139. The apostle Paul on accepting others, Romans 15:7.

Lightning Source UK Ltd.
Milton Keynes UK
UKHW040709191220
375534UK00001BA/26